Lord Buckingham's Bride

'That man is a spy – and he's looking at us,' Lord Buckingham said. 'We must give him something to watch. Kiss me, Alison.'

'Here? In front of everyone?' Alison asked.

'Do as I say,' he said softly.

Then he bent his head to kiss her on the lips, and she found herself putting her arms around him. A fleeting sliver of conscience pricked her, but then was gone as she was swept into the sheer pleasure of his kiss. She shouldn't feel like this; she had no right to respond to him, but she couldn't help herself.

He drew back slightly, his blue eyes surprised. 'You appear to be entering into the spirit of things,' he murmured, smiling, looking at her in a deliciously disturbing new way. . . .

Lord Buckingham's Bride

SANDRA HEATH

ROBERT HALE · LONDON

© Sandra Heath, 1991, 2008
First published in Great Britain 2008

ISBN 978-0-7090-8091-6

Robert Hale Limited
Clerkenwell House
Clerkenwell Green
London EC1R 0HT

www.halebooks.com

2 4 6 8 10 9 7 5 3 1

Typeset in 10½/14pt Classical Garamond Roman
by Derek Doyle & Associates, Shaw Heath
Printed and bound in Great Britain
by Biddles Limited, King's Lynn

1

Flames flickered brightly through the cold May night as the British merchant ship burned out of control at her anchorage in Stockholm harbor. A thick pall of smoke drifted on the chilly Scandinavian air, and the blaze was reflected on the still, dark water.

The fire had broken out just after twelve during the brief hours of night that prevailed at these northern latitudes, and everything had been quiet until then. The lights of the Swedish capital had twinkled across the harbor, and the distant sound of singing and laughter had drifted from the many quayside taverns. Now the air was ringing with shouts of alarm from other vessels that were in danger from flying sparks, and a noisy crowd had gathered on the waterfront to watch the conflagration that would soon take the *Duchess of Albemarle* to the bottom. All attempts to save her had failed, her crew had abandoned her to her fate, and now the final rowing boat was pulling swiftly away toward the shore.

There had only been one passenger who intended completing the ship's voyage from London to St Petersburg, and she'd been fast asleep in her cabin when the fire broke out. Miss Alison Clearwell was eighteen years old and, through no fault of her own, was traveling alone. In the panic of the fire, at first no one had remembered her, but then Captain Merryvale had burst unceremoniously into her cabin to tell her to pack what belongings she could into a small valise, as they were abandoning the ship.

Terrified, she'd flung on her fur-lined green velvet cloak over her white nightgown, snatched up what she could, including the book she'd been reading during the voyage, and then she'd stumbled along the smoky deck behind the captain, who'd handed her swiftly down into the last rowing boat.

As the little craft slid away from the blazing ship, she sat in the stern, next to the captain, who was himself manning the tiller. Her gray eyes were huge with fear, and her cloak's hood was pulled over her unruly tangle of long ash-blonde curls. Her heart-shaped face was pale and tense, and she clutched the valise close to her breast, as if it somehow gave her comfort.

Suddenly the night was filled with the splintering groan of falling timbers as the burning ship's mainmast collapsed, bringing sails, rigging, and another mast crashing to the deck where only moments before Alison had been led to safety. There were cries of horror from the shore, for everyone in this seafaring city knew that it wouldn't be long now before the doomed ship sank finally beneath the waves.

The sailors stopped rowing and everyone turned to watch the *Duchess of Albemarle*'s dying moments. Captain Merryvale looked sadly at the vessel he had commanded for the past three years. He was a lean, rawboned man with a bearded, weather-beaten face and gray-streaked brown hair, and in all his long years at sea this was the first time he had lost a ship. As he watched, the *Duchess* gave up the struggle, and with a hissing and bubbling that resembled a gigantic cauldron, she slid down out of sight. The flames were abruptly extinguished and suddenly everything seemed very dark. The pall of smoke began to drift away into the night, and all that was left of the ship was a swirl of bobbing flotsam.

Alison stared toward the scene, her heart pounding, and then she began to shiver, not only because it was so much colder far north, but also because she was so very frightened. She felt lonely and vulnerable, and with five days of journey still ahead of her before she reached St Petersburg, England seemed to be a lifetime away.

When the *Duchess of Albemarle* had left London, the daffodils had almost been over, and the lilac had been coming into bloom, but up here in these northern climes the daffodils had yet to blow and the lilac was still in the tightest of buds. Only a few weeks ago the waters in Stockholm harbor had been littered with ice, and the Baltic itself had been frozen over; it would be much colder again in St Petersburg, which was one of the most northern cities in the world. The *Duchess of Albemarle* would have been one of the first foreign ships to sail right into the Russian city after the long hard grip of winter, for until now all shipping had been able to sail only as far as Kronstadt, the huge fortress island twenty miles west of Peter the Great's beautiful city on the delta of the Neva River. With the coming of spring the ice had gone and the Baltic was free again, but the poor *Duchess of Albemarle* would no longer be able to sail past Kronstadt and into the heart of St Petersburg, for now she would rest forever at the bottom of Stockholm harbor.

Alison shivered again, for the cold seemed to seep right through to her bones. She wished with all her heart that she had never been prevailed upon to make the journey to stay with relatives she didn't even know. Everything that could go wrong with the journey had proceeded to do just that, and now this had happened. She loathed Europe, which had been at war with Britain until only two months or so before, and she resented the fact that she had been made to press ahead with the visit to St Petersburg when instead she could so easily have stayed with her friend Lady Pamela Linsey, the daughter of the Duke and Duchess of Marchington, at beautiful Marchington House, on the Thames at Hammerswith on the outskirts of London.

She turned to look toward the quay, which was much closer now as the sailors rowed strongly across the shining black water. The crowd was still gathered on the waterfront, and she could hear the low hum of their voices. At the beginning of this year of 1802, Britain had stood virtually alone against the might of Bonaparte's France, but now that a peace treaty had been signed, the frontiers were open again and everyone was indulging in an orgy of travel. But there was peace only because it suited Bonaparte and if it hadn't been for Britain's singular naval victory at the Battle of Copenhagen and the assassination of the half-mad Czar Paul I, both of which events had forced the Corsican's hand, then all those people on the quayside would still be at war with Britain. The new twenty-four-year-old Czar Alexander I was not so eager to support the French cause, and from the moment he had assumed the throne, he had made it clear that he did not intend to pursue war at any cost. Support for the French had begun to crumble away, and Bonaparte had perceived that the moment had come to sue for peace – for the time being, at least, since it was unthinkable that his ambition to be master of all Europe had in any way diminished. He was now engaged upon wooing the reluctant czar, who was showing signs of softening.

Alison lowered her eyes, staring at the bottom of the boat. If only her father had been able to return from Jamaica at the beginning of the year as originally planned, then she wouldn't have had to set out on this most loathed of journeys. As it was, it would be another six months before he returned, and now that she was eighteen, she'd become too old to remain at Miss Wright's Academy for the Daughters of Gentlefolk. The exclusive establishment in Bath had been her home for the past six years, ever since her mother had died so tragically and her father had sold everything to go to Jamaica in order to forget his grief.

Her family had been comfortably off rather than wealthy, and their estate in Wiltshire had been modest, unlike the magnificent country estates and town residences of her fellow pupils at the academy. Tears filled Alison's eyes as she recalled the dreadful events that had led to her being sent to the school. On the night of her mother's death, the family had been on a midsummer visit to friends in nearby Chippenham and, as they'd returned, a violent thunderstorm had broken out. Lightning had struck a tree just as the carriage was passing, and it had fallen on the vehicle, killing Alison's mother. Alison and her father had escaped with little more than bruises and shock, but their lives had been inexorably changed from that moment on, because her father could not come to terms with his immeasurable grief. He had loved his beautiful wife, and he was reminded of his loss every time he looked at his daughter, who resembled her so much. He had sold their home, using part of the proceeds to pay for Alison's exceedingly expensive education at the academy, and the rest to purchase a plantation in Jamaica. He had left England vowing to make his fortune, and to return to launch his daughter into London society with every possible advantage. It had taken him six long years to build up the plantation and make that promised fortune, but he had succeeded, and at the beginning of the year he had intended to come back and purchase a fine London town house for them both, but the sale of the plantation had not been smooth, a number of complications had arisen, and he had been forced to postpone his return.

Alison sighed, remembering how dreadfully unhappy she'd been when first she'd gone to Miss Wright's. She had felt so wretchedly out of place among the daughters of lords, marquesses, and dukes, but then she had been befriended by Lady Pamela Linsey, who was a year older than she and who was by far the most popular girl at the school. With Pamela's friendship she had been accepted by everyone, and her misery had gradually turned to happiness, although she had continued to miss her father, especially at vacation time, when she was the only pupil without any family in the country and had had to remain with Miss Wright. Pamela had left the school over a year before her, but their friendship had endured and they were still as close as ever.

Alison wished that things hadn't worked out the way they had. Because of the delay in her father's return, he had written to his brother Thomas in St Petersburg, whom he hadn't seen in many years, asking him to accommodate Alison for the next six months, and then he had written to Miss Wright instructing her to make all the necessary arrangements. Everything had been settled without Alison even being consulted, and when an alternative solution had appeared on the scene, it had been too late to do anything about it. The alternative solution was for her to stay instead at Marchington House with Pamela, but Miss Wright had been adamant, and the St Petersburg visit had gone ahead as stipulated by Mr Clearwell in Jamaica.

Alison wondered what her uncle Thomas Clearwell would be like. He had gone to St Petersburg soon after she'd been born, and he had more than made his fortune there, for he had become a very successful merchant with wharves and ships of his own. Now he lived in a mansion on English Quay, where most of the considerable British community were to be found. After being a widower for many years, he had recently married a much younger Russian lady by the name of Natalia Razumova, and according to his son William by his first marriage, he was devoted to her and very happy indeed.

Alison smiled a little, for it wasn't quite true that she didn't have any family in England, for she had her cousin William, who had left St Peterburg for London and who had immediately made it his business to seek out his little cousin at her school in Bath. William was very much a dashing man-about-town, with tall, sandy-haired good looks and a witty, charming nature, and Alison had been the object of

much envy from her fellow pupils when he had driven her out in his
flamboyant curricle. However, she wasn't so green that she believed
she was the sole reason for William's visits to Bath, for she'd very
swiftly become aware of his *tendre* for Pamela, who had turned his
head from the moment he saw her. At first Pamela had seemed to
return his interest, but when the matter had been brought to Miss
Wright's attention, and she in turn had acquainted the Duke and
Duchess of Marchington with what was going on, the liaison had
been very abruptly brought to an end. Pamela had left the academy
and had been guarded very carefully at Marchington House, and poor
William had been left to nurse his broken heart.

When it was felt that William had been successfully discouraged,
the Duke and Duchess of Marchington had launched their lovely
daughter into her first London Season, and she had immediately
become the belle of every ball. Pamela had everything – wealth, a title,
dark-eyed beauty, a vivacious personality, and a warmth that drew
suitors to her like pins to a magnet – and it wasn't long before her
name was being connected with that of Francis Buckingham, Lord
Buckingham, a gentleman who was not only one of the foremost
names in aristocratic horse-racing circles and a friend of William's,
but who was also reputed to be the most handsome man in England.
William Clearwell had evidently been entirely forgotten, for Pamela's
letters had been full of the handsome earl, and now the betrothal was
to be celebrated in July.

The moment Pamela had realized that Alison was being forced to
go to St Petersburg, she had written to Miss Wright telling her that
Alison was more than welcome at Marchington House, where she
could stay as long as she wished; but it had been to no avail, and the
plans for St Petersburg weren't altered by so much as a day. And so
Alison had set out on the loathed journey to Russia, and Pamela had
been left to twiddle her thumbs impatiently because Lord
Buckingham was also out of the country, visiting different places in
order to purchase new horses for his stud at Newmarket. His decision
to go had put Pamela in a considerable miff, so much so that she had
quarreled with him before his departure, and had refused to even
discuss his plans.

On a perfect spring morning in April, in the company of Mrs

Taylor, the chaperone Miss Wright had engaged, Alison had reluctantly embarked on the *Duchess of Albemarle*, which was to convey
her from London to St Petersburg by way of Amsterdam,
Copenhagen, and Stockholm. From the outset the voyage had been an
ordeal. First of all, the fine weather had changed as the vessel crossed
the North Sea, and a terrible gale had whipped up seas so mountainous that Alison had suffered the worst *mal de mer* imaginable.
Reduced to a state of utter wretchedness, she had remained in her
cabin, her face almost as green as the sea itself.

Mrs Taylor hadn't suffered at all, and had spent most of her time
flirting with the various gentlemen on board. She wasn't a suitable
chaperone, she was a predatory widow on the lookout for another
husband, and her charge's welfare couldn't have been further from
her mind. When the ship had at last entered Amsterdam harbor, Mrs
Taylor was in the company of a Prussian cavalry officer, but when it
became apparent that marriage was the last thing he intended, she
gave him his *congé* and turned her attentions to a particularly handsome and engaging American gentleman from Boston.

The *Duchess of Albemarle* sailed on to Copenhagen, where the year
before Nelson's fleet had demolished that of the Danes, and where
the American gentleman demolished the chaperone's hopes by
confessing that he had a pretty wife at home in America. Furious, the
formidable Mrs Taylor had been in a very disagreeable temper for
several days, but then her ambitious gaze happend on a widowed
Swedish baron, who, although of somewhat gloomy temperament,
was both wealthy and available. She descended upon him like an eagle
on a witless rabbit, and Alison doubted if he ever knew what had hit
him, for by the time the vessel reached Stockholm he was so firmly in
her talons that she was set to become his baroness.

When the *Duchess of Albemarle* dropped anchor earlier that very
day, the chaperone and her prey had departed for his estate on the
shore of Lake Malaren, west of the Swedish capital, and Alison had
been left entirely alone for the remainder of a journey that she hadn't
wanted to make in the first place, and that she now found both intim-
idating and hazardous. Indeed, the only good thing that could be said
about it was that Miss Wright had insisted on sending most of her
wardrobe and other belongings on ahead, so that instead of reposing

now at the bottom of the harbor, they would already have arrived at the Clearwell residence on St Petersburg's English Quay.

The rowing boat had almost reached the quay now, and Alison could see the city quite clearly. The crowd on the waterfront was beginning to disperse, but there were still many people standing around. Lights shone in windows, tavern signs were illuminated by lamps, and the sound of a little light traffic echoed through the streets near the harbor.

Earlier in the day she had seen that Stockholm was very beautiful, with a blend of magnificent public buildings, including the royal palace, facing the harbor, and an old medieval city of narrow, tightly packed houses and even narrower alleys and courts. Built where the salt water of the Baltic met the fresh water of inland Lake Malaren, the city was set on a cluster of beautiful islands that were surrounded by a mainland of tree-clad slopes.

Alison didn't realize Captain Merryvale was addressing her.

'Miss Clearwell?' he said again.

She gave a start. 'Captain Merryvale?'

'I was saying that it is my duty to see you safely on board another vessel for the remainder of your journey. The best thing would be to wait a day or so for the *Duchess of Albemarle*'s sister-ship, the *Duchess of Clarence*, but she might be delayed. A young lady on her own is obviously greatly at risk. It so happens that a brigantine by the name of the *Pavlovsk* is due in tonight, and she will leave again on tomorrow's midday tide for St Petersburg, for she only stays in port for one tide. Her captain is a friend of mine, and he owes me a favor or two. I'll see to it that you are accommodated on the *Pavlovsk* when she leaves tomorrow, but in the meantime I wish you to go to the Dog and Flute, an inn I—'

'An inn?' Her eyes widened, for Miss Wright had always instructed her pupils that they were never on any account to stay at inns.

'Miss Clearwell, I fully understand your alarm, but I promise you that the Dog and Flute is a very respectable hostelry, quite the most respectable in Stockholm, and entirely suitable for ladies. Besides, there really isn't much else I can do in the circumstances. I can hardly permit you to wait on the quayside for the *Pavlovsk* to come in, and since it is incumbent upon me to look after you to the best of my abil-

ity, the wisest thing would be to have one of my men escort you to the
Dog and Flute, which isn't far. I trust that that will be acceptable to
you?'

She knew that she really didn't have much option but to agree, for
he was doing his best under extremely difficult circumstances, and the
last thing he needed now was a foolish creature twittering about inns
not being suitable. She managed a smile. 'Of course it's acceptable,
sir.'

'Thank you, Miss Clearwell, and I promise you that passage will be
obtained for you on the *Pavlovsk* tomorrow. I'll send Billy with you
when we reach the shore, for he speaks a little Swedish and will be
able to explain to the landlord.' He nodded toward a curly-headed
young sailor in a brown jacket and baggy beige trousers who was
rowing the boat with the others.

In readiness for stepping ashore, Alison rearranged her hood,
trying to conceal her disheveled hair. She resolved to keep her cloak
closed tightly at the front, to hide the white of her nightgown.
Looking at her feet, she was thankful that she'd had the presence of
mind to put on the little black ankle boots she had bought in Bath's
fashionable Milsom Street, otherwise she'd not only be in disarray
and in her undress, but barefoot as well. Miss Wright would be
shocked to the core if she could see her pupil now, for the highly
respectable, very proper, very neat young lady who had left the academy with the odious Mrs Taylor had become a veritable ragamuffin.

The boat nudged the foot of some steps, and one of the sailors
made the rope fast. Captain Merryvale took Alison's valise and then
assisted her ashore before handing the valise to the sailor named Billy.
'Take Miss Clearwell to the Dog and Flute, Billy my lad, and see to it
that she's accommodated safely for what's left of the night. And tell
them they're to send someone with her to the quay tomorrow morning, to the *Pavlovsk*, which always comes alongside by the royal
palace. Is that clear?'

'Yes, cap'n.' Billy touched his forehead, for his hat had been lost in
the panic of the fire.

Captain Merryvale smiled at Alison. 'I trust that I will see you again
in the morning, Miss Clearwell, but if I do not, then I wish you well
for the remainder of your journey. I shall wait here for the *Duchess of*

Clarence, and will join her to travel to St Petersburg, where I must report what's happened to the shipping company. If I can be of any assistance to you there, please do not hesitate to call upon me.'

'You're most kind, Captain Merryvale. I'm truly sorry about your ship, for I know that you did everything you could to save her.'

'I did indeed, miss, but I only hope that her owners view matters in the same benevolent light. I trust you didn't lose too much,' he added, glancing at the valise.

'To be truthful, sir, I don't know what I lost, for I cannot recall what I managed to pack. All I remember is that I rescued the book I was reading, for all the good that will do.' She smiled a little ruefully, for it wasn't even a particularly good book, but was a lurid gothic tale of runaway lovers, wicked lords, and dastardly deeds. She didn't know why she had chosen it in the first place, and she doubted very much if she would ever finish it now. Still, it might serve to while away the rest of the night at the inn, for she was certain she wouldn't be able to sleep.

Billy led her up the stone steps to the quayside, where the lingering crowd parted for them to pass. She was careful to keep her eyes lowered and to hide her hair and nightgown hem as she hurried after Billy, but she still felt as if her state of undress was all too apparent.

They entered a narrow medieval alley that led at a right angle away from the harbor. The way was just wide enough for a carriage to pass, and the buildings seemed to almost meet overhead. It was a place of inns and taverns, lodging houses, and a few private residences, with only one or two shops. There were several other establishments too, of a somewhat improper nature, and Billy hurried her respectfully past them.

Almost at the end of the alley there was an inn that was larger than all the others, and outside it hung a sign showing a little white dog dancing on its hind legs while playing the flute. The hostelry was five stories high, its upper windows boasting wooden balconies, and the main doorway from the alley was approached up a flight of four stone steps. The front of the building was stuccoed in pink, and it was flanked on one side by a bright-yellow lodging house, and on the other by a dark-red chandlery. All the buildings of old Stockholm were prettily colored, and in daylight they presented a handsome sight, but in the dark the colors were strangely muted.

Billy made to go straight in, but Alison called him back for a moment so that she could glance in through the tap-room window and compose herself. The tap room stretched away from the front of the building, culminating at the far end in a doorway that seemed to lead to the kitchen, and a wooden staircase that led up to a gallery that crossed the room on the floor above. There were still a number of guests seated at the white-clothed tables, and several serving girls were bringing plates of food and tankards and bottles of drink. There was a long trestle counter on which a good selection of cold dishes had been set out, and behind it reposed a burly man who looked as if he must be the landlord. His apron was starched and very white, and his shirt sleeves were rolled up because he was standing close to the fireplace, where a roaring birchwood fire glowed in the hearth.

A rosy-faced woman in a brown-and-white-striped woolen gown bustled from the kitchen door at the rear of the building. Her faded fair hair was coiled up in plaits beneath her mobcap, and she carried two plates of hot food, which she took up the staircase to the gallery, where Alison suddenly realized that there were other tables, although only one of them was in use. A large group of young army officers was playing cards and drinking schnapps, and everything about them suggested that they were from a very elite regiment. Their elegant uniforms were black with red cuffs and collars, and bright golden braiding, and they looked very dashing indeed.

A red-haired serving girl was waiting upon them, her warm blue eyes moving time and time again to one of the officers in particular, who, although only in his twenties, appeared to be of a surprisingly high rank. He was blond and very handsome indeed, with strangely dark eyes for one who was otherwise so fair, and he lounged back in his chair without giving the adoring girl so much as a smile. She pouted, thrusting her voluptuous bosom forward as she leaned across him to pour some more schnapps into his glass. He glanced up at her for a moment. It was a cool glance, showing that he was fully aware that she was there for the plucking, and showing too that he was only mildly interested.

Billy touched Alison's arm. 'We should go in, miss.'

'Yes, of course.' She took a deep breath in readiness.

Billy hesitated. 'A word of advice, miss. When you're safely in your room, make the door fast.'

She stared at him. 'But Captain Merryvale assured me that this was a respectable place.'

'And so it is, miss,' he reassured her quickly, 'but I've just noticed that group of Russian officers up on the gallery, and they are renowned for the attention they pay to the ladies. Begging your pardon, miss, but I think it would be wise to lock yourself in. If there isn't a key, then wedge a chair under the door handle. It's better to be safe than sorry, that's what my mother always said.'

'If you really think I should . . .'

'I do, miss.'

'Then I'll do as you suggest.

'Let's go in.' Billy went up the stone steps and pushed open the door.

With some trepidation, Alison followed him inside.

2

Very little attention was paid to them as they entered, and it was a moment or so before the landlord left his place by the trestle counter to attend to them. Billy began to explain everything in halting Swedish, and as the landlord expressed astonishment to learn of the loss of the *Duchess of Albemarle*, an event that evidently hadn't reached the inn, Alison glanced discreetly around. At a burst of sudden laughter from the Russian officers, she looked up toward the gallery, and as she did, she dislodged her hood so that it fell back for a moment, revealing her tangled hair. Quickly she pulled the hood forward again, but not before she'd caught the eye of the high-ranking young officer who had been receiving so much fruitless attention from the serving girl.

Tossing his cards down, he rose to his feet, coming to stand by the balustrade to look down. He was tall and of a strong, athletic build, and his face was almost boyishly handsome. His fair hair was a little more blond than Alison had realized, and his dark eyes were more than just unusual, they were positively arresting.

His uniform was very splendid, the black tunic liberally adorned with golden shoulder knots, gold braiding, and rich crimson trimmings. The light-blue cordon of St Andrew, Russia's highest order, lay over his right shoulder. There was a miniature of the new czar at his throat and there were several heavy rings on the hands he rested on the wooden balustrade. Alison guessed that he was about twenty-five years old, and that he was very well born, for there was an air of authority and assertiveness about him that spoke of a man who was accustomed to privilege and being obeyed.

When he had appeared at the balustrade, the room had fallen quiet, so that when he suddenly addressed the landlord in what sounded like immaculate Swedish, his voice carried very clearly indeed. He obviously asked about Alison, for the landlord indicated her as he replied at some length, and then there was a stir as the *Duchess of Albemarle*'s fate was mentioned. Several men left their tables and hurried out, evidently in the hope of still seeing something of the recent spectacle, and a buzz of conversation passed around the room.

The Russian officer walked slowly to the head of the staircase and then descended, and Alison could hear the jingle of his spurs. Behind him, the serving girl came to the balustrade, her eyes stormily jealous as she realized how interested he was in the newcomer in the green velvet cloak.

Halting in front of Alison, he sketched an elegant bow and spoke to her in faultless English. 'Prince Nikolai Ivanovich Naryshky, general in the Preobrazensky Regiment of the Czar's Imperial Guards,' he said, his glance moving over her. 'May I know who I'm addressing, Miss, er?'

Alison was a little startled to find herself speaking to a prince, but although she didn't know it, she was also supposed to be impressed by the name of the Preobrazensky Regiment, which was the most senior in the whole Russian army and membership of which carried kudos like no other. Hastily she sank into a curtsy, but to her dismay her cloak parted to reveal the unmistakable frill of a nightgown hem. 'Miss Clearwell,' she replied, color rushing into her cheeks.

His dark eyes perceived the telltale white, just as shortly before they'd perceived the brief glimpse of unpinned hair. He smiled a little. 'You appear to have come ashore in something of a hurry, Miss Clearwell.'

'I think that the landlord has explained my situation, sir,' she replied, struggling to regain her poise.

'Ah, yes, what a very unfortunate accident, but then ships can so easily be set alight, can they not? Tell me, wasn't the *Duchess of Albemarle* on her way to St Petersburg?'

'Yes, she was.'

'Which means that you are also going there?'

'Yes.'

He smiled again. 'But now you have to wait here in Stockholm?'

'Only until the morning, when arrangements will be made for me to continue my journey on the *Pavlovsk*,' she replied, wishing that he wasn't so obviously probing.

'I wish that I was about to return to St Petersburg, but I fear that official duties are contriving to keep me here.'

'Official duties?'

'I have the signal honor to be the czar's representative at talks with King Gustavus Adolphus here in Stockholm, but it is an honor I would gladly forgo in order to be at home in St Petersburg.'

'I can understand that, sir,' she replied, wondering how she should be addressing him. Was he to be called 'your highness?' or 'excellency?' There were so many princes in Russia, and they weren't of royal blood, for the sons or descendants of the czars were all grand-dukes – that much she remembered from Miss Wright's interminable lessons on etiquette and correct form – but the actual matter of how to address a Russian prince had somehow slipped her memory completely. All she could do was continue to address him very politely as 'sir' and wait for him to correct her if he was in any way offended, which for the moment he didn't appear to be.

'Have you been to St Petersburg before, Miss Clearwell?' he asked, evidently being disposed to stand in polite conversation.

The color still burned on her cheeks and she wished he'd leave her alone, but she managed another polite smile. 'No, sir, I've never been there before.'

'I'm sure you haven't, for I feel certain that I would have remembered beauty such as yours,' he said softly. 'How glad I am that the war is over, for I had forgotten how very lovely English women are.'

'You're very gallant, sir,' she replied, silently wishing him to perdition for keeping all attention upon her when she wished to be as discreet as possible.

Something of her thoughts must have shown in her eyes, for suddenly he apologized. 'Forgive me, Miss Clearwell, for I did not mean to keep you talking like this.' He turned to the landlord and spoke swiftly to him in Swedish. The man bowed, took her valise from Billy, and then hurried away up the staircase, calling to the jealous serving girl to go with him.

The prince returned his attention to Alison. 'A suitable room will soon be in readiness, Miss Clearwell. Would you care for some refreshment? A light supper perhaps? Or just a little coffee?'

'I don't require anything at all, sir, just a room,' she replied, sensing that acceptance of the offer would entail taking said refreshment in his company. For all his courteousness, she didn't like him, finding his smile too easy, his tongue too glib, and his glance too knowing. He might be a prince, but he most certainly wasn't a gentleman.

He turned to Billy. 'That will be all, you may go,' he said shortly.

Billy backed uneasily away, his glance moving toward Alison, whom he didn't wish to leave to this Russian's attentions. But under the circumstances, there was very little he could do about it.

As the sailor withdrew into the alley and hurried away, the prince looked at Alison again. 'What is your opinion of Bonaparte, Miss Clearwell?' he asked suddenly.

Her lips parted in surprise, for it was a most unexpected question, but she responded as Miss Wright had firmly instructed when one was faced with such an inquiry. 'Sir, I'm afraid that I never discuss politics or religion, for it is my unhappy experience that even those who see eye to eye on the subject can somehow fall out.'

'What a very tactful and diplomatic reply, Miss Clearwell.'

The landlord and the serving girl were returning, and the prince smiled at Alison. 'Go with Agnetha, Miss Clearwell, and she will conduct you to your room. I trust that you and I will see each other in the morning, for I am staying here.'

'I'm sure we'll see each other then, sir,' she replied. 'Thank you for your kind assistance tonight.'

'Not at all, Miss Clearwell. *A bientôt.*'

She hesitated, for there was something in his voice that she suddenly found a little disturbing, but the serving girl was beckoning to her and so she followed her up the staircase. At the top the other Russian officers all gazed at her, and she saw them exchanging meaningful glances as she passed.

Agnetha paused to pick up a lighted candlestick from a table and then led her down a passage toward the rooms at the front of the inn, overlooking the alley.

Down in the tap room, Prince Nikolai remained where he was. His dark eyes were pensive, and there was a faint curve on his lips as he contemplated the undoubted charms that lay beneath the young Englishwoman's green velvet cloak. She was so very beautiful, and so delightfully innocent and untouched, just the thing to sharpen his somewhat jaded appetite. She was also so providently alone, without a maid or chaperon of any kind to protect her, and for the rest of the night she would be beneath this roof. The thought of enjoying her was far too enticing to deny, and before the dawn he meant to have possessed her.

Unaware of the dangerous desire she'd kindled, Alison followed Agnetha to the room that had been quickly prepared for her. It was a large but plain chamber warmed by a newly lit fire that still spat and crackled so much that a wire guard had had to be placed before it. A four-branched candelabrum stood on the mantelpiece, and Agnetha lit it with the candle she had brought with her.

Alison glanced around. There was a cumbersome four-poster bed hung with faded blue brocade, a heavy wardrobe, a washstand with a looking glass, and a comfortable armchair by the fireplace. The floorboards, painted brown, had been scattered with homemade rugs, and the whitewashed walls were decorated close to the ceiling with a frieze of pretty green, red, and blue flowers. Curtains of the same blue brocade as the bed were hung at the tall window and had been drawn firmly across to shut the cold night out. Everything was bathed in a warm flickering light, and would have looked welcoming had it not been for the circumstances under which Alison had arrived at the inn.

Agnetha went to the door, turning to give Alison another look of jealous loathing, and as she went out, Alison went relievedly to lock the door behind her. To her dismay there wasn't a key. Remembering Billy's advice about securing the door, she dragged the armchair from its place by the fire and wedged the back under the door handle. Then she stepped back, feeling safe at last.

Turning, she went to the windows, drawing the curtains aside to look out. As she did so, she realized that they weren't windows, but glazed French doors that gave on to one of the wooden balconies she'd noticed from the alley. Pulling the doors open, she stepped outside into the brittle night air. The balcony was flanked on either

side by those of the adjoining rooms, both of which were in darkness.
The alley below was empty. Pools of light fell across it from the tap-
room windows, and similar lights were still illuminated in other
hostelries farther toward the quay, but there weren't any people
around now. Stockholm seemed to have almost settled down for the
night, but already the first faint gray of dawn was beginning to creep
over the sky to the east. There was something strange about such brief
nights.

Drawing back inside, she closed the French doors again, but they
wouldn't close properly, and then she noticed a little wedge of folded
paper that had fallen to the floor when she had opened them. The
catch was broken and the wedge of paper was to keep them as closed
as possible. With a sigh she put the paper in the place that seemed the
most effective, then she drew the curtains across again.

Her valise had been left on the bed, and she went to look in it, to
see what she had managed to pack in the few panic-stricken moments
she had had before fleeing the ship. She took out a rose dimity gown
with long sleeves and a demure lace-filled neckline, a black-and-
white-checked wool gown with full wrist-length sleeves, and a fringed
white shawl. There was also a brush and comb, some pins, her bottle
of lavender water, a length of white satin ribbon, and a straw bonnet
adorned with artificial forget-me-nots. She hadn't thought of gloves,
stockings, her reticule, a pelisse, or her spencer, just those few things
and that wretched, wretched gothic book! Why, oh, why, had the
book come to hand instead of her reticule, which contained a pair of
scissors, a needle and thread, a vial of scent, a handkerchief, a pencil
and little notebook, and the emerald ring her father had sent to her
on her sixteenth birthday. Her breath caught in dismay, for the ring
would now lie forever at the bottom of Stockholm harbor.

Blinking back sudden tears, she set aside the dimity gown and the
shawl, meaning to change into them instead of remaining in her
nightgown, which made her feel so ill-at-ease and vulnerable. As she
had known on the rowing boat, she wouldn't be able to sleep again
tonight, not after all that had happened, and so she meant to dress,
pin up her hair neatly, and try to read the book that had managed to
take foolish precedence over other much more important items.

There was a washstand in a corner, with a cracked mirror and a large bowl and jug of cold water. She hadn't noticed it before because it had been behind her when first she had glanced around the room. As she stepped out of her cloak and nightgown, she went quickly to pour some water and give her face and hands a quick wash. She shivered, moving over to the fireplace to dry herself, and then she quickly put on the rose dimity, struggling with its interminable row of hooks and eyes, which required contortions to do up properly.

Laying the cloak on the floor near the fire so that it would keep warm and aired, she repacked the valise, after first dabbing some of the lavender water behind her ears, and then took her hairbrush, comb, and pins to the washstand to see what she could achieve with her hair, which was willful and difficult at the best of times.

She stared at her reflection in the mirror. What would Miss Wright say if she could see her now? And what would Pamela say – Pamela, who never had a shining dark curl out of place and whose clothes were always the immaculate height of perfect fashion? If Pamela had had to flee from a burning ship in the middle of the night, she would never emerge from the experience looking anything but flawless. Pamela was always faultless, always the epitome of poise and beauty, and on the day she married handsome Lord Buckingham, she would be a breathtakingly lovely bride.

With a sigh, Alison began to draw the hairbursh through her tangled hair, but as she did so, she was sure she heard a stealthy sound at the door. She turned quickly and was in time to see the door handle turning slowly. Her heart almost stopped with alarm, for as the handle then turned the other way, she knew that someone was trying to get in.

She pressed fearfully back against the washstand, the hairbrush almost slipping from her suddenly cold fingers. Her mouth ran dry and she could hear her heart beating fearfully as she stared at the door, praying that the chair would prevent it from opening.

For what seemed an age the would-be intruder kept trying the handle, but then it stopped moving. Alison's lips trembled, and her gray eyes remained large and frightened as she watched and waited for something that would tell her that whoever it was had gone away. The moments ticked by, and she went to the door, leaning past the chair to press her ear to the wood. The passage outside seemed deserted, for the only sound she heard was the distant clatter of the tap room and a burst of laughter from the Russian officers on the gallery.

Slowly she backed away from the door, going to sit weakly on the edge of the bed and dropping the hairbrush on the coverlet beside her. She pressed her trembling hands to her cheeks, trying to quell the torrent of fear that still coursed through her. What might have happened if she hadn't followed Billy's advice? What fate might she now be enduring at the intruder's hands? A sob rose in her throat. Bath seemed a million miles away, as did everything else that she knew and loved, and she wished desperately that she had stood up to Miss Wright on the whole matter of this horrid, horrid journey.

She struggled to collect herself, but as she did so, a sudden breath of breeze outside dislodged the French doors. They blew open, the curtains billowing, as if someone was standing behind them. A terrified squeak escaped Alison's lips, and she leapt up from the bed, staring at the curtains, but then she realized it was just the draft. At the same time she heard someone speaking in the alley below. It was an Englishman with a refined, well-spoken voice, and he was uttering a far-from-refined English oath, albeit in an amiable tone.

'The devil take you for a damned Swedish rogue and horse thief.'

'But it's true, my lord, I swear it upon my life,' replied another man, a Swedish gentleman by the sound of it. 'The horse got up and deliberately pushed the fellow into the river with its nose. I saw it with my own eyes, and I happen to know that that villain has never raised a crop to a horse again.'

The Englishman laughed, and it was such a comforting and reassuring sound that Alison hurried out on to the balcony.

The two men had paused outside the inn and were clearly visible in the light from the tap-room windows. The Swedish gentleman was dressed in a brown tight-fitting coat and beige breeches, with an extravagant brown-and-cream-spotted neckcloth blossoming at his throat. A matching handkerchief protruded from his hip pocket, and he stood in a rather foppish pose, flicking another handkerchief over a sleeve that appeared to be immaculate. He was of medium height and was passably good-looking, with a tall top hat tipped rakishly back on his froth of light-brown Apollo curls. He was about twenty-one years old and obviously thought himself very much the thing, but when set beside the stylishness and devilish good looks of his English companion, he was practically insignificant.

The Englishman looked as if he might just have strolled down a Mayfair pavement instead of a medieval alley in Stockholm, and his clothes were all that one would expect of Bond Street's superlative tailors. A long charcoal greatcoat with an astrakhan collar rested nonchalantly around the shoulders of his burgundy coat, and he wore a silver brocade waistcoat and a gray silk neckcloth that was plentiful without being as excessive as that worn by his companion. His skin-tight cream breeches vanished into shining black top boots, and he carried a pair of gray kid gloves in his left hand. A signet ring graced one of his fingers, a golden seal dangled from his fob, and a pearl pin nestled tastefully in the discreet folds of the neckcloth. He was the personification of masculine style and elegance, and when he removed his top hat to run his fingers through his thick coal-black hair, Alison found herself gazing down at the most devastatingly handsome man she'd ever seen.

He was in his late twenties or early thirties, and his face was fine-boned and even-featured, with a complexion that was tanned from many hours spent in the open air. He had a rugged cleft in his chin, and his firm lips looked as if they would be quick to smile. His eyes were dark-lashed and of a particularly vivid blue, a fact that she could see in the light from the tap room. He wore his rather wayward black hair a little longer than might have been expected, for in London at the moment it was the fashion for gentlemen to have their hair cut very short indeed.

Alison stared down at him. She felt as if she'd suddenly awakened from a long sleep, because for the first time in her life she was conscious of an almost irresistible feeling of attraction. She was like a moth to a flame, longing to be burned. And she didn't even know who he was.

3

Unaware of the silent scrutiny to which they were being subjected from the balcony overhead, the two men continued their conversation. It concerned thoroughbred horses, a subject on which both appeared to be very knowledgeable indeed.

The Swedish gentleman was proud of a brood mare the Englishman had just purchased from his father, and he didn't hesitate to sing the animal's praises. 'You will not regret purchasing the mare, my lord, for I promise you that the foal she carries is bred for stamina.'

'I know that now, since your father was at last persuaded to let me see the stud books,' replied the Englishman somewhat dryly. 'What dark secret is he trying to keep hidden? He's like a miser with his hoard.'

His Swedish friend laughed. 'He is a shrewd man, my lord, and keeps his own counsel. When he chose to show you the stud books, he paid you a great compliment.'

'As I paid him when I chose to buy the mare,' came the frank reply.

'That is very true. So, after a lack of success in France, Belgium, Holland, and Denmark, your expedition so far has only resulted in this one purchase. I trust that you are more fortunate in St Petersburg, although I understand that there are only one or two significant animals in the imperial stables.'

'There is one chestnut colt that is of great interest to me, since it's descended from the red Barbary stallion the czar's great-grandfather acquired in Syria. I have the promise of an audience with his imperial majesty, and I trust I will be able to, er, persuade him that the colt would be a shining example of Russian stud management if allowed to run on English turf.'

'If anyone can persuade him, you can, my lord,' replied the

Swedish gentleman, but then he shook his head doubtfully. 'I am told that Czar Alexander is an indifferent horseman, and is therefore not likely to show a great deal of interest. He is much more concerned these days with the many whims of his mistress, the Countess Irina.'

'So I understand,' murmured the Englishman.

'Well, my lord, perhaps we should adjourn to the quay, for the *Pavlovsk* may have arrived by now.'

'And she may not. No, my friend. When she arrives, my luggage will be duly taken on board and placed in the cabin reserved for me, but I mean to spend the rest of the night in a comfortable bed in a comfortable inn. This inn, to be precise.' He indicated the Dog and Flute.

The Swedish gentleman pursed his lips. 'Where it just so happens that you might encounter the czar's envoy, Prince Naryshky?'

'The possibility had occurred to me, yes,' the Englishman replied.

His friend glanced around and then dropped his voice considerably, so much so that Alison had to strain to hear. 'My lord, you would be wise to avoid him at all costs, for he is dangerous, scheming, capricious, high-handed, and always acts in his own interests. There is no one more treacherous and devious than he, and it is said that the devil would be the one requiring the long spoon were any supping to be done with this particular Russian princeling.'

Alison's eyes widened with surprise that anyone could speak so indiscreetly and unflatteringly about a man like the prince, especially in a place as public as an alley in the middle of Stockholm. If she could hear, who else might be doing just the same?

The Englishman had also lowered his voice. 'Naryshky can hardly be described as a princeling, my friend, for he is now one of the most influential men in St Petersburg.'

'Only because his sister, the Countess Irina, graces the czar's bed. If it were not for that fact, Naryshky would simply be another strutting aristocrat in the famous Preobrazensky Regiment. He owes his grand rank to her, and he wouldn't stand nearly so high in Czar Alexander's favor were it not for her constant importuning. Naryshky owes nothing to his own talents, of that you may be sure. Oh, he thinks he's set to be a great man, and his vanity is such that he even made a bid for the hand of the czar's sister, the Grand-Duchess Helen, but not even Alexander is besotted enough to bestow such grandeur upon his mistress's swaggering brother.'

'You speak as if you know a great deal about him.'

'Everyone in Stockholm knows Naryshky, my lord, for whenever he has come here, his activities have made him much despised. He is without conscience and without morals, and our authorities never raise a protest because King Gustavus Adolphus wishes to court the new czar, and the new czar is disposed to show great favor to Naryshky. Take my advice, my lord, stay somewhere else tonight, somewhere well away from Nikolai Ivanovich Naryshky, who is no admirer of the British.'

'My mind is made up, I fear.'

The Swedish gentleman shrugged regretfully. 'As you wish, my friend. So, now we must bid each other farewell.'

'Perhaps not farewell, for I would consider it a great honor and pleasure if you and your father were to visit me in England. I can promise you a very hospitable welcome, one of the best studs in the country, and some excellent days' racing.'

'Your invitation will be accepted with alacrity, my lord. I wish you *bon voyage*.'

The two men shook hands and then the Swedish gentleman walked quickly away in the direction of the quay. The Englishman watched him for a moment and then turned to look at the brightly lit tap-room windows. His blue eyes were thoughtful, then he tapped his top hat on his head and went swiftly up the steps into the inn.

Alison lingered on the balcony. The Englishman's name hadn't been mentioned at all, beyond the fact that he'd been addressed as 'my lord,' and so she had no idea who he was, but she was bound to find out, either at breakfast in the morning or certainly on board the *Pavlovsk*. She wondered if he was married. Surely he must be, for how could such a man have eluded the wiles of some determined woman? Someone as good-looking and undoubtedly charming as he must constantly receive flattering attention from the opposite sex. She gazed down at the spot where he had been, thinking that it was very doubtful indeed that such a man would so much as glance at a green girl straight out of a Bath academy for young ladies.

She shivered a little, suddenly realizing that she'd been standing out in the bitter cold for quite some time in only her gown and shawl. The gray of dawn had now illuminated the eastern sky much more, and soon Stockholm would be bathed in that pale silver light that was neither day nor night. She didn't like these short nights, for they didn't invite a deep restorative slumber, but rather filled one with an odd sort of restlessness. What she would do in St Petersburg she didn't know, for she'd been told that from the end of June until the beginning of July there was hardly any night at all, just half an hour of strangely subdued light between sunset and sunrise. It had sounded novel when she heard of it in England, but now that she had begun to experience the ever-shortening hours of darkness this far north, she didn't like it at all.

With a last glance down into the alley where she had seen the hand-some English lord, she turned and went back into her room. She closed the French doors as firmly as she could, using the wedge of paper, and then she drew the curtains. Still feeling uncomfortably cold, she hurried to the fire, holding out her hands to the warmth of the flames. Gradually she felt better and so went to finish brushing and pinning her hair, achieving a reasonably creditable knot at the back of her head. It had always been Miss Wright's policy to teach her young ladies how to attend to their own toilette, for the headmistress warned that there might come a time when a maid wasn't to hand, and a lady's hair must always be perfect. Most of the pupils had resented such lessons, for the daughters of earls and dukes would never be without the services of a maid, but now Alison was glad of the lessons, for her maid had left her in order to be married and she wouldn't have another until she reached St Petersburg.

Before going to sit on the bed with her book, she tested the armchair's firmness under the door handle. It didn't move at all, and she was satisfied that it would serve its purpose until it was time for her to go down to breakfast. Drawing her shawl more warmly around her shoulders, she propped the pillows against the back of the bed and then made herself comfortable, pulling the coverlet lightly over her knees. With a sigh she opened the book, wishing again that it was now at the bottom of the harbor instead of her precious reticule.

A serving girl hurried past the door to the next room, and Alison heard the unmistakable sound of the fire being prepared. Could it mean that the Englishman was to occupy the room? She looked up from the book, and as she did so, she was sure she heard the door of the other adjoining room open and close very softly indeed. Her eyes flew toward the other wall, but she heard nothing more; then the serving girl hurried away again, her light footsteps diminishing along the corridor.

Alison sat very still, listening carefully, but there wasn't a sound from the other adjoining room. After a moment, just as she was about to resume reading her book, voices approached, and she recognized that of the Englishman. He was conducted to the room next to hers, where the fire had been lit, and then the serving girl hurried away again. The Englishman closed the door firmly.

Alison suddenly felt much safer, knowing that a fellow countryman was in the next room. Should she approach him and tell him that someone had tried to enter her room? Putting the book aside, she got up from the bed and went to pull the armchair aside, but even as she pushed it back into place by the fire, she knew that it wouldn't do at all to approach a total stranger in the middle of the night in an inn. Indeed, such a move would be considered most improper, especially when the incident concerned had long since past, and if the truth be known, she didn't even know if the would-be intruder had meant to enter her room. What if someone had been attempting to keep an assignation and had then realized his mistake and gone away? It could be as simple as that, and she'd allowed her imagination to run away with her.

She glanced back toward the door. Should she push the wretched armchair back to wedge the handle? As she stood there undecided what to do, again she heard a soft, stealthy noise, and this time it didn't come from one of the adjoining rooms, but apparently from her balcony. A cold finger of fear touched her, and she turned slowly, her frightened gaze drawn toward the windows. As she looked, she saw the curtains tremble a little. It wasn't the slight motion caused by the breeze having opened the glazed doors, but the surreptitious movement made by someone hiding there. She'd left the tiniest crack between the two curtains, and she knew that someone was observing her through it.

With a stifled cry she fled toward the door, but before she could reach it, the curtains were flung aside and Prince Nikolai dashed across the room to seize her, forcing his hand over her mouth to silence her.

'Don't be foolish, Miss Clearwell, for I mean you no harm,' he breathed.

Terrified, she could only stare at him. Her strength seemed to have deserted her, and she couldn't even struggle to save herself. Her heart was pounding unbearably in her breast, and her whole body was ice cold with dread.

His dark eyes were intense, and his hand was still pressed roughly over her mouth. 'I don't wish to hurt you, Miss Clearwell, so I want you to promise me that you will not scream if I take my hand away. Do I have your promise?'

For a moment she couldn't respond, but then she managed to nod.

Slowly he removed his hand, but he still held her in a viselike grip from which she couldn't possibly have escaped. His lips were only inches from hers, and he held her body against his. He could smell the lavender water she used, and he found it arousing. 'How very resourceful of you to put the chair against the door, Miss Clearwell, for at first it confounded my efforts, but then I remembered that the adjoining rooms are unoccupied and that earlier today I heard the landlord mention that he would have to send for a locksmith to mend the doors on to your balcony. Dame Fortune is determined to place you in my hands tonight.'

'Please let me go,' she whispered, terrified.

'Let you go? My dear Miss Clearwell, I will only do that when I've enjoyed your charms to the full.'

'No! Please, no!' She tried to pull away.

'Don't be foolish, Miss Clearwell, for there is so much pleasure to be had. I intend to possess you, and I will do so whether you struggle or whether you consent. Of course, it would be so much better if you consented, because it would please me to introduce you to the delights of making love.'

'Please leave me alone,' she begged, tears stinging her eyes.

'Leave you all on your own? What gentleman of honor would do that?' he murmured, a sensuous smile curving his lips.

She stared at him, and then, from out of nowhere, inspiration came to her. 'I – I'm not alone, sir,' she said, the plot of her book suddenly coming to mind.

A quick suspicious light passed through his eyes, but then he gave a soft laugh. 'Oh, but you are, my dear. You're totally alone and unprotected.'

A jumble of thoughts milled in her head, and she strove with all her might to sort them into a believable story. 'I may appear to be alone, sir, but the truth is that I traveled from England with my chaperone, who left me earlier today in order to run off with a Swedish nobleman. But I am still not alone, because I've come to Stockholm to meet the man I'm to marry, and we're traveling on to St Petersburg on the *Pavlovsk* because the *Duchess of Albemarle* sank. We're running away to be married, sir, because my father wishes me to enter an arranged match with a man I detest, and in St Petersburg we are sure that my uncle will lend us his assistance.'

Nikolai was a little startled, but then his eyes narrowed. 'Your uncle? Would that be Thomas Clearwell, who resides on English Quay?'

Dismay lanced through her, for she hadn't thought that he might be acquainted with her relative, but she was trapped now and didn't dare to deny it. 'Yes,' she said. 'Do – do you know him?'

'I know of him.' His eyes were very dark and suspicious. 'Where is this so-called lover, Miss Clearwell? I do not see him, do you?' He glanced mockingly around the room.

Her heart was pounding. 'We're observing propriety, sir, and although he stayed at the quayside to assist Captain Merryvale after the ship sank, he has now joined me here and is at this very moment in the next room. Perhaps you heard him arrive? He'll be wondering why I haven't tapped the wall so signify that I am all right. I – I'm sure that at any moment he'll come to the door.'

The prince hesitated, for he had indeed heard someone arrive in the next room. She thought she had convinced him, but another slow, unpleasant smile returned to Nikolai's lips. 'Oh, my dear Miss Clearwell, how very inventive you are. First there was the business with the armchair, and now we have this string of commendably plausible lies. My respect for Englishwomen has increased immeasurably, for they are most stimulating.'

'I'm not lying,' she whispered. 'I'm telling you the truth.' Fresh terror had plunged through her, for she knew that she hadn't deterred him at all and that she was completely at his mercy.

He pressed her even closer, suddenly forcing hungry fierce kisses upon her mouth. His hands moved over her, touching her breasts and sliding down to caress her thighs, and all the time he was bearing her toward the bed. She was helpless, unable to do anything but struggle futilely in his far superior grasp.

Suddenly there was a loud knock at the door. Nikolai leapt away from her, whirling about toward the sound. Alison stumbled backward, grabbing at the bedpost to prevent herself from falling. She was so confused in that moment that she remained silent.

A voice called from the corridor. 'Alison? Are you there?'

It was the Englishman. Thunderstruck, she stared at the door. Why had he interrupted at such a providential moment, and what was more, how could he possibly know her name?

Nikolai's hand slid softly inside his uniform jacket, and she realized that he had a weapon concealed there, a pistol or a dagger. His dark eyes were filled with warning as he looked at her. 'So, you have a lover, after all,' he murmured. 'Be well advised now that it would be extremely foolish if you said or did anything concerning what has just happened. If you don't wish any harm to come to your lover, you'd better invent another plausible story to explain my presence. Do I make myself abundantly clear?'

Her eyes were huge and frightened, and she nodded.

'Then admit him.' As he spoke, he moved to stand with his back to the fireplace, his hands clasped almost casually behind his back.

Trembling so much that she felt weak, she went to the door. As she opened it, the Englishman stepped swiftly in, bewildering her still more by sweeping her into his arms and kissing her passionately on the lips, and she was too stunned to do anything but submit.

He took his time over the kiss, his fingers curling richly in the warm hair at the nape of her neck. It was the practiced kiss of a man who'd made love to many women, and who knew full well how to give pleasure. To all intents and purposes, it was also the kiss of a man who was deeply and irrevocably in love with the woman he held in his arms, and to Nikolai, who stood watching, it must have been very convincing indeed.

To Alison it was a breathless, heart-stopping moment of self-knowledge, for in spite of the danger that was still all around, she could feel herself responding to the caresses of this man whose identity was still a mystery.

4

For several seconds she was utterly powerless to resist, trapped both by confusion and by the strangely beguiling feelings that stirred through her at his touch. But then she remembered Nikolai's whispered warning, and a cold sanity swept over her. She pulled away from her rescuer's arms, turning swiftly to indicate the prince.

'Darling, we aren't alone. Please allow me to present you to Prince Nikolai Ivanovich Naryshky, who has been the very personification of gallantry ever since I arrived here. Not only did he act as my interpreter, but when a thief was apprehended in the inn a short while ago, he was so concerned for my safety that he came to see that I was all right. I am truly in his debt.' While her face gave nothing away, inwardly she marveled at the ease with which she concocted the story. It seemed that tonight she'd discovered a considerable gift for telling believable lies.

The Englishman's clear blue eyes rested lightly on the Russian. 'If Miss Clearwell is in your debt, sir, then so am I. Francis, Lord Buckingham, your servant, sir.' He sketched an elegant bow.

How Alison managed to conceal her shock she didn't know. Lord Buckingham? The man who was soon to be betrothed to Pamela? Suddenly she understood how he knew her first name. Somehow he'd overheard what was happening to her, he'd heard her addressed as Miss Clearwell, and he'd heard mention of her uncle, Thomas Clearwell. Through Pamela, and probably through William as well, he knew all about her unwanted visit to St Petersburg, and an astonishing stroke of luck had brought him to this inn when she was so desperately in need of rescue.

Nikolai hadn't noticed her reaction, for his attention was on Francis. 'I am honored to make your acquaintance, my lord, but it seems to me that your name is known to me already. Are you not going to St Petersburg in the hope of purchasing a colt from the imperial stables?'

'That was my original purpose, yes, but as you can see, I now have other reasons for going as well,' replied Francis, reaching across to take Alison's hand and draw it tenderly to his lips.

Nikolai smiled a little. 'I can think of no sweeter reason in all the world, my lord, for in Miss Clearwell you have a prize beyond compare.'

'I am daily more conscious of my great good fortune,' murmured Francis, smiling into her eyes as if he adored her with all his heart.

Somehow she managed to return the smile, but in truth she was suddenly very close to losing her nerve. So much had happened to her since leaving England that she'd been finding it a terrible strain even before the fire on the *Duchess of Albemarle,* but now she'd been forced to stay at an inn, she'd almost suffered a vile fate at the prince's hands, and finally she was having to pretend that Francis Buckingham was indeed the fictitious lover she'd invented on the spur of the moment to save herself from unwelcome advances.

Nikolai continued to smile agreeably. 'My lord, I seem to recall that you approached his imperial majesty some time ago concerning the colt; indeed, I believe your letter arrived when the peace discussions had barely begun.'

Francis nodded. 'I am a loyal Englishman, sir, but I am also a devotee of the turf, and my stud at Newmarket is acknowledged to be one of the finest in Britain. The recent regrettable war interfered most devilishly with my plans to improve my bloodstock, and the moment the whiff of peace was in the air, I wrote to every important stud in Europe. I've visited France, Belgium, Holland, and Denmark, where I was dismally unsuccessful, but here in Sweden I've acquired the sweetest brood mare imaginable, and I have high hopes of the foal she carries. Now only St Petersburg remains, and I sincerely hope that his imperial majesty will still kindly grant me the promised audience, but I know that he has so much to do that a mere Englishman's desire to purchase a thoroughbred colt cannot figure highly on his agenda.'

'On the contrary, my lord, if the czar has promised you the audience, then only exceptional circumstances will compel him to cancel it. I am close to him and believe I can boast that I know him well.'

'I am sure that he holds you in very high regard, sir, for he has entrusted you with responsibility for talks that I understand are of considerable importance.' Francis spoke with clever flattery, his tone and words astutely calculated to appeal to Nikolai's overweening vanity. Nikolai himself wasn't held in very high regard – his sister was – and the Stockholm talks weren't important, they were humdrum. But it did not harm to let the Russian believe that he, Francis, was impressed.

Nikolai gave a gracious nod that spoke volumes of his conceit, and then he came to take Alison's hand, drawing it to his lips. 'I must bid you both good night now, for I am expected at the palace in the morning and so must get what sleep I can. I trust we will meet at breakfast, but if not, I wish you both every happiness for the future.'

Alison smiled, but it was all she could do not to snatch her hand away.

He bowed to Francis, who returned the salute, and then he withdrew, closing the door softly behind him.

They heard the jingle of his spurs as he walked away, and as the sound died away, Francis suddenly clenched his fist and beat it once against the jamb. 'Damn,' he said under his breath. 'Damn it to hell and back, for Naryshky is the last man I wished to tangle with.'

Alison looked at him in bewilderment. 'But you wished to meet him. I overheard you say so.'

'Meet, yes, tangle with, no.' He turned toward her. 'So, you were eavesdropping earlier, were you?'

'Yes, as I have to believe you must have been as well, for that is the only way you could have known what was happening in here and who I was.'

He nodded. '*Touché*. When I was shown to my room, my first act was to go out on to the balcony, where I was just in time to see the prince enter your room. My curiosity being aroused I climbed over on to your balcony to listen. When it became plain that he wasn't about to be deterred, I deemed it to be time for your lover to make an appearance.' Then he smiled a little. 'I'm pleased to make your acquaintance, Miss Clearwell.'

'And I yours, my lord.'

His eyes were very vivid and blue in the mixture of fire and candle-light. 'Why are you here all on your own?'

'I'm not alone through choice, I promise you, sir,' she replied. Then she explained all that had befallen her since leaving England. 'So you see,' she finished, 'I've hardly chosen to stay in this horrid inn, and I didn't exactly lie to the prince when I said that you and I would be going on to St Petersburg.'

'Or when you said we were both going to your Uncle Thomas,' he observed.

She stared at him. 'I – I beg your pardon?'

'Surely you knew? I've been invited to stay at the Clearwell residence on English Quay during my stay. I can't imagine that Pamela didn't inform you . . .' He broke off a little ruefully. 'Perhaps she didn't, for she and I parted somewhat, er, acrimoniously, I fear. She didn't ask me where I would be staying, and I didn't inform her. So, Miss Clearwell, I am telling you now that you and I will be staying beneath the same roof in St Petersburg, thanks to the sterling efforts of your cousin William, who insisted upon it the moment he learned I was hoping to have an audience with the czar. I can only trust that that audience still takes place.'

She was confused. 'But why on earth shouldn't it?'

'Because I may just have crossed Naryshky.'

'What difference does that make? The prince is here in Stockholm—'

'But his reach is very long and very swift, I promise you. Forgive me if what I'm about to say is rather direct, but the fact is that Naryshky's desirous gaze has fallen upon you, Miss Clearwell, and thanks to my intervention, he was denied his pleasure. I trust that his agreeable manner on taking his leave is proof that he bears no malice, but if he does, then it would be very easy for him to send word to his sister, the Countess Irina, requesting her to see to it that the czar no longer gives me the time of day.'

'The countess is the czar's—'

'Inamorata? Yes, she is, and she won't need a great deal of persuading to confound any British plan, even one so insignificant as my approach concerning a colt in the imperial stables.'

'Why do the prince and his sister hate the British as much as it seems they do?'

'They are both fervent admirers of Bonaparte, and the Countess Irina regards the British as the murderers of her beloved husband, Count Axel von Strelitz, a Prussian nobleman who happened to be on board the French flagship *L'Orient* when it was blown up by Nelson at the Battle of the Nile in '98. Of the thousand men on board, only sixty survived, and although the French and British navies were engaged in battle, the countess is disposed to believe that the sinking of the *L'Orient* was a deliberate act of savagery that amounted to nothing more or less than cold-blooded murder. She happened to love her husband very much, and she's been the implacable enemy of the British ever since. She would act in a moment if her dear brother asked her to, you may be sure of that.'

Alison searched his handsome face. There was much more to all this than the mere purchase of a colt; her every instinct told her there was, but she said nothing.

He was silent for a moment, his gaze averted to the fire, but then his eyes swung to meet hers again. 'You do realize that we'll have to maintain this pretense until the *Pavlovsk* leaves?'

'I hadn't thought—'

'Well, think now. We've just pretended to Naryshky that we're runaway lovers, and so the subterfuge must be kept up until we're away from him. It will be our secret, I promise you, for no one else need ever know what passed between us here. I trust that we will both be long since back in England by the time Naryshky returns to St Petersburg, for talks such as the ones he's involved in take a notoriously long time, and he's only just begun.'

'So, what you're saying is that we behave like eloping lovers until we leave Stockholm and then resume the normal relationship that would be expected of us after having encountered each other by chance on the journey?'

'That's exactly what I'm saying. Your reputation will thus be protected, and Pamela will not hear anything that might cause her to, er, wonder.' He smiled a little. 'Is it agreed, Miss Clearwell?'

She gave a slightly resigned laugh. 'Sir, I don't suppose I have a great deal of choice, just as I haven't had much choice about anything where this wretched journey is concerned. I didn't want to leave England, I wanted to go to Pamela, but I was made to leave, and now I loathe St Petersburg before I have even seen it. Besides, I can hardly refuse to do as you ask, since it's my fault that you've been compromised.'

His eyes were suddenly very shrewd. 'Miss Clearwell, if anyone has been compromised, surely it is you.'

'That isn't what I mean and you know it,' she replied. 'There's a great deal you're failing to tell me, isn't there? I don't know what your real purpose is in going to St Petersburg, but I doubt very much if it has anything to do with horses. Whatever it is, my arrival on the scene has put it in jeopardy, hasn't it?'

'What a very odd notion, to be sure,' he murmured. 'No, Miss Clearwell, you haven't jeopardized anything, because there isn't anything to jeopardize. I'm simply on my way to try to acquire a colt from the imperial stables.'

She didn't press the point, but she didn't believe him. He was concealing something.

A breeze stirred the curtains, and she remembered suddenly that when Nikolai had burst in he'd left the windows open. She went quickly to close them, searching around for the wedge of paper, but before she closed the doors properly, she paused to look out. The sky was now pale and clear, an almost citrus yellow that softened into a delicate turquoise, and yet it was still barely three o'clock. Pushing the folded paper into place, she made the doors as firm as she could, and then drew the curtains across once more, turning to face him.

'Would it be best if we called each other by our first names from now on? After all, if we're supposed to be—'

'Lovers? Yes, Alison, I think it would be best.'

She hesitated. 'Will you tell me one day?'

'Tell you? Tell you what?'

'What you're really going to St Petersburg for?'

'You're quite determined, aren't you?'

She nodded. 'I may be inexperienced and fresh out of school, sir, but I'm not a fool, and I certainly know when I'm being humbugged.'

He turned suddenly, glancing at the armchair by the fire and deliberately changed the subject. 'I think perhaps that I should sleep here for the rest of the night, don't you? I doubt if our Russian friend will attempt anything else, but there's no need to take unnecessary chances.'

She didn't know what to say, but she could well imagine what Miss Wright would have had to say. However, she knew that his intention was only to protect her.

He smiled at the various expressions crossing her face. 'I trust you don't fear that I, too, have dark designs upon you, Alison?'

'Of course not,' she said quickly, conscious of hot color rushing into her cheeks.

'Just remember that no one of consequence to either of us will ever hear about anything that's taken place here. Good night, Alison.' With that he went to the chair and flung himself into it, his long legs stretching out toward the fire. Leaning his head back, he ran his fingers through his dark hair and then closed his eyes.

Alison hesitated for a moment and then went to the bed, where she made herself as comfortable as possible in her previous position, the book open on her lap. She reflected upon the events of the past hour or so, and upon her shameful ability to tell exceedingly plausible fibs. But then it suddenly occurred to her that one didn't have to fib to avoid telling the truth; one could also change the subject and allow a question to remain unanswered, just as Francis had done when he'd disconcerted her by suggesting that he stay in her room overnight. There was something else behind his visit to St Petersburg, she was quite certain of that, even though he had yet to admit it.

She looked at him as he lounged back in the chair. His eyes were still closed, but she didn't know if he was asleep. His lashes were thick and dark and his coal-black hair was tousled because he'd just run his fingers through it, a habit of his she was to come to know in the ensuing days. Her glance lingered on his lips as she remembered how he had kissed her. Was it really possible that in the tension and fear of that moment, she found herself responding to him? When she had looked down from the balcony and gazed upon him for the first time, something strange had happened to her, something she had never encountered before, and she knew that nothing would ever be the same again.

She lowered her eyes. She envied Pamela, she envied her with all her heart.

5

The short Scandivanian night was at an end and the sun had risen
in the sky over Stockholm, but the city was still asleep. All was
quiet at the Dog and Flute, where the guests had long since gone to
their rooms and there was as yet no activity in the kitchens. In the tap
room, the only sounds were those made by the small boy whose duty
it was to look after the fire. He was scraping out the birchwood ashes
and shoveling them into a bucket.

Up on the gallery, Nikolai lounged alone at the table where he and
his companions had whiled away the night hours. The others had
retired now, but he had too much on his mind to think of sleep.
Agnetha had been there for the taking – she had made that plain
enough – but she didn't have ash-blonde hair and big gray eyes, nor
did she possess that beguiling air of innocence that aroused his desire
to fever pitch. Beguiling indeed, for the last thing that could really be
said of Miss Alison Clearwell was that she was innocent, for her lover
had remained in her room since he, Nikolai, had left.

Nikolai's dark eyes flickered as he riffled some playing cards in his
hands. His gleaming spurred boots rested on the tabletop, where
glasses, empty bottles, dice, and cards from the night's gaming still lay
scattered. A candle burned on in its holder, the flame sunk low in a
sea of melted wax. Little daylight penetrated the gallery, and the glow
of the candle shone on his gold-braided uniform and burnished his
blond hair with hints of copper as he pondered the intriguing question of the lovely young Englishwoman and her dashing lord. They
had taken him in completely; he had really believed their story, and
he would have continued to believe it had it not been for one small

slip on their part, and one small impulse on his. He didn't really know why he had bothered to ask the landlord anything – it had simply been idle curiosity – but nevertheless it had elicited a very disturbing discrepancy in their tale. Miss Clearwell had quite definitely said that Lord Buckingham would ask for the room adjoining hers, and that was indeed what appeared to have happened – except that the landlord said that the earl hadn't asked after the lady at all, let alone which room she was occupying. How, then, had they come to be placed in adjoining accommodations? How could the Englishman possibly have known which room to ask for? It was a mystery that became even more bothersome when subsequent discreet inquiries on board the *Pavlovsk*, which now lay at her mooring in the shadow of the royal palace, revealed that Lord Buckingham had always been booked to travel on her to St Petersburg, but that very hasty last-minute arrangements had been made for Miss Clearwell, who had originally, as she said, planned to sail on the doomed *Duchess of Albemarle*. The lady had been quite emphatic that they had been traveling on the *Duchess of Albemarle* and that they'd been forced to change their plans to go on the *Pavlovsk* instead. She'd been lying.

Nikolai drew a long pensive breath. He didn't like mysteries, especially when they involved the British, for his plans were as yet far from completely laid, and he was vulnerable to discovery. What if Lord Buckingham and his ladylove were British agents? It was a possibility he couldn't afford to ignore, for there was far too much at stake. He hadn't heard anything from his contact in the British embassy in St Petersburg in recent weeks; indeed, everything had been almost suspiciously quiet. Damn that clerk in Paris! Had he been sent too late to his watery grave in the Seine? Had he somehow managed to send his information to London, after all?'

A nerve twitched at Nikolai's temple and he tossed the cards on to the table, the draft causing the candle flame to shiver. He had to be cautious, for it could still be that the English lord and the lady were what they claimed to be. There was no arguing that Lord Buckingham's approach to the czar had been made months ago, too long ago for anything of consequence to have been discovered by the British, and that was a fact that should reassure him. And yet . . . Why were they telling lies? What were they hiding? Nikolai drew a long breath. He didn't trust them, and so he had to take every precaution. He had to stay here in Stockholm, but he could have them watched, both during the voyage and in St Petersburg itself, and the moment it became clear that they were involved in any intrigue, his overseer, Bragin, could be relied upon to see that they simply disappeared.

In the meantime, he could make certain that Lord Buckingham didn't gain the imperial audience he was at such pains to achieve. All it would take was a brief note to Irina. With hindsight, it seemed a mistake had been made in allowing the Englishman's communication to reach the czar in the first place, but it had seemed so very innocent and sincere an approach that no suspicion had been aroused. There would still have been no suspicion had it not been for the inconsistencies in the story he had been told tonight. If they were indeed British agents, it had been a clever move to add the delightful Miss Clearwell to the proceedings, for she was a wonderful diversion, with her beauty, her impression of unaffectedness and inexperience, and her enchanting vulnerability. Oh, she was perfection, he could not deny her that, but now he also knew that she was quick-witted and adaptable and that if she hadn't yielded before tonight, she had certainly yielded now, for what else was she doing at this very moment if not lying between the sheets with the so-handsome Lord Buckingham?

He exhaled slowly, for it was almost as if he could touch her now, the memory of her was so real. The scent of lavender had clung to her – such an English scent, at once sweet and piquant, fresh and heady – and her skin had been so flawless, pale, clear, without blemish. He sat forward suddenly, taking up two dice and shaking them for a moment before tossing them down. When they stopped rolling, he gave a low, satisfied laugh. Double six. Luck was with him.

A door opened and closed somewhere nearby and footsteps approached. They were the steps of a man wearing spurred military boots, and Nikolai looked up with a smile as he saw the slight uniformed figure and almost feline face of one of his fellow officers.

'Ah, Sergei Mikhailovich, my good and trusted friend, how very agreeable it is to see you this morning,' he murmured, his dark eyes shining with satisfaction, for Sergei Mikhailovich Golitsin was the very person he had chosen for certain tasks.

The other paused warily, for it wasn't like Nikolai to utter such an effusive and warm greeting. Sergei was a slender young man with brown hair and almond eyes that told of Tatar blood, and he was looking a little the worse for wear after a long night of drinking and making love. 'Good morning, sir,' he said carefully, for one could never be sure if one was Prince Naryshky's friend or his social and military inferior.

Nikolai gestured toward a chair. 'What's this "sir" business? Aren't we old friends?'

'I am a mere lieutenant, whereas you—'

'This morning we are friends, Sergei.'

Slowly Sergei took the proffered seat. 'What is it you want of me?' he asked, reaching for an almost empty bottle of schnapps and pouring the clear liquid into a glass.

'We can be of assistance to each other, my friend,' replied Nikolai. 'I happen to hold a considerable number of your IOUs, do I not?'

'You do.'

'And if I were to call them all in at once, you would be in some difficulties?'

Sergei's almond eyes became alarmed. 'I'd be ruined, and you know it,' he said quickly, draining the glass.

'What would you say if I offered to tear them up and forget them?'

'I'd say that you wanted something important from me,' replied the other frankly.

'And you'd be right. Sergei, I want you to return to St Petersburg on the *Pavlovsk*, which sails on the midday tide, and I want you to observe very closely the two English guests staying here tonight. I want to know if they are indeed the lovers they claim to be, and so I want you to search their cabins for anything that might confirm their story, letters, mementos, miniatures, locks of hair, anything at all, and if you suspect that there is anything suspicious, I wish you to inform the overseer at my summer palace.' Nikolai sat forward. 'Before you leave here, I will give you two letters, one for the Countess Irina, and the other for Bragin, instructing him what action to take on my behalf. Have I made myself clear?'

Sergei nodded. It was very clear indeed, for the overseer at Naryshky Palace on the coast near St Petersburg was Nikolai's henchman, devious, ruthless, and utterly reliable. He had disposed of his master's enemies and unwanted troublemakers in the past, and they had vanished without a trace.

Nikolai's dark eyes held his gaze. 'Don't fail me in this, Sergei, or it will be the worst for you, of that you may be sure. Serve me well and your IOUs will be thrown on the fire.'

'I won't fail you.'

Nikolai leaned back in his chair again. 'There is just one thing more,' he murmured softly. 'Whether or not you find anything untoward concerning Miss Clearwell and her lord, I wish you to follow her in St Petersburg and seize the first opportunity to abduct her and carry her to my palace, where Bragin will know to keep her hidden and secure until I can return. There isn't to be any bungling, it's to be accomplished swiftly and without witnesses. Do you understand?'

Appalled, Sergei stared at him. 'Yes, I understand, but Nikolai, it is one thing to deliver letters, search cabins and spy on people, but quite another to take part in a kidnapping.'

'Just think of your IOUs, my friend, and of the ruin that faces you if I call them in. You'll do as I wish now, and you have only yourself to blame for plunging in so deep.'

'Can't your overseer be entrusted with everything, including the abduction?' pleaded Sergei.

'No, because his constant presence in St Petersburg might give rise to curiosity. Your presence there, on leave, won't attract any attention at all. The task is yours, Sergei Mikhailovich, and if you value your life, you'll accomplish it to perfection.'

Golitsin fell silent. His face was pale and his pulse had quickened unpleasantly. He was trapped, and he knew it. His only salvation lay in carrying out Nikolai's instructions.

At that moment there was a loud clatter of hooves in the alley outside and a number of horsemen in the Swedish royal livery reined in by the inn door. One of them, an official messenger, hurried into the inn and went to the boy by the fire, shaking him by the shoulder and demanding in Swedish to know where Prince Naryshky might be found.

Nikolai rose quickly to his feet and went to the balustrade. 'I am here,' he said in the same language.

The messenger hurried to the foot of the staircase and bowed, addressing him in the court French that was *de rigueur.* 'Highness, I am instructed to inform you that His Majesty King Gustavus Adolphus requests you to present yourself at the palace at nine o'clock this morning.'

Nikolai's eyes narrowed. 'Nine? The talks are due to commence at eleven.'

'Those are my instructions, highness.'

'Very well.'

'A carriage and escort will be sent in good time, highness, and his majesty will receive you without delay.'

The messenger withdrew, and a moment later the alley was again filled with the clatter of hooves.

Nikolai turned to survey Sergei, who had remained in his chair at the table. 'What do you think it's all about, eh, my friend?' he asked softly.

Sergei shrugged. 'I don't know,' he replied. He neither knew nor cared, for he was too wrapped up in his problems.

The carriage and escort came as promised, and Alison and Francis stood on the balcony watching. The escort consisted of Swedish dragoons in dark-blue uniforms, mounted on well-matched gray horses, and the gleaming carriage was drawn by a handsome team of creams. Nikolai emerged in his dress uniform, splendid white plumes springing from his helmet, and he didn't glance up as he climbed into the carriage. As the vehicle pulled away down the alley toward the quay and the royal palace, it was preceded by its Swedish escort. Then there was another clatter of hooves as Nikolai's own escort brought up the rear, looking very proud and arrogant in the black and red uniform of the Preobrazensky Regiment.

Francis went back into the room as the procession vanished from sight, but Alison lingered for a moment on the balcony, hoping that that was the last she would ever see of the prince. She was relieved that his official duties had apparently taken precedence over all else, and now she trusted that the *Pavlovsk* would have long since set sail when he returned to the Dog and Flute. She wanted to put the frightening events of the previous night well and truly behind her; she wished that she could forget them altogether, but she knew that that would never happen because no one could ever forget such dreadful things. Besides, there was one thing that she didn't wish to forget, and that was the way she had felt when Francis Buckingham had taken her in his arms and kissed her.

Taking a deep breath, she went back into the room, where he was waiting to escort her down to breakfast. His expert glance swept approvingly over her neat figure and the shining curls piled up so prettily on top of her head.

'You look very lovely, Alison.'

'Thank you.'

'Shall we go down, then?'

She nodded, but as he offered her his arm, he paused again.

'It will soon be over now, for we can leave for the *Pavlovsk* directly after breakfast, but we mustn't let the fact that Naryshky and his companions have left affect our conduct. He is staying here, and he might return before the *Pavlovsk* leaves. It wouldn't do for him to be told that we haven't been behaving like sweethearts.'

She searched his face, wanting to ask so many questions, but then she decided against it. 'I'm quite prepared to carry on as we agreed last night.'

The gallery was deserted as they approached it, but the tap room was crowded and the babble of conversation and laughter carried clearly long before they reached the top of the staircase. They paused, looking down for a moment. Sunlight shone diagonally in through the windows, and the fire crackled in the hearth. The tables were crowded and the air was heavy with the smell of coffee, toasted bread, smoked fish, and other foods that Alison didn't know.

She expected Francis to proceed on down the staircase, but instead, he suddenly put a hand over hers, turning her to face him. He drew her a little closer, tilting her face so that her lips were only inches away from his, and then he gazed into her startled eyes, for all the world like an adoring lover, but it wasn't of love that he spoke.

'Alison, Naryshky himself may not be here, but I fear that one of his cronies is, and from his furtive manner I rather fear that he's observing us.'

Her eyes widened. 'Observing us?'

'Don't make it obvious, but if you glance at the table nearest the door into the alley, you'll see a man with a newspaper he appears to be engrossed in. Do you see him?'

Her eyes slid in the direction he mentioned, and she saw a slight, uniformed figure. 'Yes, I see him.'

'Well, he was eating his breakfast when we reached the gallery, but the moment he saw us he picked up the newspaper and now he's watching us in the mirror on the wall. Do you see?'

She nodded.

'I think we should give him something to watch, don't you?'

'I don't understand—'

'Kiss me, Alison.'

She stared at him. 'Here? In front of everyone?'

'Yes.' His blue eyes were compelling. 'Do as I say, Alison,' he said softly.

For a moment she couldn't respond, but then he bent his head to kiss her on the lips, and she found herself putting her arms around him to return the kiss. She was conscious of the astonished silence that immediately settled over the tap room below as everyone looked up toward the tender but surprisingly public scene taking place at the top of the staircase.

A fleeting sliver of conscience over Pamela pricked Alison, but then was gone as she was swept into the sheer pleasure of kissing him. She shouldn't feel like this; she had no right to respond to him, but she couldn't help herself. She tried to tell herself that no one, least of all Pamela, would ever find out, and that in the future she would be able to forget the emotions this man had so effortlessly aroused within her.

He drew back slightly, his blue eyes surprised. 'You appear to be entering into the spirit of things,' he murmured, smiling.

Her cheeks became pink. 'I thought you wished us to be convincing,' she replied quickly, glancing down at the sea of upturned faces in the tap room.

'Well, I fancy that on that score we've succeeded most admirably,' he said lightly, taking her hand and pulling it over his sleeve again.

As they proceeded on down, a hum of conversation broke out again. Those who had been present the previous night when Alison had first arrived were astonished, to say the least, to have seen a transformation such as that which had taken place now.

Behind his newspaper, Sergei Mikhailovich Golitsin drew a long, thoughtful breath. There hadn't been any sign of traditional British reserve in that kiss, and if Nikolai was suspicious about the two lovers, he, Sergei, didn't for a moment believe anything untoward was about to be discovered concerning them.

His appreciative glance lingered secretly on Alison as she sat down on the chair Francis drew out for her. She was very beautiful indeed and possessed that deceptive air of innocence that a man like Nikolai was bound to find tantalizing. In spite of the kiss that had just taken place in front of everyone, it was still impossible to believe that she had just come from her lover's bed. She looked so pure and virginal, but with a hidden fire, as if she was just waiting to burn with passion.

Sergei smiled wryly, for a very sumptuous bed awaited her in the Naryshky Palace, and a very different lover from the handsome Englishman into whose eyes she was now smiling so warmly.

6

It was with great relief that shortly afterward Alison and Francis left the Dog and Flute to walk down to the waterfront and the *Pavlovsk*. The two-masted Russian brigantine was moored close to the palace; indeed, she lay in full view of the rows of symmetrical windows that faced serenely across the harbor. Named after one of the summer residences of the czars, she was a busy vessel that only stayed in port long enough to discharge one cargo and take on the next. She had arrived from St Petersburg with linen goods and she would return again with a hold full of wool, mostly from Britain, and the last of her cargo was cluttering the quayside as Alison and Francis approached. They passed the other vessels moored alongside the quay, an Icelandic whaler, a barque from Dublin, a Finnish ketch, and finally an immense Dutch East Indiaman that was so wide and tall that it almost dwarfed the *Pavlovsk*.

Captain Merryvale happened to be paying a call upon his friend, the master of the brigantine, and like the guests at the Dog and Flute, he too observed the astonishing change that appeared to have over-taken Alison. As she stepped on board with Francis, with whom she appeared to have become reprehensibly intimate in a very short space of time, Captain Merryvale was quite dumbfounded. Could this really be the shy, retiring little English rose who had hidden away in her cabin for most of the time on the *Duchess of Albemarle*? He was conscious of a deep sense of disappointment that he'd apparently been so wrong, for he would have staked his reputation upon her being the sweet young innocent she appeared to be. Evidently appearances were deceptive, for there was nothing shy or retiring about the way she leaned on the arm of her handsome escort. The captain was even more astonished when he learned that Francis was a gentleman of such rank as Lord Buckingham.

Alison was only too conscious of Captain Merryvale's disapproval, and she was a little upset. She therefore insisted that Francis be shown to his cabin first, and when she had arranged to see him on deck afterward and he had been led away by the *Pavlovsk*'s Russian captain, she turned to Captain Merryvale.

'Captain, I wish to thank you again for all you've done for me. I'm very grateful that you've shown such concern.'

'It was my duty, Miss Clearwell.'

His tone was short, and she felt the color entering her cheeks. 'I trust you do not misjudge me, Captain, for there are certain somewhat extenuating circumstances that account for my conduct.'

'It's hardly my business, Miss Clearwell.'

'But your opinion matters to me, sir, and I do not wish to go down in your estimation. I don't wish to behave as I now do, nor does Lord Buckingham, but we do have excellent and pressing reasons, I promise you. Please restore me in your good books.'

He searched her face for a moment and then softened. 'How could I refuse such a plea, Miss Clearwell? Of course you're restored in my good books.'

'Thank you.' She smiled. 'Do you still intend to go on to St Petersburg?'

'On the *Duchess of Clarence*? Yes, I do, but she will not arrive here for a day or so yet.'

'Perhaps we'll see each other there?'

'Chance might make our paths cross, Miss Clearwell, but since you are destined for the exclusive grandeur of English Quay, which is on St Petersburg's fashionable South Side, and I will be in the commercial area on Vassily Island, across the Neva to the north, I cannot imagine that we will meet again.'

'Then perhaps we should say goodbye now, sir.' She extended her hand. 'I wish you better fortune in the future, Captain Merryvale.'

'Goodbye, Miss Clearwell, I trust that whatever the, er, extenuating circumstances are, they are successfully resolved.' Touching his hat, he left her just as the Russian master returned to conduct her to her cabin.

The captain of the *Pavlovsk* was a fierce-looking, redheaded martinet with the bushiest eyebrows she had ever seen. He ruled his ship with a rod of iron, brooked no insolence or disobedience, and thought nothing of inflicting severe punishment upon wrongdoers. He spoke only the most rudimentary English, and so communicated with her by beckoning and saying '*Da. Da.*'

She followed him toward the stern and the doorway in the poop that led down to the cabins on the deck below. There were six cabins in all for passengers, and each one boasted a large airy window that looked out from the stern toward the bulky Dutch East Indiaman moored a little farther along the quay. She wondered which one was occupied by Francis; it was impossible to tell because the other doors were closed.

As the Russian left her, she looked around the cabin that was to be hers for the next five days. It seemed that one cabin was very much like another, for this one was exactly the same as the cabin on the *Duchess of Albemarle*. There was a narrow bed, a table, a chair, and a wooden chest, all fixed firmly to the floor to prevent them from moving in heavy seas, and on the wall there were several hooks and a gimbal-mounted candle-stick to provide light at night and when the window was boarded over in stormy weather.

She unpacked her valise, which a member of the crew had taken the moment she went on board. She hung her few items of clothing on the hooks and placed her hairbrush and other things on the table. She paused when she took out her book, for she could only reflect with astonishment the startling sequence of events that had resulted from her spur-of-the-moment decision to invent a tale of runaway lovers for Prince Nikolai's benefit. Still, it was nearly over now, and the moment the *Pavlovsk* set sail, she and Francis would behave much more correctly and properly toward each other.

With a deep breath she placed the book on the bed, and then she retied the ribbons of her straw bonnet before going up on the busy deck again, expecting to find Francis waiting for her. But there was no sign of him yet. She must have passed his cabin door when he was still inside, for her cabin was at the very end of the narrow passage.

She adjusted her hood, for the sea breeze was very cold, and then she wandered slowly toward the bow, where there was far less activity. She gazed around at the panoramic view of Stockholm, its harbor, and the surrounding pine-clad hills. The sunlight shone on the water, and she looked toward the point where the previous day an ill-fated *Duchess of Albemarle* had dropped anchor. Now she lay beneath those sun-dappled waves, resting forever on the bed of the sea.

Alison's gaze moved on to all the other vessels using the habor. A forest of masts and rigging swayed gently on the tide, and the flags of many countries fluttered from masts and sterns. A fishing fleet was coming in, accompanied by a screaming flock of excited gulls whose cries echoed earsplittingly all around.

Resting her hands on the bow rail, Alison looked past the *Pavlovsk*'s plain bowsprit toward the next vessel along the quay, a sleek private schooner of considerable elegance and size. She was large enough to require a crew of at least twenty men and boys, and she had a wealth of gleaming brasswork and polished wood. Her slender white hull was picked out in gold and her sails were crimson. She was facing the *Pavlovsk*, and Alison gazed at her figurehead, which was a likeness of a very beautiful young woman with a cloud of titian curls that spilled down over her naked shoulders. The schooner's name was emblazoned on her prow in bright golden letters; she was called the *Irina*.

Alison stared at the name, realization beginning to stir within her, and at that moment Francis came up behind her and read her thoughts exactly.

'Yes, Alison, she's Naryshky's vessel, named after his sister, of whom the figurehead is said to be an accurate likeness.' He stood at the bow rail next to her, looking admiringly at the schooner. 'The *Irina* is the one thing I envy the prince, for I would dearly like to possess such a craft.'

'I thought you liked horses, not ships,' she replied, smiling a little.

'The summer sailing races off the Isle of Wight interest me a great deal, and I fancy that Naryshky's schooner would see off most competition,' he said. He glanced at her. 'Alison, I fear I have something rather disagreeable to tell you.'

'Disagreeable?' She turned quickly to meet his blue eyes.

'Do you remember the fellow at the inn, the one who was surreptitiously watching us from behind his newspaper?'

'Yes. Why?'

'I was afraid that his interest in us was a little too pointed, for it suggested that he'd been set to watch us, and now I'm sure of it. He's here on the *Pavlovsk*, and he has a cabin for the voyage.'

She stared at him, a finger of unease moving slowly down her spine. 'It may simply be coincidence—' she began.

'Yes, it could, for he may simply be going home on furlough, but I don't think that's the case.'

She drew back very slowly, her gray eyes wide. 'What are you saying?' she asked, the disquiet deepening within her.

He put a hand quickly over hers. 'Alison, it could simply be that Naryshky's interest in you is great enough for him to want to learn all he can about you.'

'Or? Francis, what else might it be?'

'All we have to do is persist with our pretense, convince his spy that we're genuine, and all will be well,' he replied, ignoring her question.

She searched his face. 'That's *all*? It's been hard enough pretending for only this short time, but to do it for five days more is simply too much.'

'It's very important,' he said quietly.

'What's very important?' she demanded. 'You've been very careful to avoid answering any of my questions, but it's still patently obvious that you're hiding something. Well, it may amuse you to keep me in the dark, but it doesn't amuse me in the slightest.' Her disquiet was suddenly replaced by a tremble of emotion that was very akin to panic. For all her bravado at the inn, and her storytelling and acting, she was naive and unused to the ways of the world. Too much had happened to her in too short a time, and all of a sudden she didn't feel up to carrying on. She wanted to go home, to Pamela, where it was safe and comfortable.

Tears suddenly filled her eyes and she pulled her hand away from his. 'I can't go on with any of this, I really can't,' she whispered. 'I want to go home to England.'

For a moment he didn't say or do anything, but then he removed his top hat and ran his fingers through his hair. 'And how do you propose to return? All by yourself without a chaperone? Surely your adventures thus far have taught you the foolishness of that!'

'My experiences with a chaperone were hardly elevating.'

'Perhaps not, but if you insist upon going back to England, you'll be placing me in a quite impossible position. I feel responsible for you, Alison.'

'I'm not a child.'

'No, as I recall your own words last night, you're inexperienced and fresh out of school.'

'I can't help that, any more than I can help being frightened by something I don't understand. Can you imagine how it feels to know that someone is keeping a secret from you, and to also know that that someone expects you to behave as if all is well?'

'Alison, there's nothing to be alarmed about and there's certainly no reason for you to be told anything.'

She held his gaze. 'So, at least you now admit that there is something.'

He nodded. 'Yes, I admit it.'

'And you still expect me to go through with five more days of pretending without the benefit of knowing what it's all about?'

He drew a long breath and said nothing.

She shook her head. 'It's not good enough, Francis. If you want me to continue to St Petersburg, then you have to tell me exactly what all this is about.'

'Alison . . .'

'I can be very stubborn and determined when I choose to be.'

Irritation shone in his eyes and then he looked away for a moment. 'Very well, you leave me no choice but to explain, but before I do so, I want you to give me your word that you'll never divulge any of it to anyone at any time in the future.'

'If that is your wish, then of course . . .'

'It's a very strict wish, Alison, and I'm thinking particularly of your close friendship with Pamela. I love her very much, but I'm aware of her faults, one of which is her great capacity for chitter-chatter. I don't want my activities, present or future, compromised by an idle, unguarded comment in the wrong ear. Do I still have your word?'

She nodded. 'Yes.'

He paused for a moment, glancing up at the palace windows. 'Alison, my visit to Europe was originally planned in all innocence, but as you've now guessed, its purpose is now no longer greatly concerned with the acquisition of horses. I'm a government agent, and I have to place some very secret and sensitive documents in the czar's hands.'

She stared at him. 'A government agent?' she repeated.

'Yes. I was drummed into service just before I left England. A dinner invitation from Lord Hobart, the Secretary of State for War and the Colonies, turned out to be something more than a social nicety, for I found myself being quietly enlisted over the mulligatawny and fully instructed by the time the fruit and liqueurs were on the table. It seems that these documents are very vital indeed and that the usual diplomatic channels cannot be trusted at the moment. The documents prove that not only are the French perfidious in their present overtures to the czar, but also that someone in Russian high places is a traitor working for Bonaparte.

'The fact that I was so providently on my way to a promised audience with the czar was the very thing as far as his majesty's government was concerned, and as a loyal Englishman I was required to do my duty. I am now doing that duty, Alison, which is why it is so important that you and I continue with our story. Naryshky is an ardent Bonapartist and his interest has been aroused, and that is bad enough, but to then arouse his suspicion that we might pose a danger to the French cause would be very undesirable indeed. He and his sister between them wield immense power in St Petersburg, and one word from either of them would prevent my audience with the czar from ever taking place. I involved myself in events at the inn last night, for you had to be saved from his advances, but in doing so, I lent myself to the tale you'd invented. I thought we would only need to keep up the subterfuge until the *Pavlovsk* sailed, but now it's plain that we must continue until we reach St Petersburg. My mission must be accomplished smoothly, Alison, and that is why, when I learned that Naryshky was here in Stockholm, I made it my business to seek him out. I meant to act the genuine horse bore, as I thought it would be beneficial if my name were to figure in his communications, albeit as a tedious devotee of the British turf.' He smiled a little. 'If it hadn't been for that decision on my part, I wouldn't have been there to save you last night,' he reminded her.

'And now I've become a necessary millstone?'

'That's one way of putting it. We've lied to him, Alison, and that's a fact that he must not discover, or he'll write to the countess and that will be the end of my audience. Would that the usual diplomatic channels were still safe, but they aren't.'

'Why? What happened?'

'Certain secret information was somehow getting out of our embassy in St Petersburg and reaching Bonaparte. We have a new ambassador there, Lord St Helens, and he notified London that one of his subordinates – he didn't know which one – was working on behalf of the French. The documents I have to deliver to the czar contain proof of certain very dangerous and secret French activities against Russia, and that is why the usual diplomatic routes have to be circumnavigated. Bonaparte is endeavoring to woo Alexander, whose support is vital if the Corsican's ambition to be master of Europe is ever to be realized. We have now discovered that while Bonaparte is flattering the czar on the one hand, on the other he's gathering as much information as he possibly can to launch an invasion of Russia, not by the expected overland path, but from the Baltic, by taking Kronstadt and then St Petersburg itself.'

Alison stared at him. 'But, isn't Kronstadt. . . ?'

'A virtually impregnable fortress island that straddles the sea approaches? Yes, it is, but when all its secrets are known to the enemy, it becomes far less of an obstacle. We have agents in Paris, and one of them, a clerk who works close to Bonaparte himself, has sent copies of certain papers to London. These papers, which include detailed maritime charts of the Baltic and the Gulf of Finland, the name given to that part of the Baltic closest to Russia and Finland, give full and accurate information about Kronstadt's defenses, both military and naval. They list the full complement of men, the guns and artillery, the standing orders, complete details of the ironworks and shipbuilding yards on the island, and contingency plans. The maritime charts show all sandbanks, channels, currents, tides, and any hazard that might impede an invasion. The waters there are very treacherous indeed because they're so shallow, and that means that all conventional naval vessels would have to sail dangerously close to Kronstadt and thus be in firing range.

'Bonaparte intends to build a huge fleet of shallow draft vessels to transport troops, horses, guns, and everything else necessary to an invasion force. This fleet could sail out of range of Kronstadt and with the night tide skim over the sandbanks, et cetera, and the defenses on the island could then be successfully eliminated by the full French navy, which would have complete knowledge of every likely retaliation and maneuver on the Russians' part. There is even the suggestion that the military and naval commanders at Kronstadt, who we believe to be the traitors who've supplied the French with the information, would lead their men into changing sides and thus give Kronstadt over to the French intact.

'Alexander is at this moment hovering on the brink of believing Bonaparte's silken words of friendship, but he wouldn't be such a fool if he knew what the Corsican was really up to. We can't risk the usual diplomatic approaches, which would mean the high possibility of the French learning that we've rumbled them, and so I've been dragged into it all. Perhaps "dragged" is the wrong word to use, for I'm doing it willingly enough.'

He smiled a little sadly. 'Bonaparte can never be satisfied with peace, Alison, not until he's realized his overwhelming ambition to be lord of Europe and beyond; and to embark upon that course, he first needs the support of Russia, whose territories stretch into the infinity of the East. When Czar Paul was alive, the Corsican was assured of Russian favor, and as a result, Britain found herself standing alone. But Paul's death put a stop to all that, because Alexander had a healthy mistrust for the French. We have to see that that mistrust is maintained, Alison, because for Britain's sake, as well as Russia's, Alexander mustn't be seduced by Bonaparte.'

She lowered her eyes, finding it difficult to absorb everything.

His fingers tightened over hers. 'Alison, I must beg you to reconsider about going back to England. If you return, not only will I be unable to escort you safely there, but I'll also be placed in a very awkward position *vis-à-vis* the delivery of the documents. Naryshky is, I'm sure, keeping us under surveil-lance, and even if it is only because of his unwelcome interest in you, that doesn't alter the fact that he's bound to notice anything untoward in our conduct.' He gave a wry laugh. 'And let's face it, it would be somewhat odd if you dashed off back to England and I not only allowed you to do so but also left you to do it all on your own. Last night and this morning we've been aping the tender lovers, and then you suddenly make a bolt for home? He'd be bound to wonder why I put a visit to Russia before my love for you, and he'd think it suspicious enough to put paid to my meeting with Alexander. At least, he might think it suspicious enough, and that's the possibility I have to avoid at all costs. Please stay with me, Alison – play my adoring sweetheart for a few days more, that's all I ask.' His fmgers were still warm and persuasive over hers. 'Just until St Petersburg, by which time we'll have convinced everyone on this brigantine that we're head over heels in love.'

'And what then? What if something else happens and we're forced to keep up the pretense even then? We'll have to offer some explanation to my uncle and step-aunt and—'

He put a finger to her lips and shook his head. 'Don't find problems that aren't there,' he said softly. 'If such a thing should happen, then I'll think of something, but at this precise moment all I'm concerned about is the next five days. I can't emphasize enough how important my mission is and how important it is that you stay with me now that circumstances have flung us together.' He glanced at the quayside, where the final bales of wool were being loaded. 'The time's come for you to decide, Alison, because in a minute or so we'll be under way. What's it to be? Do you still mean to go back to England, or will you stay with me?'

'I have no real choice but to remain with you, do I? I've caused the problem and it's my duty to do what I can to put matters right again. I'll stay with you, Francis, and I'll do whatever is necessary to help you deliver the documents to the czar.'

The smile he gave her was proof of his immense relief. He drew her hand to his lips and kissed the palm.

It was a gesture that set her foolish emotions spinning again. She shouldn't feel like this about him; she mustn't feel like this about him. She suddenly thought of Pamela again, and pangs of fresh conscience stabbed through her.

'Is there something else?' He looked at her in some concern, for her eyes were troubled.

'Wrong? No, of course not,' she replied quickly. 'I was just wondering something, that's all.'

'Wondering?'

She gave him a brisk smile. 'Where do you keep the documents hidden?' she asked, for it was the first thing that came into her head.

He laughed a little. 'They never leave my person, Alison, I carry them in a leather wallet next to my heart.'

About a quarter of an hour after that the *Pavlovsk* left her moorings and followed a pilot skiff across the crowded harbor toward the more open water of the island-dotted sound that led east to the Baltic. Pinewoods swept up from the shore, and forts were silhouetted above the treetops, their guns trained upon the water over which any invader would have to come. Like those to St Petersburg, the approaches to Stockholm were very well defended indeed.

Alison and Francis remained on the brigantine's deck as she sailed away from the Swedish capital. Alison glanced up at the forts, wondering if Bonaparte was as well informed about them as he was about Kronstadt. Perhaps he had been able to gather vital information about the defenses of many more countries, including Britain. What if he knew exactly how to invade and take London itself?

Turning, she looked back toward Stockholm, still bright and colorful in the May sunshine. She could just make out the royal palace. Was Prince Nikolai still there, conducting the talks on behalf of Czar Alexander? She didn't really care where he was, she just hoped that she would never see him again.

As the *Pavlovsk* stood out toward the sound, Nikolai himself was observing her from one of the palace windows. His face was unsmiling as he watched the vessel grow smaller. God help Sergei Mikhailovich Golitsin if he missed anything of importance where Miss Clearwell and Lord Buckingham were concerned. There had to be a clue somewhere, something that would confirm his suspicions that the two so-called lovers weren't lovers at all. The discrepancy in their story was all the proof he needed that things were not as they should be, and he meant to get to the bottom of it.

With an impatient sigh, he turned from the window to resume his restless pacing of the antechamber, for, contrary to the message he'd received at the inn, King Gustavus Adolphus hadn't been waiting to receive him at nine; indeed, there was still no sign of the cursed Swedish monarch. He, Prince Nikolai Ivanovich Naryshky, had been kept loitering like a common petitioner.

The antechamber was an uncomfortably high-ceilinged room, with portraits of past monarchs gazing down from walls that were rich with swags of gilded plasterwork. Liveried footmen stood on either side of all the doors, and beside the velvet-decked windows where golden fringes and tassels adorned the sumptuous curtains.

Nikolai's fellow officers remained wisely at the far end of the room, watching him as he paced angrily up and down. They hoped the King of Sweden wouldn't delay for much longer, because Nikolai's temper was a fragile thing at the best of times, and there wasn't one among them who relished the prospect of his foulest mood.

Suddenly the doors of the audience chamber opened and one of the king's aides-de-camp came in. He was splendidly attired in black velvet and his head was encased in a powdered white bagwig. His manner was diplomatically polite as he bowed low to Nikolai.

'I must beg your forgiveness for this inexcusable delay, highness, but I fear I have unwelcome news as far as the talks are concerned.'

'Unwelcome news?' Nikolai had stopped pacing and his dark eyes were suddenly sharp.

'His majesty was unwell on rising this morning, and although he meant to see you in person, I fear his condition has worsened somewhat and he has been obliged to retire to his bed. His doctors say that it will be some time before he's well again, and so his majesty feels that it would be wise to postpone the talks for the time being, until he is sufficiently recovered to preside over them again. You are, of course, more than welcome to remain here in Stockhohn, but perhaps you would prefer to return to St Petersburg until the talks can be resumed?'

Stay in Stockholm? Who in their right senses would wish to stay in this godforsaken place? A smile had begun to play on Nikolai's lips. 'Please convey my sympathies to his majesty and tell him that I trust he will recover with all swiftness. I will return to St Petersburg until such time as the talks are reconvened.'

With a relieved bow, for he had expected a display of high-handed Russian temperament, the aide-de-camp withdrew into the audience chamber again. A murmur of conversation broke out among the other officers, and Nikolai went to the window again, staring across the shining water toward the *Pavlovsk*, which was now a mere speck on the horizon. Suddenly he was free to return to St Petersburg, free to keep a watch in person on the movements of Lord Buckingham and the delightful Miss Clearwell.

He glanced down at the *Irina*. There were arrangements to make, so that he wouldn't be able to leave until the next tide now, but that didn't matter. The schooner was swift and would reach Kronstadt before the brigantine, so that he'd be waiting there when his intriguing new English acquaintances arrived.

7

Just as had happened to the *Duchess of Albemarle* soon after her voyage had commenced, the *Pavlovsk* found herself sailing into worsening weather. On the second day out, when she was on the exposed water of the Baltic, a gale picked up from nowhere, and as the long Scandinavian evening drew in toward the brief hours of darkness, the brigantine battled against mountainous seas. Ominous clouds raced across the dimming sky, and the gale howled relentlessly through the rigging. The vessel plunged and rolled, her timbers groaning, and such a heavy spray lashed across her deck that it ran in rivulets along the slippery boards. A door banged constantly somewhere, left unattended as the crew strove to keep the ship facing into the storm.

Night fell, and still the seas battered the *Pavlovsk*. The cabin windows had long since been boarded over to keep the waves out, and the passengers had been confined to their accommodations. Alison lay uneasily on her bed, gazing up at the trembling shadows cast by the gimbal-mounted candle. Her hair was brushed loose because she had had a headache a little earlier, and she wore the black-and-white-checked gown. The cabin felt curiously humid and unpleasant, and she looked longingly toward the boarded window, wishing the night was calm and the window open just a little.

Francis was seated at the table, his head resting on his arms as he snatched a few minutes' sleep. He had joined her the moment the storm became heavy enough for the cabin windows to be made secure, and he had managed to keep her relaxed by talking about Pamela and future plans. But as the hours passed and there was no sign of a lessening of the storm, he had persuaded her to try to sleep. She had lain there restlessly, and it had been Francis himself who had fallen asleep.

Her breath caught as another huge wave sent the brigantine soaring upward to a peak, left her hanging there for a moment, and then plunged her down with sickening speed into the deepest of troughs. On the *Duchess of Albemarle* Alison had fallen early victim to seasickness, but evidently she had found her sea legs during that voyage, for now she didn't feel sick at all, just frightened by the sheer force of the weather outside.

She heard the captain shouting orders and then the pound of footsteps on the deck overhead, but as she listened, she heard something else, something that struck terror through her, for it took her back to that dreadful night more than six years before when her mother had been killed. A rumble of thunder spread through the darkness, soft and distant at first, but then rolling closer before dying away on an echo. Her face was suddenly drained of color as she sat up quickly, staring toward the boards over the window. As she looked, there was a flicker of lightning between them, followed almost immediately by a thunderclap that seemed to split the night.

She was terrified of thunder, irrationally filled with dread because of her mother's tragic death. Her heart had begun to pound in her breast, and she no longer felt the cabin's humidity because she was suddenly as cold as ice. She was twelve years old again, and the cabin had become a swaying carriage. She could hear her mother's teasing, reassuring voice telling her that the thunder was only God moving his furniture around. The creaking of the ship changed into the clatter of hooves and wheels upon a rough country road, and the constant banging of the distant door was the crack of the coachman's whip. There was another jagged flash of lightning, another reverberating clash of thunder, and she heard her mother's single scream.

Suddenly she could bear it no more. The cabin seemed to be stifling her and she couldn't breathe. Getting up from the bed, she fled toward the door and flung it open; she ran out along the narrow passage toward the steps that led up to the door on to the deck above.

She was so panic-stricken that she almost lost her footing, but she still scrambled up, dragging the door open at the top. The fury of the storm rushed in on her, snatching at her hair and gown. Rain stung her face, and a wash of seawater rushed past.

A vivid flash of electric blue lit the darkness, and for a split second the night was day. She saw the huge waves towering all around, and a cry of fear escaped her as the *Pavlovsk* began to surge upward toward the sky. Another thunderclap exploded through the darkness, and as the brigantine reached the heart-stopping peak of the wave and remained motionless for a moment, a further brilliant burst of lightning lit the seas for miles around. Alison stared across the waves and saw another vessel, a sleek white schooner with crimson sails. The *Irina*!

Then the *Pavlovsk* was plunging downward again, the lightning was extinguished, and suddenly she could hear Francis' anxious voice as he dashed up the steps behind her. He grabbed hold of her, pulling her close with one arm as he strove to close the door with the other. The gale hurled itself against his efforts, but at last he forced the door to and then held Alison with both hands, looking incredulously into her eyes.

'What in God's name were you doing? One step out on that deck and you'd almost certainly have been washed away,' he cried, shaking her angrily.

Her lips trembled and her gray eyes were huge in the weak light thrown by the passageway's gimbal candlestick.

His anger died away. 'What is it, Alison?' he asked more gently, realizing that something had happened.

Thunder rumbled across the night outside, and with a stifled cry Alison flung her arms around him, hiding her face against his shoulder. He held her close and felt how her whole body quivered with fear.

'It's only thunder,' he whispered, stroking her hair gently. As he did so, something made him turn his head to look back down toward the cabins. One of the doors, that of the cabin occupied by Nikolai's spy, closed very softly, and Francis knew that the entire incident on the steps had been observed.

Quickly he swept her from her feet and carried her down the steps toward her cabin, and once safely inside, he kicked the door to behind them before laying her gently on the bed. Then he sat by her, taking her cold hands in his.

'What happened, Alison?' he asked quietly and firmly.

'I saw the *Irina*,' she replied, 'and she was sailing east as we are.'

'It must have been a trick of the light, the *Irina* is still in Stockholm.'

'No, Francis, I saw her. The prince isn't in Sweden anymore; he's on his way to St Petersburg, I know he is.'

Francis didn't attempt to argue the point, but she knew that he didn't really believe her. And why should he? She had been very distressed and almost hysterical, and in a flash of lightning she had become convinced she had seen the schooner. In his place she would probably have doubted as well, but she knew she'd seen the *Irina*, for the image was sketched indelibly on her memory.

The storm gradually abated the following day, and the *Pavlovsk* skimmed eastward before a very brisk breeze. She made such good time that although the wind died away on the fourth day she still reached Kronstadt at dawn on the fifth, dropping anchor among the flock of merchant vessels lying in the lee of the island, outside the massive harbor walls.

Kronstadt rose awesomely out of the ice-cold water, its silhouette black against the eastern horizon, where St Petersburg lay some twenty miles farther on. The sky was clear, but still there were snowflakes drifting aimlessly through the brittle cold. Kronstadt was a little farther north than Stockholm, and the difference was tangible.

Huge granite ramparts and a dangerously narrow harbor mouth protected a wooden-built town of some thirty-five thousand inhabitants, and apart from the impressive fortifications that bristled with artillery on all sides, the only building of any consequence was the cathedral, dedicated to St Andrew, the bell of which echoed through the dawn as Alison and Francis went up on deck.

Flames flickered eerily in the ironworks on the shore, and from the shipbuilding yards there came the sound of hammering. Men at the harbor mouth shouted as they guided a sloop through the constricted entrance, and the sea gulls were beginning to call as they stirred from their roosts to accompany the first fishing boats out to sea.

Among the merchant vessels lying at anchor offshore there was a line of naval frigates, all safe under the protection of the great guns of the fortress. The deep channels were secure and guarded, but farther out to sea, where the shores of the mainland could just be seen, the shallow water was free of all shipping except fishing boats. Alison gazed at it all, thinking that it didn't require a military or naval expert to perceive that this place was unassailable unless the attacker had very precise and secret intelligence, such as that now in Bonaparte's clever and ambitious hands. With the information he now possessed he might easily be able to incapacitate Kronstadt and then sail on with his vast fleet of shallow-draft landing craft to take St Petersburg itself.

She shivered as she stood with Francis on the deck, for the bitter cold had swiftly crept through her clothes to touch her skin. Francis wore his greatcoat, with his top hat pulled well down on his head, and the cold didn't seem to affect him so much, but she felt chilled to the core in her black-and-white-checked gown and fur-lined cloak. Her hood was raised and she had on her straw bonnet, but nothing seemed to repel the rawness of the northern air.

They had both glanced around the moment they came on deck, wondering if they would see the *Irina* among the other vessels, but there was no sign of the schooner. Alison knew that this merely confirmed Francis in his belief that she had imagined everything on the night of the storm.

A rowing boat was making its way toward the brigantine, rowed by a single sailor, and a flight of wooden steps was being lowered against the *Pavlovsk*'s side in readiness. As Alison and Francis watched, the little boat nudged the foot of the steps and the sailor made fast. Then he climbed quickly out of the rocking boat and came up to the deck, where the captain and first officer were waiting.

An American merchantman nearby was weighing anchor. Her sails filled gently as the almost imperceptible breeze caught them, and slowly she slid away toward the west. As she left her place, another vessel was revealed beyond her; it was the *Irina*.

Nikolai's beautiful schooner swayed gently on the slight swell left by the departing merchantman, her white hull reflecting in the calm water. Her crimson sails were furled and the elegant figurehead looked so lifelike that it was almost as if the Countess Irina herself was languishing there and would at any moment stretch down a graceful arm to dip her fingers in the sea.

Alison's lips parted in dismay. 'You see?' she whispered. 'It was no trick of the light.'

Before Francis could reply, there was the sound of footsteps on the deck behind them, and they turned quickly to see the captain and first officer approaching. The two men halted before them, and the captain nodded at the officer, who spoke adequate English. He cleared his throat awkwardly.

'My lord,' he said to Francis, 'Prince Naryshky sends his compliments and wishes you and Miss Clearwell to join him on the *Irina*. He would like to extend his hospitality and convey you for the remainder of your voyage to St Petersburg. The boat will return for you in half an hour. Your luggage can stay here and we will see it safely to your address.'

Alison kept her eyes lowered to the deck, silently praying that somehow Francis would find a way of politely declining.

He gave a smile and the merest suggestion of a courteous bow.

'The prince is most kind, but we would not wish to impose upon his kindness,' he replied.

Alison crossed her fingers in the folds of her cloak.

The officer cleared his throat again. 'It is no imposition, my lord, of that you may be sure; indeed, you would not be wise to decline. The prince is a very powerful man; he stands very close to the czar, and to refuse his generosity would be to court his displeasure.'

'Then what can I say but that we gladly accept,' Francis answered without so much as a flicker of unease.

Alison could barely conceal her consternation, but still kept her eyes downcast.

The first officer nodded. 'A prudent decision, my lord. As I said, the boat will return in half an hour.' He indicated the rowing boat, which was pulling away from the *Pavlovsk* toward the *Irina*. There were two men in it now, the sailor who had rowed it across and the army officer who had been spying upon the brigantine's two English passengers.

As the captain and first officer withdrew again, Alison turned anxiously to Francis. 'Don't we have any choice?'

'We have to go, Alison. The first officer meant it when he warned us against declining. Naryshky isn't a man to toy with.'

She was silent for a long moment. 'We're in a scrape, aren't we?' she said then.

'We may not be, for it still might be that his sole purpose is to pursue you, and if that is so, then I can protect you merely by my presence. Naryshky may be many things, but I doubt if even he would attempt anything in front of me, and believe me, I don't intend to leave you on your own with him.'

She looked toward the *Irina*, where the rowing boat was now coming alongside similar steps to those that had been placed against the *Pavlovsk* a short while before. 'We're still in a scrape,' she said, 'for now we'll have to keep up with our act even when we reach St Petersburg. And to do that we'll have to confide in my uncle and step-aunt, for it's impossible to behave politely and properly beneath their roof and then like lovers outside in case the prince's spies are watching us. Besides which, we don't know if the prince is acquainted with my uncle or not. He certainly knows his name and that he lives on English Quay.'

Francis took her hand and squeezed it gently. 'I can see the problems as clearly as you, Alison,' he said softly. 'Indeed, perhaps I can see them even more clearly.'

'What do you mean?'

'It doesn't matter for the moment. What does matter is that we carry this off with style now. Naryshky's creature can only report that we've billed and cooed appropriately since leaving Stockholm, and that he went through our cabins with a fine tooth comb and found nothing.'

'Went through our cabins?' she gasped.

'Yes. I noticed that things in mine had been disturbed, and then I actually saw him leaving yours when you were up on deck. He won't have found anything because the documents never leave my person. So, all we have to do is continue our loving display when we go on board the *Irina*. What happens in St Petersburg is a bridge we'll cross as and when we come to it, for I must take everything step by step and be careful at all costs to protect my real purpose. The documents I carry with me are of the utmost consequence in all this, and I have no choice but to put their safety before everything else. Just bear with me, Alison, stand by your promise in Stockholm, and I will do the right thing by you.'

'The right thing? I don't understand.'

He smiled, taking her face in his hands for a moment. 'No, I really don't think you do. You are the sweetest of innocents, Alison Clearwell.' His lips brushed over hers.

Her heart turned over with the surge of feeling that rushed through her, and all anxiety and fear fled into the cold, almost arctic air. Stand by her promise to him? She would stand by him no matter what, because she was beginning to fall in love with him. He would never be hers – he belonged to Pamela – but she, Alison Clearwell, wished to her very soul that it could be otherwise.

Sergei alighted from the rowing boat as it nudged the steps against the *Irina*'s hull. Pausing for a moment to adjust his uniform, he then went quickly up to the shining, spotless deck and along toward the stern of the vessel, where he knew Nikolai's private quarters were to be found.

He stepped through an elegant doorway into a sandalwood-scented passage and then halted as he saw the prince coming toward him wearing a peacock silk floor-length dressing gown over his white shirt and uniform breeches, for he hadn't dressed properly since being awakened the moment the *Pavlovsk* had arrived. His blond hair was tousled and uncombed and his valet had yet to shave him, but his dark eyes were sharp and alert.

'Well, Sergei Mikhailovich, what have you to report concerning our two lovebirds?'

'Simply that in my opinion that is exactly what they are, sir, love-birds.'

'Sir? But we are still friends Sergei. Now, then, what makes you so certain about Lord Buckingham and his ladylove?'

'Everything about them. Nikolai, before they came down to break-fast at the Dog and Flute they indulged in a very public embrace that only a fool would think was a pretense, and on the *Pavlovsk* they've spent every available moment together.'

Nikolai pursed his lips thoughtfully. 'Did you manage to search their belongings?'

'Yes.'

'And?'

'And nothing. I found absolutely nothing.'

Nikolai smiled a little. 'No loving mementos?'

'No.'

'And you don't think that that is a little odd?'

Sergei drew a long breath. 'Well, possibly, but—'

'There's no "possibly" about it, my friend,' interrupted Nikolai, 'it's very odd indeed as far as I'm concerned. Here we have two passionate lovers, and yet they have no love tokens, no love letters to read and read again, no miniature of their sweetheart's face, and no lock of hair to place in a locket. They may have gulled you into believing them, Sergei, but I am not so easily convinced.'

'But why are you so interested in them Nikolai?' asked the other, his curiosity suddenly getting the better of him.

'That is no concern of yours, especially if you wish to see the end of your IOUs.'

'Forgive me,' said Sergei quickly. 'Is there anything else you wish me to do for you?'

'Well, since I am now going to be in St Petersburg myself, I mean to attend to most things personally, but there are still two particular tasks I require of you.'

'Yes?'

'One of my tenants at Novgorod, Leon Razumov, has a daughter named Natalia who about a year ago married Thomas Clearwell.'

'Clearwell? Is he a relative of. . . ?'

'The Miss Clearwell on the *Pavlovsk*? Yes, he is her uncle. As soon as you arrive in St Petersburg, I wish you to inform the new Mrs Clearwell that I wish to see her without delay. I will give you the time and place.'

'Very well.'

'Do it as quickly as possible, for I don't want any unnecessary delay, and see to it that she says nothing to anyone. When I've finished with her, she'll gladly tell me everything she knows about our two so-called lovebirds.'

'I'll do as you ask.'

'I'm not asking, my friend, I'm ordering,' said Nikolai quietly.

'I understand.'

'See that you do, or it will be the worse for you.'

Sergei nodded. 'Shall I return to the *Pavlovsk* now?'

'Not so fast, my friend, for I haven't finished yet. There is still the small matter of seizing Miss Clearwell for me.'

Sergei's heart sank, for he had been hoping against hope that the abduction would no longer fall to him. 'Nikolai, I—'

'Don't be foolish now, Sergei, for it will not do for you to try to get out of this. I intend to have her, and you are the instrument I mean to use. There is no longer any need to remove her to my summer palace. All you need do now is bring her on board the *Irina*, which will lie at anchor on the Neva directly opposite English Quay. I don't care how you go about kidnapping her, just as long as you're discreet. There mustn't be any hint of my involvement, I just want her to mysteriously disappear.'

'But Nikolai, it's so very risky,' pleaded Sergei, sick with anxiety.

'Not so risky as having to survive once I call in your debts, my friend. Now you may go back to the *Pavlovsk*.'

Resignedly Sergei inclined his head and then turned to retrace his steps out on to the deck.

Nikolai followed him to the doorway and then stood watching as he went down to the waiting rowing boat. As the little craft pulled away from the schooner, Nikolai drew a long and very thoughtful breath. He hoped that Sergei was right and that Miss Clearwell and her lord were all they professed to be, but he still couldn't run the risk. Lord Buckingham must not be allowed to speak privately with the czar; indeed, he mustn't get anywhere near the czar, just in case that clerk in Paris had dispatched his information before meeting his death in the Seine. It wouldn't do to take any chances just yet, not when plans were still in their infancy. The truth would come out in the end, but only when it was too late for Alexander, Czar of All the Russias, to do anything but surrender.

Nikolai's face was cold and bitter. The day Alexander had taken the Countess Irina von Strelitz as his mistress had been the day he had made an implacable and unforgiving enemy of Nikolai Invanovich Naryshky, for by that single act the Romanovs had declared to the world that a daughter of the house of Naryshky wasn't good enough to be the czarina, but was good enough to be the czar's whore. And this had been after he, Nikolai, had been turned down for the hand of the Grand-Duchess Helen, Alexander's beautiful eighteen-year-old sister. That refusal had stirred resentment; the resentment had become hatred when Irina had been taken to Alexander's bed. No man, not even the czar, could be allowed to deal so many monstrous insults, and now Alexander would pay dearly for his actions. The new czar would have been better advised to show appreciation for the loyalty and support he, Nikolai, had given, but in the absence of such appreciation, there was another who was more than prepared to bestow favor where it was due. Bonaparte knew how to reward those who deserved it, and no one had rendered more service recently than Prince Nikolai Naryshky of the czar's Preobrazensky Regiment.

Nikolai looked away from the rowing boat toward the massive fortifications of Kronstadt. His gaze encompassed the batteries and harbor, the naval base, and the fleet of warships lying at anchor among the merchant shipping. What price all this when the French possessed all the necessary knowledge to crush it? Eh, Alexander, my czar? And all because you thought a Romanov grand-duchess was too good for a Naryshky, but a Naryshky princess by far too inferior to become a Romanov. Nikolai smiled coldly to himself, for no one, not even Irina, knew how he really felt. They would know in the end, though. Oh, yes, they would know in the end.

8

The rowing boat's oars dipped strongly into the clear Baltic water as Alison and Francis were conveyed toward the *Irina*. Nikolai's schooner looked almost seductively beautiful, her white and gold hull shining and her crimson sails furled tightly as if slumbering.

A sailor was waiting to conduct them up to the deck, and they followed him through the same doorway where earlier Sergei had gone to report on them. At the end of the passage there was another door, this one inlaid with silver and mother-of-pearl, and the sailor opened it and then stood aside for them to enter. When they had done so, he closed the door behind them and they were alone.

They found themselves in a very warm, deserted stateroom of such sumptuousness that it might have been removed in its entirety from an Oriental potentate's palace. Rich folds of crimson and gold damask had been draped against the walls, and there were brightly colored carpets on the floor. The chairs and ottoman couches were uphol-stered with sable and quilted gold satin, and there were low tables with tops of chased silver. In one corner there was a high gilded cage containing a brightly plumed macaw, and nearby there was a side-board on which had been placed an array of exquisite refreshments, from bottles of champagne, vodka, and ruby-red wine, to caviar, walnut cheese, candied fruit, nuts, and other delicacies. The room was very efficiently warmed by an ornate black stove that stood in the center of the floor, with a chimney pipe that passed up through ceil-ing.

There were two other doors apart from the one through which they had entered, and both were closed. A line of splendidly glazed windows afforded a prime view over the crowded water behind the schooner, and beneath them there was a long window seat that was liberally scattered with crimson and gold silk cushions.

Alison glanced around in admiration, for she wouldn't have believed such luxury could exist on board a ship. The air was so warm that she had to toss back her hood, and as she did so, she became aware of the scent of roses from an open potpourri jar standing on the floor next to the stove.

Francis removed his greatcoat and then teased off his gray kid gloves, dropping them into his upturned top hat and then placing the hat on the window seat with the greatcoat. Then he too paused to glance around, toying with the frill of shirt that protruded from the cuff of his sage-green coat. There was a simple gold pin in the knot of his neckcloth, and the frill on the front of his shirt disappeared into his lilac paisley waistcoat. His long legs were immaculately clad in tight cream cord breeches, and the shine on his boots was very commendable indeed, considering he was traveling without a valet.

One of the other doors opened suddenly and two rather strange figures entered. One was a dwarf, extravagantly clad in a golden robe and plumed turban like a tiny sultan, and the other was a tremendously tall muscular black man who wore baggy white pantaloons and a crimson sleeveless jacket. They both remained absolutely silent and took up positions on either side of the only door that had yet to open. They stood with their arms akimbo, gazing straight in front of them.

Francis had turned to observe them the moment they entered, but Alison, who had been standing much closer to them, found their presence a little disturbing, and she moved instinctively toward him. He smiled reassuringly and relieved her of her cloak, for the heat from the stove was almost unbearable. Suddenly the macaw gave a series of earsplitting shrieks and Alison started so much that Francis quickly put an arm around her waist.

'Courage now, for it's only a dratted bird,' he murmured.

Somehow she managed to smile at him, but then the other door opened and Nikolai entered. He wore his uniform, and at his side, held by a golden chain and a collar studded with amethysts, was a lynx with tufted ears, spotted fur, and cold amber eyes.

Alison had never seen a lynx before and she shrank still closer to

Francis, her gaze fixed upon the animal.

Nikolai smiled a little. 'Khan will not harm you, Miss Clearwell, but if he frightens you, I will have him removed.' He handed the chain to the black man and the lynx was led away. Nikolai turned to her again. 'I was forgetting that the lynx is no longer to be found in Britain, and so you will not be used to such things.'

Relieved that the animal had been removed, Alison summoned the will to smile a little foolishly. 'You must forgive me, sir, for in England a gentleman might be seen with a dog or hound, but never with a wild animal.'

He came toward them. 'It is you who must forgive me,' he murmured, and then inclined his head. 'Welcome on board my *palais flotant*, my friends. I am only sorry that King Gustavus Adolphus's illness came too late to spare you the rigors of five days on a vessel like the *Pavlovsk*.'

'The king is ill?' asked Francis.

'I fear so, and the talks have been postponed for the time being, which leaves me at liberty to extend my hospitality. Please be seated, my friends.'

Francis conducted Alison to one of the couches and then waited for a moment in order to sit down at the same time as Nikolai, who was at pains to be the gracious and attentive host.

'Have you breakfasted yet?' he asked.

Francis nodded. 'Yes. At least we took what passes for breakfast on the *Pavlovsk*. I fear that cold pork sausage, goats'-milk cheese, and vodka are hardly appetizing first thing in the morning, especially to a lady.'

Nikolai smiled. 'I can well imagine. Allow me to provide you with something more suitable.'

'I'd appreciate a cup of coffee,' said Alison quickly, for in truth the breakfast had put paid to her appetite for the time being.

The prince nodded and then looked enquiringly at Francis. 'And for you, my lord?'

'Coffee would be most agreeable,' he replied.

Nikolai clapped his hands to the dwarf, who immediately hastened away.

Alison glanced out of the line of windows and to her surprise suddenly realized that the *Irina* was already under way. She hadn't heard the sound of any running feet or shouted orders, she hadn't even detected the rattle of the anchor chain, but nevertheless the schooner was gliding away from Kronstadt and a white wake was beginning to foam behind her. As the island slipped farther away astern, the schooner's sails suddenly caught the westerly breeze and she seemed to leap forward eagerly, skimming over the water toward St Petersburg.

Prince Nikolai watched Alison as she gazed at the scene beyond the windows. His glance took in the sweetness of her profile, the soft silver-fair of her hair, and the slenderness of her figure, outlined so perfectly by the soft folds of her black-and-white wool gown. She still seemed so untouched, like a rose that was about to uncurl its matchless petals to the sun, and yet she had lain in Lord Buckingham's arms and allowed him to possess her. Was it really possible that she wasn't to be trusted? Could someone of such angelic and virginal beauty be the accomplice of a British agent, or even be the agent herself? Dear God, how he would like to know whether that clerk in Paris had died too late. If only information had still been forthcoming from the British embassy in St Petersburg . . . But there hadn't been anything useful from there for months now. Every instinct told him something was wrong, but when he looked at the exquisite loveliness of this young Englishwoman, he found it impossible to believe that there was anything amiss at all.

If it hadn't been for that one small discrepancy in the story she and her handsome lord had told in Stockholm, he, Nikolai, wouldn't suspect anything at all. Now there were other things, such as the strange absence of any mementos in their belongings and the fact that while Lord Buckingham had all along been booked to sail on the *Pavlovsk*, the fascinating Miss Clearwell's name hadn't appeared on the manifest until after the sinking of the *Duchess of Albemarle*. If the Englishman and his lady were trying to pull the wool over his eyes, then they would pay the price of their folly. The lady would pay another price first, however, when she was forced to submit to advances that she had repulsed in Stockholm.

Realizing that he'd been studying her a little obviously, Nikolai suddenly turned to Francis. 'Tell me, my lord, will you and Miss

Clearwell be marrying as soon as you reach St Petersburg?'

Alison looked around quickly.

'Yes,' Francis replied in an even tone, 'for Miss Clearwell's reputation has been compromised enough by the simple fact of our elopement. She will become Lady Buckingham as soon as I am able to arrange the necessary special license.'

Alison marveled at how matter-of-fact and convincing he sounded. It was as if they were indeed about to become man and wife.

Nikolai smiled. 'I trust that you will invite me to the ceremony, my lord?'

'We would be honored to do so, sir.'

The dwarf returned with a silver tray upon which stood a Turkish coffee pot and some delicate gold porcelain cups and saucers. He placed the tray on a table and proceeded to pour the coffee, bringing them each a cup in turn, commencing with Nikolai, to whom he bowed very low indeed.

The dwarf then retreated to his position by the door, where the black man had also reappeared. Standing with their arms akimbo again, they commenced to stare straight ahead as if they were statues and could not hear a word that was said in the stateroom.

Conversation didn't again touch upon anything concerning wedding plans, but ranged instead upon topics concerning Prince Nikolai himself. He told them of his magnificent summer palace on the coast of the Gulf of Finland, some fifteen miles west of St Petersburg, of his town residence in the capital itself, and his meteoric career in the famous Preobrazensky Regiment. They also learned that his family possessed a castle near Florence, a villa in Fiesole, and an estate of many thousands of hectares in Finland. It wasn't by accident that the conversation centered upon Nickolai, for Francis saw to it that the prince's immense vanity was constantly flattered. Alison knew why Francis was doing it, for while Nikolai was waxing lyrical about himself he couldn't ask awkward or downright difficult questions about anyone else.

Their conversation was interrupted at last when the schooner's captain came to the stateroom to say something to Nikolai, something they didn't understand because he spoke in Russian. When he had withdrawn, however, Nikolai explained. 'Come to the windows, my friends, for I wish you to see my summer palace. We're passing very close to the shore now.' He got up, beckoning them toward the windows.

Alison rose in some surprise and spoke without thinking. 'Close to the shore? But isn't the gulf far too shallow for a vessel like this to risk sailing near the coast?' As the words slipped from her lips, she knew she had made an error, for it wasn't expected that a lady should be so knowledgeable.

Nikolai paused, looking a little curiously at her. 'How very well informed you are, Miss Clearwell. I confess I'm surprised to find a lady who is so aware of things nautical.'

For the space of a heartbeat she was at a loss, but then she smiled. 'You shouldn't really be surprised, Prince Nikolai, because when I was on the *Duchess of Albemarle* Captain Merryvale himself told me that the gulf is so shallow at times that only the very lightest of vessels can sail right up to St Petersburg, and then only under the guidance of a pilot. He said it more than once, even hinting that the *Duchess* might have to halt at Kronstadt and transfer her cargo and passengers, well, passenger, to a galliot.' She knew that yet again she had managed to sound completely plausible.

Nikolai smiled a little. 'Ah, yes, Captain Merryvale and the *Duchess of Albemarle*. But tell me, were not both you and the earl to have sailed on to St Petersburg on that unfortunate ship?'

'Yes.'

He smiled a little and went to the windows without saying anything more.

She guessed that she had said something else wrong, and glanced uneasily at Francis. His rather troubled eyes were already upon her. She had somehow made another error, and he knew what it was. She could have bitten her tongue out for allowing herself to be drawn too much, but it was too late now, and what was done was done.

With a heavy heart she allowed Francis to assist her from the couch, and although he squeezed her fingers reassuringly, she still felt wretched. What had she said?

Francis drew her hand over his arm as they joined Prince Nikolai by the windows. The schooner was making speed now, the wake stretching far behind her, and sea gulls swirled excitedly, dipping low over the water and then soaring high again. The southern shore was only about two hundred yards away, and Alison could clearly see the shingle beaches with fringes of birchwoods, and the hinterland of undulating tree-covered hills. It was very lovely countryside, and obviously very fashionable, for dotted among the trees were many fine mansions and summer palaces. Some were classically elegant, taking their inspiration from France, Italy, and England, but others were much more Russian, with gilded domes and cupolas. From time to time there were glimpses of armorial gates and magnificent parks that swept right down to the water's edge. There were formal gardens that rivaled Versailles itself, and everywhere there were fountains, cascades, waterfalls, and ornamental lakes. Little hermitages and pavilions had been placed facing the sea, and they seemed much resorted to even this early in the morning, for frequently she saw carriages waiting by them or saddle horses. In England at this time of year all the flower beds would be bright with wallflowers, petunias, polyanthus, and lilac, and the first roses of summer would be budding, but here there was nothing, just the delicate white of thousands of snowdrops growing in sheltered spots.

A group of horsemen was riding wildly along a beach, their mounts' hooves splashing through the shallow waves that broke against the shingle. Alison watched them and her gaze was drawn inexorably to one palace in particular. It was an astonishing sight, topped by a cluster of blue, green, and gold domes and with a facade that might have come directly from Byzantium. Never before had she seen such a palace, and it was viewed as if in a dream, for she gazed at it through the spray and mist of countless fountains, some of them dancing as high into the air as the palace's domes.

Nikolai glanced at her. 'What do you think, Miss Clearwell? Do you admire my palace?'

'Your palace? How very fortunate you are. It's very beautiful indeed,' she replied honestly.

'I am flattered that you think so,' he murmured, his dark eyes upon her. 'One day soon I will take you there, you have my word upon that.'

She looked quickly at him, thinking she detected an odd note in his voice, but he just smiled and indicated the shoreline again.

'You see? It is possible to sail close to the land, but only if the master of the vessel knows the channels and sandbanks like the back of his hand. The captain of the *Irina* is the finest pilot in these waters, and he is the only man who would dare to take such a large schooner this close to the shore, and do it at speed. We will soon be in St Petersburg, but the *Pavlovsk* will not reach there until tonight.'

A lookout shouted from his post, and his call sounded faintly in the stateroom.

Nikolai smiled again. 'St Petersburg has been sighted, Miss Clearwell. I am sure that your stay there will be an experience you will never forget.'

Again she glanced uneasily toward him, but there was nothing in his eyes to suggest that he spoke with any hidden meaning. All the same she was glad when Francis rested his hand over hers, so much so that she couldn't help curling her fingers tightly in his.

There was nothing to add depth to the scene as the *Irina* sailed from the Gulf of Finland into the beautiful city that Peter the Great had founded a hundred years before on the Neva delta. The river only flowed the forty-five miles from inland Lake Ladoga, and as it reached the sea, it divided into four main arms that were joined by countless other streams and tributaries. Peter the Great hadn't been satisfied with what was already a vast amount of water and had ordered the cutting of many canals to further enhance the capital that was to be his 'Window to the West,' the glittering achievement that would win the envy of the modem world. As glorious as Venice itself, but on a much grander scale, the new capital was so low-lying that the presence of so much water always made it vulnerable to flooding, and so the inhabited islands were all protected by immense Finnish granite embankments that kept out all but the severest of floods.

The city was an incomparable sight as the *Irina* sailed up the main artery of the Neva. Classical facades shone yellow, pink, white, and pearl gray in the bright midday sun; blue, green, and gold domes pierced the sky; and reflections shimmered on the dark-blue water. There were many green pleasances, for every palace and mansion had a garden, every square had walks that would soon be shaded by spring leaves, and every street was lined with trees. Spires, pillars, statues, and monuments gleamed in the crisp northern air, and there was a sense of grandeur and spaciousness such as Alison had never encountered before.

The Neva was a quarter of a mile wide where the *Irina* dropped anchor just before the crowded pontoon bridge, known as the Isaac Bridge, which was put in place every summer to connect Vassily Island to the north with Admiralty Island to the south, where the administrative heart of imperial Russia was situated. There was no need for bridges in the winter because the river froze so firmly that it was easily possible to walk across from island to island. There were other pontoon bridges where the channels of the Neva were wide, but where the waterways were narrower, there were permanent stone or wooden bridges connecting the various different parts of the delta.

Vassily Island was the largest of the islands, and was also the commercial and academic center of the city. As well as the Academy of Arts and the Academy of Sciences, there were crowded quays where many vessels were discharging and loading cargoes. These quays were busy again after the long hard winter, and the foreign vessels moored there were some of the first to enter the city after the Neva had melted. This was where the *Duchess of Albemarle* would have come alongside and where the *Pavlovsk* would arrive tonight; it was also where the *Duchess of Albemarle*'s sister ship, the *Duchess of Clarence*, would tie up in a day or so's time.

The cobbled wharves were cluttered with crates, sacks, and bundles, and a constant flow of carts drawn by heavy horses was to be seen passing to and fro. Winches shrieked and men shouted, but these sounds were drowned suddenly in an ecstatic pealing of bells as the churches and cathedrals of the capital rang out for midday.

On Admiralty Island, or the South Side, as Captain Merryvale had said it was called, the pontoon bridge joined the land in front of St Isaac's Square, where a bronze equestrian statue of Peter the Great had been placed on a huge block of stone. On the far side of the pontoon bridge, away from the *Irina*, the South Side stretched away along the waterfront in a superb line of administrative buildings, including the soaring gilded spire and weathervane of the Admiralty itself, the czar's Winter Palace, and the Hermitage, where so many priceless treasures were on display that it took days to inspect them all. Facing the Neva across St Isaac's Square was newly completed St Isaac's Cathedral, which was considered unsatisfactory and was already to be rebuilt to an entirely new design, while on the nearside of the square, closest to the *Irina*, the South Side became the one-and-a-quarter-mile embankment of English Quay, one of the finest residential streets in St Petersburg.

Palatial mansions with balustraded roofs faced northward over a wide paved avenue toward the river and Vassily Island directly opposite. There were symmetrical windows, tall porticoes, grand pilasters, and walled gardens where the sheltered trees were already in leaf. More trees graced the embankment above the water, and were interspersed with elegant three-branch streetlamps which at night shone on both street and river. English Quay was a very fashionable place to be seen, and on summer evenings the cream of society, including the imperial family, were to be found strolling its length. Fine carriages drove past the mansions, all drawn by no fewer than four horses because distances were so vast in St Petersburg that two horses would soon have tired. Ladies and gentlemen as stylish as their counterparts in Paris or London were taking the air along the pavements, and many small boats and several elegant private barges were moored at jetties from which wide flights of stone steps led up to the street above.

Nikolai stood watching from the deck of the *Irina* as Alison and Francis were rowed toward the steps that were nearest Thomas Clearwell's residence. His dark eyes were half-closed and his lips a set line. After unwittingly telling the truth by correcting herself over whether the *Duchess of Albemarle* was to have had passengers or a single passenger for the last part of her voyage, she had then deliberately lied again. She had insisted that she and Lord Buckingham were both to have sailed to St Petersburg on the *Duchess of Albemarle*, and yet, he Nikolai Ivanovich Naryshky, knew that Lord Buckingham had booked passage on the *Pavlovsk*. And then there was her unusual knowledge of the shallow waters of the gulf. In spite of her ready explanation, there was something disquieting about the incident. It all confirmed his suspicion that there was more to the two English lovebirds than met the eye, and it made him all the more determined to get to the bottom of it all. He couldn't afford to let them outwit him, and now that they were here in St Petersburg, where his power and tentacles reached into every corner, it wouldn't be long before the whole business had been satisfactorily settled.

A thin smile played on his lips as he thought of Alison. Yes, soon everything would be settled to his complete satisfaction.

9

The rowing boat was still some way from the steps leading up to English Quay, and Alison shivered as she sat in the stern next to Francis. She glanced back toward the *Irina*, which gleamed very white out on the dark-blue water of the Neva, and she could quite clearly see Nikolai standing on the deck watching.

She looked uneasily at Francis. 'I've made a bungle of it, haven't I?' she asked frankly, keeping her voice in a whisper for fear that the man rowing the boat might understand English.

'It can't be helped,' replied Francis with equal frankness.

'But what exactly did I say that was so wrong? I know I was foolish when I mentioned the shallow navigation in the gulf, but there was something else, wasn't there?'

He nodded. 'It was when he prompted you about us both sailing from Stockholm on the *Duchess of Albemarle*. I fear he has already checked and knows full well that I was never booked to sail on any vessel other than the *Pavlovsk*.'

She stared at him. 'Then that must mean that he now truly suspects we're being less than honest with him?'

'I would if I were he.'

She was appalled to think that she'd given them both away. 'I'm so sorry,' she said in a small voice.

He put an arm quickly around her shoulders. 'I think the damage was done long before now, Alison. Since he asked you so pointedly about our sailing arrangements, I've been considering everything that happened from the moment you arrived at the Dog and Flute. If he was curious enough about us to inquire concerning the passage we'd booked, maybe he was also curious enough to ask certain questions at the inn itself.' He met her eyes. 'There was a flaw in our story, Alison, and I wish I'd seen it before now, because I think that that flaw is the reason for his great interest in us. You told him that I had asked to be placed in the room next to yours, but I didn't ask any such thing; indeed, it would have been quite obvious to anyone making inquiries that pure chance was the only reason I was in the adjacent room.'

Tears suddenly filled her eyes. 'And that was my fault as well, wasn't it? If I hadn't said—'

'You had to say it once you had embarked on your story. I don't blame you for any of this, please believe me. Circumstances dictated what happened, and you said what you had to get away from him. It didn't work, and so I had to intervene.'

'But it's still because of me that the prince is so intent upon what we do. You have to see the czar, but the prince can put a stop to that in a moment if the whim takes him, which it might do easily now that he's found us out in mistakes of my doing, and now that he's here in St Petersburg—'

'He can still be fobbed off,' Francis interrupted quietly. 'There is one obvious way to get ourselves out of this scrape, and I've known we must take it ever since I saw the *Irina* at Kronstadt.'

'Obvious way? I don't understand.'

He smiled a little, putting his gloved hand to her cheek. 'I know you don't, Alison, but I said that I'd do the right thing by you, and I meant it.'

She flushed slightly, remembering the moment he had said those words to her. He had also called her the sweetest of innocents, and he had kissed her. 'I still don't understand,' she whispered.

'I wasn't jesting when I told Naryshky we would be married as soon as the necessary special license could be obtained. I intend to make you my bride as soon as possible.'

She stared at him and then drew back sharply. 'What are you saying?' she breathed incredulously.

'Simply that I must do the logical as well as the honorable thing.'

'Have you taken leave of your senses?' she cried, and then realized she had allowed her voice to rise sufficiently for the sailor to look curiously at her. She lowered her tone again. 'Francis, I know that your mission here is vital, but to go to such inordinate lengths—'

'I don't mean to do this simply because of the reason I'm here,' he interrupted, putting his hand to her cheek again, 'although I admit that it must be my most immediate consideration. So let us take that point first. Our government has been forced to use me in order to place vital information in Alexander's hands. He has to receive those documents if Bonaparte is to be thwarted and peace is to continue. Naryshky and his sister admire Bonaparte, and do all they can to promote his cause, which naturally means preventing any possible approach from Britain. Naryshky now has reason to doubt that I'm simply a devotee of the turf, and he's obviously wondering if we're also more than just the ardent and besotted lovers we've pretended to be. We've made some slipups, but they're not insuperable, especially if we do indeed go through with the marriage.'

She stared at him. 'You make it sound so simple.'

'No, Alison, it isn't simple, I'm just saying that I think Naryshky's suspicions could be allayed if we go through with the marriage, expecially if he's there to witness the ceremony.'

'But you love Pamela, Francis,' she said. 'You love her very much, far too much to want to have me as your wife.'

He met her eyes. 'I did say that delivery of the documents isn't my only reason for wishing to do this. Another reason is that I've compromised you, a fact that is bound to get out now that Naryshky is also here in St Petersburg. As far as he is concerned, we've been behaving like man and wife, for we've spent nights alone together. We don't yet know how well acquainted he is with your uncle and step-aunt, which means that there is a very real possibility that he will tell them about us. What do you imagine will happen then?'

'I don't know, I haven't thought about it.'

'Then think about it now. If we say nothing, can you imagine their reaction on hearing what he has to say? And if we take the precaution of acquainting them with all the details, they'll undoubtedly back us up, but they will also see that your reputation and virtue have been grossly jeopardized. Your uncle will find himself responsible for a niece who has yet to be launched into London society, but whose chances of a good match have been ruined by her involvement with a man who could quite easily do the right by her if he so chose. Under those circumstances, he is bound to insist that I marry you, and he would be justified.'

'My reputation may be ruined here in St Petersburg, I can see that, but no one in London is going to know about it.'

'No? Alison, St Petersburg is a city of some two hundred and thirty thousand inhabitants, of which nearly one thousand are British. Those British citizens have family in England and have friends and relations who visit them here. Look at your uncle's house. Do you see that carriage and four drawn up outside?'

She looked toward the imposing mansion. It had a colonnaded porch and finely proportioned windows, and on one side of it there was a walled garden that extended to the boundary of the neighboring property. The garden wall was pierced by an elegant wrought-iron gateway through which could be seen leafy paths, fountains, and statues. The double front door was painted dark blue, and a maid was busy polishing the lions-head brass knocker. The carriage and four of which Francis had spoken was waiting at the curb outside.

'Yes, I can see the carriage,' she said, 'What about it?'

'I saw it arrive a moment or so ago, and I saw the lady who emerged and called at the house, which can only mean that she is acquainted with your uncle and step-aunt. Her presence has put an effective end to my prospects of ever marrying Pamela.'

Alison's lips parted in astonishment. 'But who is she?'

'Her name is Mrs Arabella Fairfax-Gunn; she's the most notorious and dangerous gossipmonger in England, and she also happens to be a confidante of Pamela's mother, the Duchess of Marchington. She'll go around with a bell the moment she sniffs anything out, and she *will* sniff it out, you can be sure of that. Her instinct is unerring where possible scandals are concerned, and at the very least she will discover that you and I met in Stockholm and then traveled here together, without so much as a maid to make things proper. She mixes very thoroughly in high society and never turns down an invitation, which means that sooner or later she is bound to come into contact with the prince, whose knowledge of our activities is titillating, I think you'll admit. One way or another, whether we marry or not, news of what we've been doing is going to travel back to England, and the moment the Duke and Duchess of Marchington get wind of it, they'll put a stop to the betrothal. And if you were Pamela, Alison, would you believe my protestations of innocence? Here I am, on the loose in Europe and surrounded by all manner of tittle-tattle concerning goings-on with her best friend.'

'But if she loves you—'

'You're very beautiful, Alison, very beautiful indeed, and even Pamela will think there is no smoke without a certain amount of fire. By the time Mrs Fairfax-Gunn has finished embroidering the tale with all manner of lascivious detail, you may be certain that the whole of London will believe you and I to have indulged in a very passionate and torrid affair.'

'What if you're mistaken and it wasn't Mrs Fairfax-Gunn?'

'Alison, no one else on earth could possibly look like that. She's just under five feet tall and almost as wide, and she always wears the brightest shade of vermilion because her late husband once foolishly told her that it made her look youthful. There's no mistake, the person who just entered your uncle's house was Mrs Arabella Fairfax-Gunn.' He took her hands. 'We're almost at the steps now, Alison, and so we must decide right now what story we intend to tell when we enter the house. For all the reasons I've just given, I want you to marry me, Alison, and I want the ceremony to take place as quickly as possible. I must protect my mission here and I must protect your good name; I cannot hope now to marry Pamela, as I think you must realize.'

'But you don't want me,' she whispered, tears filling her eyes.

'If you imagine I'm indifferent to you, I think you underestimate yourself,' he said softly. 'I find you very attractive indeed, Alison Clearwell, sometimes far too attractive for my peace of mind.'

'But you don't love me.'

He didn't say anything.

'Francis—'

'If the reasons I've already given don't persuade you, perhaps you should consider your father. When he returns from Jamaica, he hopes to use the fortune he's made to launch you into society with every possible advantage. If you refuse to marry me now, you'll be at the center of a scandal that will cause your father a great deal of unnecessary distress. He'll return to find his daughter's name ruined and her chances of ever making a good match spoiled beyond redemption. Is that what you want for him?'

'That isn't fair, Francis.'

'I don't mean to be fair, I mean to make you see sense. Marry me, Alison, and spare everyone an endless number of difficulties.'

'But, what of Pamela? She's my closest friend.'

'Pamela will never be my wife now, make no mistake about that. Please, Alison, for all our sakes.'

'I don't know what to do . . .' Confusion swirled through her.

'It's very simple, Alison, just say yes.'

'Francis, we'll be marrying for all the wrong reasons.'

'Many marriages have succeeded on far less than we have.'

She looked into his eyes. 'Is this what you really want?' she asked softly.

'Yes, Alison, it's what I really want.'

Her lips trembled. Briefly she saw Pamela's accusing face, and her conscience cut through her.

'Just say yes,' he whispered, his fingers closing persuasively over hers.

She found herself nodding. 'Yes,' she breathed. 'Yes, I'll marry you.'

He exhaled slowly with relief. 'You won't regret it, I swear it, Alison.' The boat nudged the foot of the steps, and he glanced up toward the top of the embankment far above. 'When we go into the house, we'll tell your uncle and everyone else exactly what we've told the prince. And since your uncle is bound to agree in order to protect your good name, I think we can consider the matter settled. I'll also tell the same story at the British embassy when I report there. No one need ever know that we aren't a love match.' He stepped ashore and then turned to hand her out of the boat.

She hesitated for a moment, for she felt as if she was being swept helplessly along. 'I wish there was another way.'

He drew her closer, tilting her face toward his. 'Alison, do you find the thought of marrying me totally abhorrent?'

'No, no of course not,' she said quickly. Abhorrent? She was halfway to loving him, but she didn't want to win him this way.

'I don't intend to make you my wife and then discard you. I mean to do the right and proper thing by you in every way, but first I must attend to the reason I'm now here in St Petersburg. That must come before all else, you do understand, don't you?'

She nodded. 'I promised in Stockholm that I would do what was required of me, and I still stand by that.'

He smiled a little wryly. 'But I'll warrant you didn't think so much would be expected of you,' he murmured.

'That will teach me to make promises to strange gentlemen,' she replied, attempting to disguise her true turmoil by making light of it.

'And it will teach me to take on the mantle of St George,' he said, smiling, but then he became more serious. 'I'm truly sorry to have forced all this upon you, Alison. In Stockholm you wanted to flee safely home to England, and if I'd allowed you to, then none of this would be happening now.'

'And maybe your subsequent decision to press on to St Petersburg on your own would indeed have incurred much more suspicion from the prince.'

His eyes were very blue. 'Who knows indeed?' he said softly, then he turned to indicate the steps. 'Let us enter the fray.'

He offered her his arm and they proceeded up toward the tree-lined waterfront above. Behind them the *Irina* still shone on the wide Neva, her crimson sails furled and her beautiful figurehead gazing toward the crowded pontoon bridge.

They crossed the wide paved street toward the Clearwell residence, and a light breeze blew in from the sea, stirring through the trees. Alison's heart began to beat more swiftly as they passed the waiting carriage and beneath the colonnaded portico to the door, where the maid had now gone in after polishing the lion's-head knocker until it sparkled. As they waited for the door to open in response to Francis's authoritative knock, Alison glanced back down at Mrs Fairfax-Gunn's carriage and four.

Suddenly the door opened, and they were confronted by a stern-faced butler in a dark-brown velvet coat and beige knee breeches. His complexion was sallow and his eyes were set together above an aquiline nose, and on his head there reposed a powdered wig. He didn't look Russian, as indeed he wasn't, for he spoke with a Scottish accent and his name was Mackay.

On hearing who they were he immediately admitted them,

murmuring a welcome to St Petersburg and saying that they hadn't been expected to arrive together. They stepped into an entrance hall of great splendor, with a shining parquet floor, walls hung with exquisite green silk, and a lofty ceiling from which hung no fewer than eight crystal chandeliers. A marble staircase swept up between Corinthian columns toward the floor above and the main reception rooms. Then it continued on up to the next floor and the bedrooms. Paneled mirrors on the walls gave a cunning illusion of endless vistas, and the only item of furniture was a golden couch placed before the huge fire burning in the wide marble hearth to their right. Two portraits hung on either side of the chimney breast, one of Catherine the Great and the other of King George III. There were a number of foliage plants standing in polished brass bowls, some of them climbing up the columns and others over treillages. The Russian winters were long and harsh, and so summer was recreated indoors. The scent of hyacinths was everywhere, for vases of the heady spring blooms stood all around; it was a perfume that ever afterward would remind Alison of the moment she entered her uncle's house in St Petersburg.

Mackay relieved them both of their outdoor clothes and then paused, a little perplexed. 'Begging your pardon, sir,' he said to Francis, 'but isn't there any luggage? Perhaps Miss Clearwell's maid has remained with it on board the ship?'

'It's a long story, Mackay, but Miss Clearwell has no maid or chaperone, and only a single valise, and all my luggage will arrive tonight when the *Pavlovsk* gets in.'

The butler looked mystified. 'Very well, sir. Mrs Clearwell is out at the moment because her father is returning to Novgorod today, but Mr Clearwell is in the grand salon. Mrs Fairfax-Gunn has called, so if you would be so kind as to remain here, I will inform him of your arrival.'

'That's quite in order, Mackay. Proceed as you wish,' replied Francis.

'Thank you, sir.' Bowing, the butler spirited their outdoor garments away to where a footman was discreetly waiting, then the footman melted away into the shadows while the butler went slowly up the staircase.

Francis drew Alison toward the fireplace and ushered her on to the sofa. Then he smiled down at her. 'Journey's end at last.'

She glanced around. 'It feels very odd to be in this house, for although it belongs to my only uncle, it's still the house of a complete stranger.'

'Surely not a complete stranger, for you know his son, William, well enough.'

'William and I aren't that well acquainted; indeed, you most probably know him better than I.' She looked away as the thought crossed her mind that Pamela too knew William a great deal better than she. She wondered if Francis knew about Pamela's close friendship with William, for the Marchingtons had gone to considerable lengths to conceal what they saw as their daughter's indiscretion.

Mackay was coming back downstairs, and at the bottom he hastened to stand in readiness by the front door, thus indicating that Mrs Fairfax-Gunn's brief visit was at an end. The voices of a lady and gentleman echoed from the floor above as Mr Clearwell politely escorted his guest, and what they were saying carried very closely down into the hall below.

'My dear Mr Clearwell, I'm so disappointed that your wife isn't at home as expected, but of course I understand that she must put her father before me. Now, then, you will come to the opera tonight, won't you? And now that your niece, Miss Clearwell, is here, to say nothing of dear Lord Buckingham, I simply insist that they come as well. I know it isn't the thing to fill one's box, but I think five is quite acceptable.'

'Er, I'm sure they'll be delighted to accept, Mrs Fairfax-Gunn, for the cream of St Petersburg society is bound to attend now that Czar Alexander is to be there.'

'Mr Clearwell, do you think that the Countess Irina will attend? I've been in St Petersburg for more than a week now and I've been so longing to see her, but I fear she hasn't left her residence on Crustoosky Island—'

'Krestovsky Island,' said Mr Clearwell.

'I beg your pardon? Oh, yes, I'm afraid my command of these Russian names is too dreadful for words. Where was I? The Countess Irina. Do you think she will attend?'

'It is her custom to attend first nights, Mrs Fairfax-Gunn, and I happen to know that she is particularly fond of Mozart.'

'Oh, I do hope you are right, for I'm dying to see her. I'm told she's quite the most beautiful woman in the whole of Russia.'

'Well, since I haven't seen the entire female population of Russia, I cannot presume to comment,' Alison's uncle replied, 'but she most certainly is very striking.'

'Red hair, I understand.'

'Titian hair,' replied Mr Clearwell.

'Red, titian, what's the difference?' remarked Mrs Fairfax-Gunn, obviously a little miffed at being put right a second time. Then she forgot her mild annoyance and bubbled irrepressibly on. 'I'm so excited now that the countess's brother has returned. You are certain that the schooner belongs to him?'

'Quite certain, for the *Irina* is very distinctive, and the view from this house is quite superb.'

'Such an elegant vessel,' agreed Mrs Fairfax-Gunn. 'Oh, I can't wait to meet the prince; indeed, I shall do my utmost to win an introduction. They say he's devastatingly handsome.' She sighed wistfully. 'I was so afraid that I wouldn't even see him because he was in Stockholm, but now he's back, and—'

'Madam, it could be that the schooner sailed without him, and he's still in Stockholm,' Mr Clearwell pointed out patiently.

'Oh, no, I'm certain he's here,' she declared. 'Do you think he will be at the opera tonight?'

'I really have no idea, Mrs Fairfax-Gunn.'

'I certainly hope he will be, for I absolutely refuse to return to England without being able to boast that I've met the most important man in St Petersburg after Czar Alexander himself.'

The voices were almost at the top of the staircase now, and Alison turned to stare up for her first glimpse of her uncle and the infamous Mrs Fairfax-Gunn. But at the precise moment that a splash of bright vermillion came into view, Francis suddenly stepped forward and took her hand, bending as he raised it to his lips. He lingered over the moment, enclosing her hand in both his, and it was a deliberately intimate gesture, fully intended to be witnessed by the two people who had just arrived at the head of the staircase.

Alison's breath caught and color rushed into her cheeks. She tried to snatch her hand away, but it was too late, and anyway Francis held her too tightly. She looked accusingly into his eyes, for she hadn't expected his action, and she didn't like having such a gesture forced upon her in front of the uncle she had never met and in whose house she was to stay.

His eyes were very blue and compelling. 'We've chosen our course and we're going to follow it to its conclusion, Alison,' he said softly, then he slowly relaxed his hold upon her fingers.

At the top of the staircase Mr Clearwell and Mrs Fairfax-Gunn had come to an astonished halt, taken completely by surprise by the apparently loving scene they had just witnessed by the fireplace.

10

lison's cheeks were crimson with embarrassment as she turned unwillingly to look up. Her uncle was so like her father that he might have been his twin instead of his elder by six years. He had the same tall, lean, courtly good looks, and his gray hair hadn't thinned at all. His indigo wool coat boasted a black velvet collar, and the gold buckles on his white silk knee breeches matched the buckles on his black shoes. A starched neckcloth burgeoned at his throat, and the lace adorning the front of his shirt protruded from a partially buttoned waistcoat of fine old-rose brocade. His hazel eyes, mirrors of her father's, were at first just astonished, but they then darkened with anger as he began to descend.

Mrs Arabella Fairfax-Gunn simply couldn't believe her eyes, or her good fortune, in having happened upon a scene as intriguing as the one she had just observed. Could it really be that she had seen handsome Lord Buckingham, who was soon to be betrothed to dear Lady Pamela Linsey, tenderly kissing the hand of an unmarried young lady with whom he had apparently been traveling alone? The scandalmonger's clever eyes cast swiftly around the hall, but found no sign of a maid or a chaperon, or even of any luggage. How very, very curious. For a moment she hesitated, but then swept on down the staircase in Mr Clearwell's wake.

She was as short and round as Francis had said, and her porcine figure was clad in the most unbecoming vermilion pelisse and matching gown. Even the plumes springing from her wide-brimmed hat had been dyed vermilion, and they quivered like the antennae of a monstrous insect that had just detected a delicious tidbit nearby. Her brown eyes glittered as they rested appraisingly on the two new arrivals. Something was afoot, her every instinct told her so.

Alison felt quite dreadful as her uncle reached them. His bright glance encompassed her for a moment and then moved to Francis. Lowering his voice so as not to be heard by the swiftly approaching Mrs Fairfax-Gunn, he spoke very briefly. 'I trust you have a suitable explanation at the ready, sir.'

He said no more, because Mrs Fairfax-Gunn swept up in an eager rustle of costly silk. Her expert gaze moved calculatingly over every inch of Alison's appearance, her lips twitched shrewdly and then she beamed at Francis. 'Why, dear Lord Buckingham, what a delightful and unexpected pleasure it is to see you here. Until a few moments ago I had no idea at all that you were coming to St Petersburg.' She extended a plump vermilion-gloved hand for him to kiss.

'Mrs Fairfax-Gunn,' he murmured, obliging with the hand, 'I have to confess that I had no idea you would be here either.'

Her smile was sleek. 'I'm quite sure you didn't, sir,' she said, glancing pointedly at Alison, who still sat on the sofa, her gaze downcast because she hadn't yet regained her composure. Mrs Fairfax-Gunn's eyes flickered cleverly. 'Lord Buckingham, do introduce me to Miss Clearwell.'

Again Francis obliged. 'Mrs Fairfax-Gunn, may I present Miss Clearwell. Alison, this is Mrs Fairfax-Gunn.'

He used Alison's first name quite deliberately, as Alison herself knew full well, but to Mrs Fairfax-Gunn and Mr Clearwell it sounded like a very telling slip of the tongue.

Mr Clearwell's hazel eyes darkened still more, and he was about to speak when Mrs Fairfax-Gunn turned once more to Francis. 'Lord Buckingham, do tell me how dear Lady Pamela is. Is she well?'

'She was when last I saw her.'

'Which was when?'

'Some time at the beginning of March.'

'So long ago?' murmured the other, her tone suggesting that he had obviously been busying himself since then.

Mr Clearwell decided that the moment had come to bring the meeting to an end. He was fully aware of Mrs Fairfax-Gunn's reputation, and he had no desire to present her with any more ammunition to spread around the drawing rooms of St Petersburg. Giving her a gracious smile, he took her hand and drew it determinedly over his sleeve. 'Thank you so much for calling today, Mrs Fairfax-Gunn, I'm sorry that Mrs Clearwell wasn't at home, but as I've explained, she is saying goodbye to her father.'

The woman reluctantly allowed herself to be led toward the door, where Mackay was waiting. She halted suddenly, turning to look back at Francis. 'You and Miss Clearwell are invited to share my box at the opera tonight, Lord Buckingham. Mr and Mrs Clearwell are coming, and I'm sure it will be an excellent evening. It's *Don Giovanni*, you know.'

Francis smiled. 'Miss Clearwell and I gladly accept your kind invitation, Mrs Fairfax-Gunn.'

Triumphant in the knowledge that she would now be able to pry and pump much more, she permitted the discreetly exasperated Mr Clearwell to conduct her to the door, then swept out to her waiting carriage. The door closed behind her and Mr Clearwell walked swiftly back to the two by the fireplace.

His wrath fell initially upon Alison. 'Well, missy? I'm deeply disappointed that our first meeting should take place under such unfortunate circumstances. What were you thinking of? How could you indulge in such an unguarded display of affection in front of that infernal woman! Indeed, how could you indulge in it at all! I begin to wonder what manner of lessons you've been receiving at that so-called academy for young ladies. I am appalled that you should consider it fit not only to travel unchaperoned, but also in the company of a gentleman who is not even remotely related to you.'

Mr Clearwell turned to Francis. 'As for you, sir, I trust you're well pleased with yourself for having supplied the town crier with chitter-chatter to broadcast up and down the Neva. William's letters led me to believe you to be an upright man of honor, but your conduct here so far hasn't been in the least honorable. Have you no sense of propriety?'

'Sir—'

'And don't think to fob me off with idle excuses, my lord,' interrupted Mr Clearwell before Francis could say anything. 'I want to hear what you have to say in mitigation – in short, I want a good defense of your actions. Do I make myself clear?'

'Abundantly so, sir, and in my defense I can only say that I love your niece and that my actions haven't been in the least frivolous. I realize that I have compromised her in front of Mrs Fairfax-Gunn, but I fear she has been compromised far more in front of Prince Naryshky. Please don't misunderstand, for I haven't taken advantage of her – I care for her too much for that – but due to circumstances that were indeed extenuating, I fear that much damage has been done to Alison's reputation.'

Mr Clearwell stared at him. 'Do you intend to elucidate upon this?' he asked after a moment, his tone frosty.

'It's a long story, sir.'

'Then let us adjourn to the grand salon. Please follow me.' He led the way to the staircase.

The grand salon deserved its name, for it was a very handsome high-ceilinged room on the floor above, occupying one entire side of the mansion. There were tall windows on three walls, some overlooking the Neva, some the walled garden at the side, and the rest facing toward the grounds at the rear and the coach houses and stables that backed on to the properties in Horseguards Boulevard, running parallel with English Quay.

Its walls were hung with sumptuous blue-and-silver brocade, and like the hall below it positively glittered with chandeliers. The Russians had an immense liking for brilliantly lit houses, and so most rooms possessed an abundance of chandeliers, candelabra, girandoles, or just simple candleholders. Gilt-framed paintings hung on the walls, the furniture was upholstered in sapphire-blue velvet, and the heavy blue silk curtains were tied with silver ropes. The only wall without windows was taken up with an impressive line of display cabinets and with a wide white marble fireplace. Flame light danced over the rich furnishings and cast moving shadows over the contents of the display cabinets: jade, porphyry, ivory, and exquisite porcelain figurines. The air was again heady with the scent of hyacinths, for there were bowls of the sweet-smelling flowers on every table. There were more plants everywhere, and a beautiful telescope was on a stand by the windows, through which it was possible to observe the Neva and Vassily Island opposite.

Francis conducted Alison to a chair close to the fireplace and then remained standing as he waited for her uncle to be seated.

Mr Clearwell made himself comfortable in what was obviously his favorite chair and then surveyed Francis. 'Well, sir? I await your story.'

'Mr Clearwell, please believe me when I say that the last thing I ever wished to do was damage Alison's good name, but I fell in love with her from the moment I saw her, and I'm afraid my interest was beginning to be remarked upon in England. I was naturally anxious to protect her, but with her father's return delayed for so long, and with her understandable wish to obtain his consent, it wasn't acceptable to simply go ahead with a clandestine match. Then, completely by coincidence, arrangements were made for her to come here to St Petersburg, and since I knew that you were in fact the head of her family and that you were acting in her father's absence, I made arrangements to come here as well, to seek your permission to marry.'

Alison stared into the fire. If only he were speaking the truth, if only he did love her as he claimed . . .

Mr Clearwell took a long breath. 'Proceed, sir.'

'It was necessary for me to leave England before Alison, and we arranged to meet in Stockholm. She traveled with a chaperone who was engaged for her by Miss Wright in Bath. The chaperone was entirely unsuitable and deserted Alison the moment the ship dropped anchor in Stockholm. Then, that very night, a fire broke out on the ship and Alison only just escaped with her life. It wasn't possible to find another vessel before morning, and so we were forced to stay overnight at an inn. Naturally we took separate rooms, but Alison was already distressed after so much going wrong, and when a thief was apprehended on the premises, she became very upset indeed. It was all too much for her, sir, and I decided that she should not be left alone. I slept in the armchair in her room for the rest of the night.' He paused, waiting for Mr Clearwell to say something, but he remained silent.

Francis proceeded. 'We didn't think that this impropriety would ever come to light because it happened in Stockholm and we were on the point of coming on here to St Petersburg. Unfortunately, Prince Naryshky was staying at the same inn and we made his acquaintance.

He was to have remained in Stockholm, but to our dismay he has also returned to St Petersburg, and he knows about that night in the inn. He has displayed considerable interest in us, so much so that he wishes to attend our marriage, and he went so far as to meet our ship at Kronstadt and convey us here on his schooner. Our luggage is still on the other vessel and will not arrive until much later today.

'Mr Clearwell, that is why I fear that Alison has already been gravely compromised, and now that Mrs Fairfax-Gunn is here and has made it clear not only that does she guess there is something going on but also that she intends by hook or by crook to gain an introduction to the prince, you must see that the situation is quite impossible. You must permit me to marry your niece, sir, and to do so without any delay at all; otherwise, her name will be bandied over St Petersburg and then over London as well. I wish to do all in my power to protect her from that.'

Alison still gazed into the heart of the fire. It was fact, and yet it wasn't; it was the truth with a clever sprinkling of untruths here and there.

Her uncle exhaled slowly. 'You haven't behaved prudently, have you? If your conduct in England had been what it should be, none of this would have arisen.'

'On that count I'm to blame,' Francis replied with a nod. 'I wish it were not so.'

'Before I say what I intend to do, I wish you to answer a question, my lord.'

'Please ask it.'

Mr Clearwell rose slowly to his feet. 'It concerns the existence of a prior arrangement between you and Lady Pamela Linsey, the daughter of the Duke of Marchington.'

Francis paused for a moment. 'I didn't know you knew about that, sir.'

'I know of it because William mentioned it in his last letter. Knowing my son as I do, I can read between the lines and guess that he too is enamoured of that particular lady.'

'Yes, sir, he does.'

Alison looked up quickly. So he did know about William and Pamela.

Francis spoke again. 'Mr Clearwell, if the truth be known, Lady Pamela regrets having allowed her parents to separate her from your son. The Duke of Marchington wished her to marry someone with a title, and William wasn't considered to be suitable enough. She's fond of me, as I am of her, but we don't love each other. She loves your son, and I love your niece.'

Alison stared at him. How could he say such a thing! Pamela loved him and he loved her, and if his other untruths could be justified, this one couldn't.

Her uncle pursed his lips. 'Well, that may or may not be so, my lord, but what I need to know is whether or not you are free to many Alison. Was there a binding agreement between you and Lady Pamela?'

'The betrothal was to have taken place in July, sir, but there is no longer any question that it will still take place. My dealings with Lady Pamela will in future be those of a friend, not a suitor.'

'I see. Do I have your word upon that?'

'You do, sir.'

Mr Clearwell nodded. 'Very well, you have my consent. Indeed, I have no real option if I wish to act as my brother would. Alison must be shielded from any odium or gossip, and that has to be my prime consideration. I have to tell you, sir, that if you hadn't expressed a desire to do the right thing by her, I would have insisted that you did.'

'I wouldn't expect you to do anything else, sir.'

'The marriage will take place as soon as the appropriate special license can be obtained. The English church is closed at the moment, as it is soon to be demolished and rebuilt, which means that you must marry here in this house. The new British ambassador is an agreeable fellow, and I'm sure he can be prevailed upon to speed things up. With luck, all should be accomplished in a few days.'

'I trust so, sir, for although I've mishandled things to a certain extent, I do love Alison with all my heart. May I now ask you a question, sir?'

'By all means.'

'How well acquainted are you with Prince Naryshky?'

'If it were up to me, I'd avoid him like the plague itself. I think him a most disagreeable fellow, thoroughly unscrupulous and a

Bonapartist to boot. He and his sister dislike the British and do all they can to promote the French cause. Do you know of his sister?'

'The Countess Irina von Strelitz? Yes, I do.'

'Suffice it that at the moment Czar Alexander pays heed to her every slightest wish. He's completely devoted to her, and for all I know, she may be equally devoted to him, but I doubt it. She's Naryshky's sister and undoubtedly as scheming and treacherous as he.'

Francis looked closely at him. "You said "if it were up to me".'

'Yes, because although I would have nothing to do with him, I'm afraid that my wife isn't in any position to follow such a lead. Her father is the prince's tenant on one of his estates at Novgorod, which is about one hundred miles south of here on the road to Moscow. In Russia to be a man's tenant is tantamount to being his property, and Leon Razumov, Natalia's father, although a wealthy man, is entirely in Naryshky's grip. Why, I even had to approach Naryshky for permission to marry Natalia.' He drew a heavy breath. 'I will be honest with you, Leon has been here in St Petersburg for the past week or so endeavoring to see Naryshky's overseer, who is a man with even fewer scruples than the prince himself. It seems that the overseer, whose name is Bragin, has a nephew whom he wishes to see in Leon's place at Novgorod, and that when Naryshky returns he is to be approached on the matter. Naryshky pays great attention to Bragin, who is invaluable to him because he'll carry out any order, no matter how ruthless, and it's therefore rather doubtful if Leon's cause will receive any sympathy at all. Natalia is naturally very upset about it all, for she loves her father and still has brothers and sisters on the estate where the family has lived for more than two hundred years.'

'I'm very sorry to hear all this, sir, especially as my opinion of Narshky more than equates with yours,' replied Francis sympathetically.

'Perhaps a wedding would be a welcome diversion for Natalia, for she feels so helpless where her father is concerned. She adores weddings and is still young enough to think that love is wonderful.' Mr Clearwell smiled fondly. 'For many years she nursed a broken heart because her fiancé was killed in a hunting accident, and at thirty-five she believed she was destined to remain a spinster. I thought I was too set in my ways to marry again, but when we met, we hit it off immediately. She is the most precious thing in my life, and so perhaps I can understand how you and Alison feel about each other. I know that in giving my consent to your marriage I am doing what my brother would do if he were here, for although we haven't seen each other in many years, I'm still sure I know how he would react to these circumstances.'

'I'm very grateful for your understanding, sir.'

'Understanding your situation is one thing; enduring the wretched Mrs Fairfax-Gunn at the opera tonight is quite another. But I think we must press ahead with it. She was going from here to the British embassy, where there is apparently a gathering of wives to hear some unutterable fellow sing Russian folk songs. She'll have been clacking away for some time by now and everyone will already be whispering about you two. The sooner we brave them all, the better, I fancy.'

'I agree, sir.'

'Besides, *Don Giovanni* is my favorite opera, and Count Vorontzov's private box is one of the best placed in the opera house.'

'Count Vorontzov? The Russian ambassador in London?' Francis asked.

'Yes, it seems that he and the late Mr Fairfax-Gunn, who most probably went to his grave to escape from his wife, were very good friends, the count having been ambassador since the eighties. Anyway, when Vorontzov learned of the lady's desire to visit St Petersburg, he arranged for her to use the house of a friend who is away in the country for the time being, and he gave her full use of his family's private box at the opera house, there not being a Vorontzov in St Petersburg until September. At this precise moment I cordially wish Count Simon Vorontzov in perdition, you may be sure of that.' Mr Clearwell looked at Francis. 'By the way, was there any foundation in this business of your purchasing a colt from the imperial stables?'

'Foundation? Why, yes, of course. Why do you ask?'

'Because it seemed probable on reflection that it was simply a ploy to be here with Alison.'

'My business with Czar Alexander is genuine, I promise you. Indeed, one of my first priorities must be to leave my name at the Winter Palace and trust that I will soon be summoned.' Francis's glance moved briefly to meet Alison's.

Her uncle didn't notice. 'I will drive you to the palace in my carriage this afternoon. We'll stop at the British embassy on the way and see about that special license.'

'By all means, sir. Thank you.'

A carriage drew up outside and Mr Clearwell went to the window. 'Ah, here is Natalia now. I'll go down to meet her and tell her all about you. I do hope that your arrival will take her mind off her father.' He hurried out, closing the door behind him.

Alison immediately got up, looking accusingly at Francis. 'Did you have to say those things about Pamela and William? We're wronging Pamela enough already without suggesting that she—'

'Are we?' he interrupted, stiffening because he was caught off-guard by her anger.

'Yes, of course we are.' Her guilty conscience was weighing very heavily in that moment.

'And what do you know about Pamela and your cousin? Anything at all? Did you ever see them together after she left Bath? No, you didn't, which means that you know absolutely nothing on the subject.'

'I know that she loves you.'

'Really? And how, exactly, do you know that?' he asked cuttingly.

For a moment she stared at him; then she turned away because she had to battle against the tears that again brimmed to the surface.

He closed his eyes for a moment and then went to her, turning her to face him. 'What is it?' he asked gently.

'I feel so terribly guilty,' she whispered, the tears shining in her large gray eyes. 'I keep thinking about Pamela, and I feel dreadful.'

'Then don't.'

'That's an impossible instruction to obey.'

'Alison, I know that all this has been a great strain for you and that it's far from over yet, but I promise you that the moment I can, I'll take you home to England.'

'Home? And where will my home be, Francis?' she asked quietly.

'With me, because you'll be my wife.'

'Yes, the wife you don't want because Pamela is the one you love.'

'I'm marrying you because I want to.'

She shook her head. 'You're marrying me because you feel obliged to and because you wish above all to protect your true purpose here. Don't lie to me, Francis, for I know full well that you don't want me.'

Her uncle and step-aunt were approaching the door, and she drew away from him to return to her seat. She avoided his eyes because she was afraid that he would realize how she really felt about him. She had to shield herself from hurt, for loving him was already bringing her heartbreak.

11

The second Mrs Thomas Clearwell was petite and instantly likable, with rich brown hair, friendly green eyes, and an open countenance. She wore a mustard-colored pelisse trimmed with sable, and beneath a sable hat her hair was coiled up in two plump plaits. It was evident that she was as devoted to her husband as he was to her, but it was also evident that she had been crying, for her eyes were tearstained. She endeavored to conceal it, however, hastening forward immediately to take Alison's hands.

'Ah, my dear, what a surprise you have caused!' She had a pleasant voice with a heavy Russian accent. She turned to Francis. 'And you, my lord, we thought you wished only to purchase a horse from the czar, but instead you've come to steal my husband's niece.'

'I've come to do both,' he replied, kissing the little hand she extended to him.

'Practical and passionate? Sir, that is Russian, not British,' she said lightly.

Mr Clearwell hastened to effect the necessary introductions.

'My lord, may I introduce my wife, Mrs Clearwell. Natalia, this is Francis, Lord Buckingham.'

Francis still held Natalia's hand, and he drew it to his lips a second time. 'I am honored to make your acquaintance, Mrs Clearwell.'

'And I yours, sir.'

Natalia then turned to Alison, and once again Mr Clearwell introduced them formally. 'Alison, this is your Aunt Natalia. Natalia, my niece, Alison.'

Natalia smiled into Alison's eyes. 'I am truly delighted that you have come to stay with us, my dear, for it will be so good to have a little company. Your uncle says that you have no maid or chaperone. Is this so?'

'Yes.' Alison quickly explained.

'You shall have Katya to attend you. She is from here in St Petersburg and is very good. I know because she attended me when my maid was indisposed. Your luggage arrived safely several weeks ago, and all your clothes have been aired and smoothed in readiness. How provident it was that your headmistress chose to send every-thing ahead, for if she hadn't and it had all been with you on that ship in Stockholm . . .' Natalia broke off, looking concernedly at her. 'It must have been a very frightening experience for you, my dear.'

'Yes, it was.'

'But at least you were not alone, for you had his lordship to comfort you.'

'Yes.'

'Well, all that dreadfulness is over now, Alison, and you are safely here with us. We will make this stay a very happy one, I promise you, and I will see to it that you are the most beautiful of brides.' Natalia paused again. 'Your uncle tells me that Prince Naryshky is not only well disposed toward you, but also that he wishes to attend your wedding. Is this true?'

'Yes, he has expressed such a wish.'

Mr Clearwell looked anxiously toward his wife. 'Natalia, I trust that you do not intend to use the occasion to approach the prince.'

'I must do something, Thomas.'

'He is an upredictable, contrary, and unpleasant man, my dear, and my advice is that you simply leave well alone. Bragin has a great deal of influence with him, but if Naryshky is in a bad mood when even his most trusted henchman approaches him, then any request will be turned down flat. Your father stands a better chance if things are simply left as they are, believe me.'

'But if I just stand aside and do nothing, I will feel that I have failed my father.'

'He knows that you support him, my dear,' said Mr Clearwell, putting his arm lovingly around her shoulder.

'He was so sad when he drove away. I have never seen him brought so low and unhappy.' Fresh tears filled Natalia's eyes.

Mr Clearwell kissed her forehead. 'I know, my dear, I know. Now, then, you must put all that from your mind and attend to your duties where Alison is concerned. Show her the room you have taken so much trouble to prepare for her, and perhaps you can begin to discuss the wedding plans. Lord Buckingham and I intend to go to the embassy this afternoon to seek the special license, and after that, the wedding will take place as quickly as possible.'

Natalia took the handkerchief he pressed into her hand, and then she managed a brave smile. 'You are right, Thomas. I must try to think of something else, and what better diversion could there be than a wedding.' She looked apologetically at Alison and Francis. 'Please forgive me, for I do not wish to dampen everything. Come, Alison, let me show you to your room. I do hope you will like it, for I have given it much thought.'

She went to the door and Alison began to follow her, but then Francis stepped quickly forward, taking Alison's hand and drawing it to his lips. His blue eyes were warm and intense as they gazed into hers, and he whispered softly so that only she could hear.

'Don't feel guilty anymore, Alison, I beg of you. Go to your room now and rest for a while, and when we meet again, know that I really do wish to make you my wife.'

Then he nodded toward Natalia, who was waiting at the door. 'Go with your aunt,' he said more audibly.

Alison did as he bade, and as she and Natalia walked away from the grand salon toward the staircase that led up to the floor above, Natalia smiled at her. 'Lord Buckingham quite obviously loves you to distraction, my dear, and I could not be more happy for you. To have the love of a fine man is the most wonderful thing in all the world, but if that man is also so handsome that he stops your heart, and if he is wealthy and has a title, what more could any woman ask of fate? God is disposed to smile upon you, Alison, there is no mistake about that.'

Alison summoned a smile. 'I love Francis with all my heart,' she replied simply, and knew that it was true.

Her room was at the side of the house, facing east toward the heart of St Petersburg. The two tall windows looked out over the walled garden beside the mansion, and the view extended over the Neva to the left, and the rooftops of Horseguards Boulevard to the right, parallel to and behind English Quay. Isaac Bridge could be seen stretching across the river's shining dark-blue water, and the *Irina*'s beautiful white silhouette still rocked at anchor in the same place.

Gray-and-gold silk adorned the room's walls, and heavy gray velvet curtains hung at the windows. There was a large four-poster bed draped with dull gold silk and an elegant fireside chair upholstered in the same gray velvet as the curtains. Flames flickered warmly in the pink marble hearth, and there were more hyacinths to fill the air with perfume. Several luxuriant ferns stood in big brass bowls, and a bay tree in a terra-cotta pot had been placed against the wall between the two windows. Chandeliers were suspended from the high ceiling, their crystal drops moving gently in the heat from the fire. A gray, white, and gold carpet had been placed in the center of the parquet floor, the fringe combed so carefully that there wasn't a single strand out of place. All around the edge the wooden floor shone with polish, reflecting the dancing light from the fire.

Through an adjoining door there was a large dressing room containing a muslin-draped dressing table with a looking glass, a row of large white-and-gold wardrobes, a washstand behind a lacquered Spanish screen, and a handsome full-length cheval glass in which one might examine every inch of one's appearance.

Natalia stood by the four-poster bed, looking anxiously at Alison as she glanced around. 'I do hope you like it, my dear.'

'It's very beautiful,' replied Alison, smiling warmly at her. 'You have indeed taken care of everything, and I'm very grateful.'

Natalia relaxed. 'I did not know what you would like, Alison. I know the sort of things that young Russian ladies appreciate, but when it comes to someone from England . . .'

'I couldn't be more delighted with everything, Aunt Natalia.'

'Thank you, my dear. You must forgive the hyacinths that are everywhere, only they are my favorite flower, and on my birthday last week your uncle had what seemed to be every hyacinth in St Petersburg delivered to the door.'

'I am very fond of hyacinths.'

'My dear, at the moment you will have to be,' said Natalia, laughing a little. 'Ah, it is good to have another woman to talk to. At home I have sisters, and I miss them . . .' Her smile trembled a little. 'I mustn't think about home,' she said briskly, walking to the window and looking out. 'I understand we are all to go to the opera tonight.'

'Yes.'

'It wasn't entirely accidental that I chose to be out today when I knew that that terrible woman might call. She is an incorrigible troublemaker, and if she could make something of the fact that I have married an older man, I vow that she would. She is bound to stir up all the scandal she can where you and Lord Bucking-ham are concerned, you know that, don't you?'

'Yes. Francis knows her from England.'

'She is quite horrid, but since your uncle has accepted her invitation, I fear we must go. Still, it is Mozart, and that at least I will enjoy.' Natalia turned to look at her. 'Are you really up to a visit to the opera, my dear? You look so pale and tired.'

'I'll be all right when I've rested for a while, Aunt Natalia.'

'Then rest you shall, and this afternoon you and I will begin to discuss the wedding. It will be small, I know, for such things must be of necessity, but we must still make you the most delectable of brides, must we not?'

'We can try.'

'My dear, you are hardly a plain little mouse,' declared her new step-aunt with a warm smile. Then she sighed. 'I know that your uncle has advised me not to say anything to the prince, but if he is here in this house and I have the opportunity speak to him, I don't think I will be able to hold my tongue. I am so afraid that my father and the rest of my family are about to be turned out of the estate they've cared for for the past two hundred years. There have been Razumovs in charge at the Naryshky estate in Novgorod ever since the present prince's ancestor first purchased it. Indeed, it is said that the Razumovs were placed there because that ancestor had not only enjoyed the favors of Razumov's wife, but had also fathered her child. I have to admit that sometimes it seems that there is foundation in the story, for every generation of Razumovs possesses at least one member who has the Naryshky blond hair and brown eyes. My brother Alexei bears a more-than-passing resemblance to Prince Nikolai.' She smiled ruefully at

Alison. 'I'm sorry, my dear, for I'm sure that you have no wish to hear the somewhat shocking story of my family's history.'

'Aunt Natalia, there are many families in England with similar tales to tell, and some of those families are very highborn indeed,' replied Alison, thinking of several earldoms and a dukedom or two that owed everything to a king's desire for someone other than his queen.

Natalia nodded. 'Yes, I suppose there are, my dear, but they aren't about to be thrown out of their home because an overseer has too much of the master's ear.'

Alison didn't reply, for the injustice of Leon Razumov's situation was only too plain.

Natalia came to her, giving her a warm hug. 'Welcome to this house, Alison. I'm sure that you and I will get on famously. But for the moment I will leave you to rest. Do you wish for any refreshment? A little light luncheon perhaps?'

'No, thank you. Perhaps later on. . . ?'

'I will send Katya to you in a few hours' time. Rest well, my dear.'

As the door closed upon her step-aunt, Alison went to the window to gaze out. She stared toward the *Irina*, thinking about Nikolai. So much trouble and difficulty had come about simply and solely because he had noticed her. She was afraid of him and wished that she didn't have to see him again.

She looked down into the walled garden below and the criss-cross of paths patterning the lawns. The wall gave shelter enough for the daffodils to be quite advanced, their almost open buds nodding in the light breeze that came in from the Neva. There was a little white summerhouse against the wall, just beyond the wrought-iron gate from the quay. The summerhouse nestled among lilac bushes that must look very lovely indeed when in full bloom.

She stared at the garden, and it seemed to blur before her eyes. She could see Francis's face and hear his whisper. 'Don't feel guilty anymore, Alison, I beg of you. Go to your room now and rest for a while, and when we meet again, know that I really do wish to make you my wife.'

She would be his wife and he would be her husband, but he would never be hers. Although his ring would grace her finger, he would always belong to Pamela.

*

As Alison stood at the window of her room at English Quay, three miles to the north across the city, on secluded Krestovsky Island, the Countess Irina von Strelitz was returning from a ride along the canals and waterways of the delta. She wore a crimson riding habit trimmed with deep white fur, and there was a white fur hat on her magnificent titian hair. Her soft brown eyes were radiant from the ride in the brisk spring air, and her pale cheeks were flushed. She had a curvaceous figure that was outlined exquisitely by the clever cut of the habit, and she rode with the accomplishment that was expected of highborn Russian ladies. Her mount was still impatient after the ride, capering a little as she reached the road that led across her estate to the stables, but she urged it on and the sound of its hooves carried clearly across the park, where fountains played among the lime trees. She was happy because tonight she was going to the opera, a diversion she always enjoyed, and afterward, when St Petersburg slept, the czar would leave his retreat on nearby Kamenny Island, cross over the wooden bridge, and come to be with her. She would lie in his arms between scented sheets, and when he left at dawn, he would love her more than ever, for only she knew how to make him happy and relaxed and, above all, how to satisfy his every and most secret desire.

Her house came into view and she reined in for a moment. It was a lovely house, with a green cupola and a Roman portico on white columns, and it faced across the park toward the wooden bridge leading to Kamenny Island. An elegant conservatory was built against the southern wall, its many glass panes catching the sunlight as she rode toward it. She always returned from her rides to take a little refreshment in the almost tropical surroundings of the conservatory, and accordingly a groom was waiting by the door to take her horse.

As he led the horse away, she paused to tease off her gloves. Her wedding ring shone on her finger, a constant reminder of the great love she had had for her dead husband. She would never forget Axel von Strelitz, and she'd never forgive the British for murdering him.

Pushing open the conservatory door, she stepped from the cold into the sweet-scented humidity inside. Flourishing green leaves pressed all around, and exotic flowers bloomed brilliantly, sometimes white, sometimes a vivid salmon-pink or scarlet, and sometimes mauve or pink. Vines climbed up trellises, vases of cut flowers stood waiting on the red brick floor, in readiness for taking into the house, and tiny birds fluttered among the branches high overhead. There was a tinkle of water as fountains splashed into marble basins where fish darted beneath lily pads and the soft buzzing of insects among the blooms. The air was almost stiflingly hot after the crisp May air outside, for the conservatory was heated by a number of large stoves that were kept constantly stoked to make everything as warm as possible.

There was an alcove at the far end of the conversatory, a secret place where a white-painted wrought-iron table and several chairs had been placed, and it was there that she always liked to sip a small cup of sweet Turkish coffee after her rides. Gathering the skirt of her riding habit, she made her way quickly toward it, for the maid would have put the coffee there the moment her mistress had been seen riding toward the house. Her light footsteps sounded on the pathway leading between the towering greenery, and a small chattering call greeted her as her pet monkey jumped excitedly up and down on its perch, knowing that it was about to be fed some delicious strawberries from the little bowl that was just out of its reach.

Smiling, Irina hurried past the table and chairs without looking and took one of the strawberries to hold it out to the little creature. As the eager little paws snatched at the fruit, someone coughed very deliberately behind her.

Irina whirled about and found herself staring at a dashing figure in the uniform of a high-ranking officer in the Preobrazensky Regiment. 'Nikolai,' she cried delightedly, hurrying to him and flinging herself into his arms.

He laughed, holding her close. 'Irina, Irina, how very good it is to see you again.' He spoke in French, the first language of all highborn Russians.

'But when did you return? I thought you would be in Stockholm for weeks yet.'

'King Gustavus Adolphus is ill, thank God.' He smiled at her, his gaze moving over her lovely face. 'You grow more beautiful each time I see you. I trust that his imperial majesty still pays you every attention?'

'Of course he does. I will see him tonight, first at the opera and
then afterward, when he comes here to be with me.' She drew back.
'Will you come to the opera as well, Nikolai? You know how I hate it
when I have to sit alone in my box, and the czar sits alone in his box.
If you were with me, it would be much better.'

'If you wish it, then of course I will come with you. Irina, how have
things been in my absence?'

'Things?' She went to the table to pour the coffee into the two little
cups that the efficient maid had placed on the tray. 'What things?'

'Political things. Is Alexander more favorably disposed to France
than he was when I left?'

'Yes. I do my best.'

'I'm sure you do.' He smiled as he accepted the cup she held out to
him. 'I trust that the new British ambassador hasn't too many oppor-
tunities to exert his charm upon him?'

'Upon Alexander? No.'

'Good, because if there is one thing our dear czar responds to it is
the cultured and engaging manner of a gentleman like Lord St
Helens.'

Irina's smile faded a little. 'Don't talk about the czar like that.'

'Like what? Oh, Irina, don't be silly, I didn't mean anything.'

She went to the table and sat down, sipping her coffee for a
moment. 'I don't like it when you refer to the czar in that way,
Nikolai.'

A light passed through his eyes and then he nodded. 'Forgive me, I
didn't mean to offend you. Very well, you have my word that I will
be more respectful in future.'

'He has advanced you, Nikolai. If it were not for his assistance, you
would not be of such a high rank in the regiment, would you?'

'And if it were not for his intransigence, I would by now be married
to the Grand-Duchess Helen,' he replied sharply. 'It is good enough
for him to bed you outside his marriage, but it isn't good enough for
me to make his sister my princess.'

Irina's brown eyes swung toward him in surprise at the force of his
bitterness. 'Nikolai, I had no idea you felt so strongly. You've never
given any sign of it before now.

A nerve twitched at Nikolai's temple, for he hadn't meant to let her

realize so much. 'Don't let us argue, Irina, for all this is old ground.'
He looked pointedly at the wedding ring on her finger. 'Perhaps now
is not the time to mention this, but . . .' He allowed his voice to trail
away.

She saw the way he looked at her ring. 'To mention what, Nikolai?'

'Well, knowing how you feel about the way Axel was killed—'

'Was murdered,' she interrupted. 'What do you want to tell me?'

He sat down, ignoring her look of disapproval as he raised his legs
and rested his spurred heels on the edge of the wrought-iron table.
'Do you recall an approach made to the czar by an Englishman called
Lord Buckingham? He wishes to purchase a colt from the imperial
stables.'

She nodded. 'Yes, I remember. What about it?'

'I've now met Lord Buckingham; indeed, I made his acquaintance
and that of his bride-to-be while staying in Stockholm.'

'And? Oh, do get to the point, Nikolai!'

'I was agreeably surprised by them, and when I learned that I was
to come back to St Petersburg, I waited for their ship at Kronstadt and
conveyed them here in the *Irina*.'

'I can only imagine that the lady is very beautiful,' Irina murmured.

'I will ignore that remark,' he replied.

'Which means I'm right. Do go on.'

'Well, during conversation on the *Irina*, I learned that until very
recently Lord Buckingham had been in the British navy and that he
commanded one of their vessels at the Battle of the Nile.'

Irina looked steadily at him. 'Are you sure?' she asked softly.

'Very sure indeed, and what's more, I happen to know that his
vessel was responsible for the final explosion on the *L'Orient*. Irina,
Lord Buckingham may as well have put Axel to death with his own
hand.'

Slowly she put her cup down. Her hand was trembling and her face
had gone pale. She rose to her feet and turned away. 'Why did you
tell me?' she asked in a whisper, going to give the monkey another of
the strawberries.

'Because I happen to know how very much the Englishman desires
that colt from the czar. It means a great deal to him, something to do
with bloodlines and a red Barbary stallion from Syria. It occurs to me

that although it would be small revenge to you for losing Axel, it would nevertheless be quite a blow to his lordship if you were to thwart his plans to see Alexander. All you have to do is whisper in the imperial ear tonight and Lord Buckingham will be denied his dearest wish.'

'Does the acquisition of this colt really mean so much to him?'

'My dear Irina, he's an Englishman, a devotee of the turf, and a passionate breeder of the finest horses. He has set his heart on this colt because he has worked for years to perfect the thoroughbred. It would cut him to the quick to be denied not only that particular colt, but any other from the imperial stables. Indeed, the severest blow you could deal him would be to see that he is denied any prospect of access to the czar, for that would humiliate him as well.'

'Humiliate him?' She turned, a third strawberry in her fingers.

'He's a braggart and has been telling all and sundry that he will be able to persuade the czar to do as he wishes.'

She gave the strawberry to the delighted monkey. 'Lord Buckingham will not see the czar,' she said softly, 'you have my word upon that. When I see Alexander tonight, I will tell him it would hurt me if he received the Englishman who killed my husband.'

'It is wise to ask Alexander a favor that concerns your late husband?'

'The czar understands and respects my feelings for Axel, just as I understand the fondness and respect he has for the czarina, even though he comes so often to my bed. He will grant my wish, make no mistake about that.'

Nikolai smiled and got up from his seat. 'Well, I think I'd better be going.'

'I hoped you might stay,' she said quickly.

He went to her, kissing her on the cheek. 'I've already ignored my duty by coming to see you before I reported to the Winter Palace, and after I've conveyed the situation with Gustavus Adolphus, I'll be expected to go straight to the barracks.'

'But you'll still come to the opera with me tonight?'

'Of course. And you will be sure to put a stop to Lord Buckingham's hopes?'

'Oh, yes, I'll be certain to speak to Alexander tonight. The

Englishman will never be received.'

Smiling again, he turned to go, but Irina spoke once more.

'What is her name, Nikolai?'

'Whose name?'

'Lord Buckingham's bride-to-be. She is what all this is really about, isn't she? You desire her?'

'You wrong me, Irina.'

'I know you, Nikolai.'

He smiled a little. 'Her name is Miss Alison Clearwell.'

'And do you think you will succeed with her?'

'Oh, I mean to succeed with her, Irina,' he replied softly.

'Then I wish you well,' said Irina, taking up a fourth strawberry and holding it out tantalizingly toward the monkey's quick little paws.

Nikolai left the conservatory, and as he returned to the landing stage where a boat was waiting for him, he hummed lightly to himself. Soon Lord Buckingham would be thwarted, whether or not he was a British agent; and if he were to disappear in the near future, it was going to be highly unlikely that Alexander would order an investigation. Alexander would be afraid that Irina was behind the disappearance and would stay his hand in order to shield her.

Lounging back in the stern of the boat, Nikolai smiled a little. He was beginning to feel safe again now that he was able to take control of things himself, and soon he would be as completely secure as ever. In the meantime, however, before his ultimate aim came to rewarding fruition and Alexander paid the price for the insults of the past, there was the delightful prospect of possessing Miss Alison Clearwell. His desire for her had increased rather than lessened, and she was constantly on his mind. Her perfume permeated his dreams, a seductive blend of lavender and innocence to torment his senses, and the need to make her his grew stronger with each passing hour.

12

Alison looked at her reflection in the tall cheval glass, for her preparations were now almost complete and it was nearly time to leave for the ordeal of the opera and Mrs Fairfax-Gunn. Outside, the long northern evening was still light, even though the hour was late, and it would be some time yet before the lamps were lit along the embankment. The *Pavlovsk* had arrived an hour or so before, and now lay at her mooring on Vassily Island, just a little downstream from the *Irina*. Francis's luggage and her valise had been brought straightaway to English Quay.

The new maid Natalia had provided for her had proved to be very talented indeed. Katya was small and slight, with dark hair worn in coiled plaits that were almost completely concealed beneath a large white mobcap, and she wore a sturdy beige linen gown, with a neat white apron to protect it. She had a rather flat face and would have been quite dull had it not been for her lustrous dark-brown eyes, which shone as appealingly as those of a spaniel.

Language had proved something of a problem, for Katya spoke only Russian, with a spattering of French learned from the young tutor from Lyons with whom she had had a brief liaison. French was therefore the only common ground between maid and new mistress, and it was in this language that they had endeavored to get by. After a few initial misunderstandings they had managed quite adequately, so much so that Alison was able to tell Katya exactly how she wished her hair to be dressed and describe to her the sort of posy of fresh violets she wished to wear on a ribbon around her wrist. Now Katya had gone to purchase such a posy, and she would be back in a few minutes.

It had been very satisfying to again have the choice of her full wardrobe, instead of just the rose dimity or the black-and-white-checked wool. Her father had always provided amply for clothes, knowing that it wouldn't have done at all for his daughter to be at a disadvantage among her titled fellow pupils, and so she had had a number of suitable gowns from which to choose for the opera. She had decided upon a simple low-necked silver silk with long diaphanous sleeves that were gathered in a lacy frill at the wrist. It had a pretty amethyst buckle on the high waistband directly beneath her breasts, and so she wore with it the amethyst earrings and necklace that had been her mother's and that thankfully hadn't been among the few pieces of jewelry she had carried with her on the journey, for those pieces now lay at the bottom of Stockholm harbor. It was because of the amethysts that she had thought a posy of violets would look perfect tied around the gathered frill at her wrist. It was a fashion that she had first seen when Pamela had returned from a Christmas vacation at Marchington House, and soon all the girls at the academy had adopted it for special occasions. It was eye-catching and pretty, and not exorbitantly expensive, provided one was sensible about the flowers one chose. Here in St Petersburg it was early spring, and there were always violets in spring, no matter where one was in the world. She regretted that she didn't have any violet scent, and so used her customary lavender water.

Her hair was pinned up into a knot on top of her head, with a few wispy silver-blonde curls framing her face. The knot was twined with silver satin ribbons that fluttered at the slightest movement and gave the knot an almost temporary appearance, as if at any moment a cascade of hair would tumble down to brush her naked shoulders.

There was a discreet tap at the bedroom door, and she left the dressing room. 'Come in, Katya,' she said.

The door opened and Francis stepped in, smiling slightly.

'I've been called many things in my life, Alison, but Katya isn't one of them.'

'I thought it was my maid.'

'So it seems.' He paused, his gaze moving slowly over her. He wore a black velvet evening coat, white satin waistcoat, white gloves, a frilled white silk shirt, white silk pantaloons and stockings, and a ruby pin of some size adorned the lacy folds of his neckcloth and there was a *chapeau-bras* tucked under his arm. He looked the picture of formal elegance, and Alison doubted if there was another man in the world who could match him for style and looks.

His blue eyes met hers and he smiled again. 'You look very lovely, Alison.'

'Thank you.'

'When St Petersburg society sees you tonight, it will understand full well why I wish you to be my bride.'

'You don't have to pretend, Francis.'

'I'm not. I thought I'd made that quite clear.'

She turned away, going to the window to look down into the walled garden. 'Did you and my uncle go to the Winter Palace?'

'Yes. I left my name as is the custom, and now I can only wait and hope that Alexander sends for me without delay. I know he's going to Memel soon, for a meeting with the Prussian emperor, so I trust that he will attend to as much as he can before he leaves.' He studied her. 'Aren't you going to ask if I also called at the embassy?'

'Did you?' She faced him again.

'Naturally. There will be a slight wait before the special license can be issued, something to do with documents, but it will be granted in just under a week. I had hoped that it would be a little more swift, but it can't be helped. Your aunt isn't too displeased, however, for now she has time to issue a few more invitations than had initially seemed possible.'

'Invitations? I thought it was to be a very quiet affair.'

'And so it will be, but it isn't going to be hole-and-corner. Alison, I think you're laboring under something of a misapprehension where this wedding is concerned. There isn't going to be anything under-handed or shameful about it; it's going to be a proper ceremony, and at the end of it you will be Lady Buckingham. Your conscience may make you feel guilty about it, but I swear to you that there is no need to blame yourself for anything.'

'How can you say that! How *can* you,' she cried. 'At this very moment Pamela is at home in England planning for her marriage to you. She loves you, she wrote to me time and time again to say so, and yet here we are, calmly planning to face her with a shocking and unkind *fait accompli*!'

'Well, one of us is planning calmly,' he replied dryly. 'Very well, let me explain again why I think it is essential that we go through with this. First, there is the need to keep Naryshky's suspicions at an absolute minimum, and the way to do that is to give him proof that we are the runaway lovers we say we are. Next, there is the far-from-inconsequential matter of your reputation, which has been greatly harmed by events so far. From your manner now, I begin to wonder if you wish to be known as a woman of no virtue. Then there is the shame that will fall upon your family – upon your father in particular – if we decline to tie the knot and you are left with a considerable stain upon your character. And now we have the further complication of your aunt's father and his difficulty with Naryshky. Do you imagine that Leon Razumov's situation is going to be improved if Naryshky's wrath falls upon the occupants of this house? Well, do you?'

'I – I . . .' She couldn't reply.

'Put all these things on the scales of justice, and try to balance it with your damned conscience, and I don't think there's a very even case, do you?'

'And in the future, when we're married—'

'The marriage will be what we make of it, Alison,' he interrupted quietly.

There was another tap at the door, and this time it was indeed Katya. She had the posy of violets in her hand, but she looked strangely pale and uneasy.

Alison was concerned. 'Is something wrong?' she asked in French.

'No, madam,' replied the maid, but it was obvious that she was lying. Something was wrong.

'Are you sure?' pressed Alison, not liking to see the girl so disquieted.

'Everything is all right, madam,' insisted the maid, hurrying to a drawer to select a suitable ribbon with which to fix the posy to Alison's wrist, but as she found one and came to tie the flowers in place, Francis shook his head.

'That isn't where they'll show to best advantage. Here, let me.' He put his hat on the bed and then teased off his white gloves before taking the violets from the maid. 'Bring a hairpin, if you please,' he said to her in French.

'Yes, my lord.' Katya hurried into the dressing room and returned with the pin.

Francis took it and slid it carefully over the stems of the violets; then he stood in front of Alison, gently pinning the posy to the knot of hair on her head. When he was satisfied that it was in the right place, he moved slowly around her, examining her from every side, and then he halted in front of her again. 'That's much better,' he said, suddenly taking her face in his hands, moving his thumbs against her cheeks.

Her breath caught a little, and she felt telltale color warming her skin. She knew he was going to kiss her, and her lips trembled. She wanted him, she wanted him so much that her whole body ached.

Katya went out discreetly, and he drew Alison gently toward him, kissing her softly at first, but then holding her closer as the kiss lost its gentleness and became more urgent. She could feel the firmness of his body against hers, and her own body quivered with forbidden excitement, stirring with the desire that he could always awaken. Her skin tingled at his touch, and the stuff of her gown was so thin that it was as if she were naked in his arms. Her secret was betrayed in that intimate moment. She wasn't capable of hiding the truth any longer: she loved him, and that love was revealed in all its pain.

He cupped her face in his hands again, gazing down into her guilty eyes. 'Oh, Alison, Alison,' he whispered, 'at this moment I can see into your very soul.'

'No . . .'

'Yes, Alison, because what you try to hide with your eyes is given away by your lips. Your guilty conscience is as much due to your feelings for me as it is to your remorse over Pamela.' His blue eyes were dark and intense, and he didn't intend to allow her any quarter. 'Be honest with me, Alison,' he said softly.

She pulled away in confusion, moving to the window and looking down into the garden. The shadows were slowly beginning to lengthen, but as she gazed at the summerhouse, all she could see was Pamela's tearstained, accusing face. The vision seemed to shimmer in the evening light, and it brought a touch of ice to the heat of passion.

She stared out and despised herself. Why was he doing this? What reason could he have for pressing so unfairly? Indeed, what reason was there, except the obvious one, that his secret mission must be safeguarded, no matter what the cost?

'Alison, there is no need to feel guilt—' he began.

'Why? Because you feel none?' she cried, all the emotion suddenly bursting forth. 'Oh, it's quite clear that you have no conscience, Francis, for your sole motive in all this is the protection of those documents you carry with you. They are the be-all and end-all for you, and you don't really care about my reputation, about my family's feelings, or about Natalia's father. Those things are just levers that you don't scruple about using in order to achieve your purpose.' Was she really saying all this? The words seemed to be spilling out from lips over which she had no control.

For a moment he was silent, but his eyes had frozen. 'Is that what you really think?' he asked at last.

'Yes, for how else am I to think about a man who so lightly accuses his innocent love of still having a *tendre* for her former suitor?'

'You sincerely believe that I am shabby and calculating to that degree?'

'Aren't you?'

'No, madam, I am not, but I don't intend to lower myself to explain to you. If you choose to think that the documents are all that matter to me, then think it. Proceeding on that sole assumption, I must ask you if you intend to renege on your promise to me or if you mean to stand by it and go through with the match?'

His cold anger cut through her like a knife, and it was all she could do to meet his icy gaze. 'I'll stand by my word.'

'I'm all gratitude,' he murmured acidly, sketching her a derisory bow. 'Very well, madam, now that we understand each other so well, I suggest that we go down in readiness for the joyous evening ahead.'

'Francis—'

'Oh, don't be alarmed, madam, for I don't mean to go on in this vein when we are in company. I shall keep it contained until our private little moments together. When we are with others, I will be the tender and adoring lover, make no mistake of that.' Coldly he offered her his arm.

She felt numb and confused as she picked up her shawl, gloves, and reticule, which Katya had put out in readiness on the back of the fireside chair, then she hesitated. 'Francis, I didn't mean to—'

'But you did all the same, madam,' he interrupted frostily.

Tears stung her eyes, but she overcame them, placing a shaking hand over his black velvet sleeve. He said nothing more as they left the bedroom and made their way to the head of the staircase.

When Katya withdrew from the room several minutes before, she didn't linger by the door but made her way quickly toward Natalia's room, outside which she hesitated, pressing her hands nervously against the crisp folds of her apron. Her tongue felt a little dry in her mouth and she tried to compose herself because she knew that what she had to say would be received with alarm. Taking a deep breath, she knocked at the door.

After a pause it opened and Natalia's maid looked out. 'What is it?' she asked in Russian, her tone superior because she and not Katya was maid to the mistress of the house.

'I must speak with *madame*.'

'She is very busy getting ready.'

'Please, it's very important.'

Natalia called out. 'Who is it, Maria?'

'It's Katya, *madame*. She says she must speak urgently with you.'

'Come in, Katya.'

Giving the other maid a toss of her head, Katya entered the blue-and-gold bedroom and then went on through into the little dressing room, where Natalia sat at the muslin-draped dressing table. She wore a turquoise silk tunic over a white undergown, and there was a turquoise turban on her head. Strings of fine pearls were looped over the turban and more pearls graced her throat. A turquoise-studded bracelet encircled the wrist of one of her long white gloves, and her shawl trailed carelessly over her lap to the floor. She smiled at Katya in the mirror as the maid entered the dressing-room.

'What is it, Katya? Is there a problem?'

Katya glanced over her shoulder to where Maria was standing by the brocade-hung four-poster bed, then she looked uneasily at Natalia. 'I must speak alone with you, *madame*.'

Natalia was a little surprised, but spoke to Maria. 'Wait outside, Maria.'

Giving Katya a resentful look, the other maid withdrew, and Natalia smiled. 'Very well, Katya, what is it you wished to say?'

'*Madame*, a short while ago Miss Clearwell sent me out to purchase her a posy of violets to wear tonight, and when I was leaving the house, I noticed a man standing under the trees by the river. He was watching me, and I was a little frightened. Anyway, he didn't follow me, and so I hurried to the florist and then came back. I looked out for him, but he didn't seem to be there, but just as I reached the gate into the garden, he stepped out in front of me. He'd been lying in wait.'

Natalia's lips parted. 'Who was he? A robber?'

'Oh, no, *madame*, for he was an officer in the Preobrazensky Regiment. He said his name was Sergei Mikhailovich Golitsin, and he asked me if I worked in this house. When I said that I did, he told me I was to deliver a message to you.'

'To me? But I do not know this Sergei Mikhailovich Golitsin,' said Natalia.

'No, *madame*, but you know the person from whom the message comes.'

'And that is. . . ?'

'Prince Naryshky, *madame*.'

Natalia's green eyes widened a little and her face became paler. 'The prince? What is the message?'

'That if you have any regard for your father, you will meet the prince tomorrow at noon by the bronze horseman in St Isaac's Square, and that neither you nor I is to mention any of this to anyone else.'

'Did he say anything else?'

'Not concerning you, *madame*.'

'But he did say something?'

Katya nodded. 'He asked me about Miss Clearwell and the English lord. He wished to know what their plans were tonight, and so I told him that you were all going to the opera to hear *Don Giovanni*. He pressed to know if everyone was traveling together, or if anyone would be following alone, and I told him that you would all go in the same carriage.'

Natalia rose slowly to her feet, her shawl slipping to the floor. 'Are you quite sure that's all he said about my father? Just that if I had any regard for him I would meet the prince at noon tomorrow?'

'By the bronze horseman. Yes, *madame*.'

'Thank you, Katya, that will be all. You may return to Miss Clearwell.'

'Yes, *madame*.'

As Katya withdrew, Natalia rested her trembling hands on the dressing table, her head bowed for a moment. What did this mean? Did it bode well or ill for her father? Oh, how was she going to endure until noon tomorrow?

She raised her head again, gazing at her face in the mirror. And why had this Golitsin person asked about Alison and Lord Buckingham? What did they have to do with something concerning her father?

Maria came to the dressing room. '*Madame*? *Monsieur* is ready, and the carriage is at the door.'

'Very well.'

Mackay waited in the entrance hall with the ladies' fur-lined evening cloaks and the gentlemen's greatcoats. Alison, Francis, and Mr Clearwell were ready.

Thomas Clearwell smiled admiringly at his wife as she descended the staircase. 'My dear, you look charming.'

'Thank you, Thomas,' she replied.

He couldn't help but notice her subdued tone. 'Are you quite well, my dear?'

'Yes, quite well. Don't fuss, Thomas,' she replied, giving him a quick smile as she turned for Mackay to place her sable cloak around her shoulders.

A moment or so later they all four emerged into the cold evening air, where the sun was still well above the horizon even though it was now very late indeed. A carriage and four was waiting at the curb, and as the door closed upon the small party, the bearded coachman cracked his whip and swiftly brought his team up to a smart trot along the broad pavement of English Quay.

As the carriage drove past the river side of St Isaac's Square, Natalia looked toward the great bronze equestrian statue of Peter the Great, by which she would meet the prince the next day. What did he want of her? Did he merely wish to inform her that the estate at Novgorod was going to Bragin's nephew and that her father and family were to be turned out? Her lips trembled and she swallowed, toying with the strings of her reticule.

The carriage halted at the crowded curb outside the magnificent opera house, and several liveried footmen immediately hastened forward to open the door and lower the iron rungs. Francis and Mr Clearwell alighted first, pausing to tuck their hats under their arms.

Alone in the carriage with Natalia for a moment, Alison leaned concernedly across to her. 'Are you sure you feel quite well? You seem very pale,'

'I'm quite all right,' repeated Natalia, glancing quickly at her as she wondered again why the man named Golitsin had asked about this young woman and her husband-to-be. Then Mr Clearwell was leaning in to assist his wife from the carriage, and in a whisper of turquoise and white silk Natalia alighted.

Francis then Caine to the carriage door, extending his hand to Alison. True to his promise, he had been all that was attentive and apparently natural when they had been with her uncle and step-aunt.

A throng of people was already crowding the noisy gold-and-white vestibule, moving in a sea of jewels, plumes, velvet, and uniforms beneath an array of brilliantly illuminated chandeliers. Little black boys in splendid Eastern attire hurried about selling programs, and a number of liveried footmen were at hand to relieve the new arrivals of their outdoor garments, spiriting coats, top hats, cloaks, and mantles away to the vast cloakroom that was already filled to overflowing, for tonight's performance was very well attended indeed.

Of Mrs Fairfax-Gunn there was no sign, because she had long since proceeded to the box, but of her activity there was already evidence, for most of the British persons to whom Alison and Francis were introduced had quite obviously been acquainted with with certain shocking facts concerning them. The quickly exchanged glances, the fans raised to lips, and the awkwardly cleared throats were very eloquent. The very first time it happened, Francis took the matter in hand and announced that he and Alison were in St Petersburg to be married. It was an announcement that Mr Clearwell and Natalia immediately confirmed and that Alison herself gave weight to by smil-

ing and leaning a little closer on his arm. It was a first-night performance of her own, one that she had had to steel herself to go through
with now that things had deteriorated so much between them. She
wished she had held her tongue, but she hadn't; she had allowed her
guilty conscience to overwhelm her and said things that would have
been better left unsaid.

The announcement of the impending wedding had to be repeated
numerous times as they made their slow way up the sweeping marble
staircase to the inner vestibule on the floor above, from where
passages and smaller staircases gave admittance to the various tiers of
private boxes.

Alison half-expected to see Nikolai, to meet his eyes suddenly, but
he wasn't anywhere to be seen. Nor was there any sign of a woman
with titian hair who might be his sister, the countess Irina.

The inner vestibule was an impossible crush, but no one made
much of an effort to pass hurriedly through, for convention
demanded that such a crush was to be endured. Alison and Francis
became separated from her uncle and aunt for a moment or two, but
before they could rejoin them, something happened that reminded
Alison very forcefully indeed that Francis's secret purpose here in St
Petersburg was very important to Britain.

A studious-looking young man in formal but plain clothes pushed
his way through the press toward them. He had straight brown hair,
a beaky nose, and a wide mouth, and his watery blue eyes met Francis's
for such a brief moment that if Alison hadn't been looking she would
never have noticed it. The young man paused, toying with his cuff
and glancing around as if looking for someone, and he didn't appear
to be paying any attention at all to Francis, but he spoke to him all the
same, and in a low, discreet tone that revealed him to be a fellow
Englishman.

'Something's up, and it's important you have new information
about a certain highness. Be in the Clearwell coach house before first
light and I'll meet you there.' Then he walked on, still appearing to
be looking for someone and still not seeming to have spoken to
Francis at all.

Alison put a quick hand on Francis's arm. 'Who was that?'

'The British ambassador's private secretary.'

'A certain highness – does that mean Prince Naryshky?'

'I imagine so.'

'What do you think it's about?'

'I really have no idea and I certainly don't intend to indulge in a discussion in a place as crowded and public as this,' he replied sharply.

She recoiled a little. 'As you wish,' she said stiffly.

At that moment her uncle returned for them. 'Ah, there you are, we thought we'd lost you. Come, for everyone is about to adjourn to the boxes. Natalia is waiting for us in the passage.'

13

Several glittering candlelit passages extended from the inner vestibule, and Mr Clearwell led his small party along the one that gave on to the grand tier, or *bel étage*, of boxes. The passageway was lined on one side by gilt-framed mirrors interspersed with doors to private rooms, and on the other by the rich crimson velvet curtains that gave on to the boxes themselves.

Count Vorontzov's private box was at the very end, almost directly above the stage, and a box-opener in golden livery was waiting to admit them. The box was crowded with people, for Mrs Fairfax-Gunn was holding court among her new St Petersburg acquaintances, all of whom were much impressed by her connections in London's high society. Thus the four new arrivals, who were the only guests she had actually invited to share the box throughout the performance, were able to enter without being particularly noticed.

Alison managed to squeeze her way to the front of her box and look out over the sumptuous crimson, gold, and white auditorium. It was ablaze with chandeliers, each one shimmering and flashing in the warm air, and the chatter of refined voices echoed all around the vast horseshoe-shaped hall, where tiers of elegant golden boxes stood out against pure white scagliola walls that were exquisitely painted with wreaths of flowers.

The stage was immediately to Alison's right, its immense gold-adorned crimson velvet curtains moving barely perceptibly in a hidden draft, and the orchestra pit was directly below, the sound of the musicians' tuning-up exercises almost drowned by the babble of the audience. The tiers of boxes swept regally away to her left, reaching all around the auditorium to end directly opposite with the imperial box, where Czar Alexander himself would soon be seated.

Garlands of flowers decorated the imperial box, which was larger and more luxurious than any of the others. Magnificently draped with swathes of golden velvet, it contained several elegant crimson sofas and chairs, but at the front, in splendid isolation, was the gilt chair that the czar would occupy. It was beautifully carved and upholstered, and its back was topped by a likeness of the imperial crown. It drew glances, as if Alexander were already seated there.

Mrs Fairfax-Gunn's box thinned a little as people began to adjourn to their own places elsewhere, and at last she perceived that her four special guests had arrived. She gestured to them to join her on the seats that had been placed in readiness, patting the one next to her to indicate that that was where she wished Alison to take her place.

The scourge of London society wore the inevitable vermilion, satin this time, with three enormous dyed ostrich plumes soaring above her head. Her gown plunged low over her ample bosom, and its tiny sleeves exposed an expanse of dimpled upper arm before the wealth of flesh vanished into long white gloves that looked uncomfortably tight. There was rouge on her cheeks and lips, and her brown eyes had a predatory look as they lingered for a long moment upon Alison. It was quite obvious that she was wondering how susceptible Mrs Clearwell's intriguing little niece might be to some subtle prompting.

Alison reluctantly took the indicated seat and Francis positioned himself at her shoulder. Natalia sat on the other side of Mrs Fairfax-Gunn, and Mr Clearwell stood by her, as was expected of the gentlemen until the performance commenced, at which point they too would be seated.

After a little polite conversation, comments upon the splendor of the gathering, the chill of the St Petersburg spring, the regrettable absence so far tonight of both Prince Naryshky and the Countess Irina, and soon, Mrs Fairfax-Gunn was just about to embark upon a minute interrogation of Alison when Francis took the wind completely from her piratical sails by coolly informing her of the impending marriage.

The woman's rouged lips parted in utter amazement. 'I beg your pardon, my lord? I'm afraid I don't quite understand, so would you mind—'

'Repeating it? Why, of course, Mrs Fairfax-Gunn. Alison and I are here in St Petersburg to be married; indeed, we hope to be man and wife before another week is out.'

She gaped at him, her mouth resembling that of a codfish Alison had once observed at a fishmonger's shop in Bath. Come to that, Alison's thoughts went on, the protruding astonished eyes added to the overall impression of a codfish.

London's most feared scandalmonger was at a complete loss for words. She had spent her entire life snooping and prying, trying to sniff out whatever morsels of gossip she could, and now, quite out of the blue, she was handed on a platter the most startling tidbit imaginable. The match between Lord Buckingham and Lady Pamela Linsey had been set to be the highlight of the 1802 London Season. Everyone who was anyone was to be invited to the nuptials, and now here was his lordship, calming announcing that he was on the point of rushing into marriage with an unknown. Why all the secrecy? Why the haste? Mr Clearwell quite obviously hadn't known about the match before Lord Buckingham and Miss Clearwell had arrived, so it all smacked of an elopement. Why elope? Had the handsome bridegroom been a little remiss? Had vows been anticipated, with unfortunate results? Oh, what a cat to set among the London pigeons. This was going to be the *cause célèbre* of the year. There wouldn't be a drawing room in England that didn't ring with the story.

But first, a few pertinent questions had to be asked. Recovering apace from her shock, Mrs Fairfax-Gunn leaned forward, turning to look directly into Francis's blue eyes. 'Tell me, my lord, before I left England I heard no announcement that your betrothal to Lady Pamela was no longer to take place. I take it that such an announcement has now been made?'

'One is usually made under such circumstances,' he replied noncommittally.

'Yes, but—'

'Aren't you going to offer us your congratulations, Mrs Fairfax-Gunn?' he interrupted politely.

'Congratulations? Why, er, yes, yes of course.' The bright brown eyes moved to Alison. 'I'm truly delighted for you, my dear, for it isn't every day that one comes across what is quite obviously a love match of the highest order. Earlier today I guessed that there was something going on, when his lordship let slip your first name. Tell me, my dear, did you and he travel alone together all the way from England?'

'No, Mrs Fairfax-Gunn, and we would not have been alone together at all if it hadn't been for my chaperone's disgraceful conduct. She deserted me at Stockholm in order to go off with a new suitor, and so I'm afraid my reputation has been gravely compromised. That is why Lord Buckingham and I wish to be married as quickly as possible, for it would hardly do for the new Lady Buckingham to be subjected to spiteful gossip, would it?' Alison was astonished at the cool composure that was enabling her to carry this moment off so successfully.

The woman looked suspiciously at her, for these were not the words of an innocent green girl. 'Spiteful gossip? Why, my dear, I'm quite sure no one would wish to spread untruths about you.'

'I'm so glad that you agree, Mrs Fairfax-Gunn, for to be sure I've been brought quite low at the thought of being the center of scandal. I've been anxious that people might wonder if I'd been less than virtuous and that Lord Buckingham has been less than a gentleman. He has been all that's honorable and loving, Mrs Fairfax-Gunn, and I would be most upset if unkind talk spoiled our happiness. So would Prince Nikolai—'

'Prince Nikolai?' The woman sat up. 'What has he to do with it?'

'He has expressed a wish to attend the wedding. Oh, he's been so kind and gallant—'

'The prince is to attend?'

Alison nodded. 'I'd be so happy if you would come too, Mrs Fairfax-Gunn.'

The brown eyes shone with eager delight. 'Oh, my dear, nothing would give me greater pleasure.'

Alison smiled. 'I'm so glad.'

Natalia had been seated quietly throughout the exchange, her fan moving gently before her face. When Alison described the prince as kind and gallant, the fan hesitated for a moment and Natalia looked at Alison, wondering again why Golitsin had asked so specifically about Thomas's niece and her lordly suitor. Observing Alison now, so delightful in her silver silk gown, amethysts, and posy of violets, her pale silver-blonde hair piled up so sweetly on her head, perhaps it was not so strange that Prince Naryshky's creature should be inquiring about the movements of the two new arrivals at the house on English Quay. The prince was a womanizer of the worst kind, and a young woman like Alison would be bound to catch his eye.

At that moment there was a fanfare, and everyone in the opera house rose to their feet. Silence fell expectantly over the auditorium and all eyes were upon the imperial box. Several ladies and gentlemen in court dress appeared there, standing respectfully aside in readiness for the arrival of the czar. Throats were cleared and someone in the orchestra dropped his violin, but then quite suddenly Alexander stepped into view and the whole opera house began to applaud.

Czar Alexander I, the fourteenth Romanov emperor of Russia, was twenty-four years old, with a round face, delicate features, dreamy blue eyes, and a fine head of sandy-gold curls. He was dressed in the uniform of the Preobrazensky Regiment, of which he was comman-der-in-chief, and he made a very impressive figure as he stood acknowledging the applause of the glittering gathering.

As he took his seat at last and the audience began to follow suit, Alison moved discreetly aside from the place next to Mrs Fairfax-Gunn, whose attention was momentarily diverted by something that Mr Clearwell was saying. Having parried the scandalmonger's first foray, Alison had no wish to be further exposed, and her eye was therefore upon a chair slightly behind the others, close to the curtained entrance of the box. If she could sit there, she would be safe from everything.

Francis observed her movement and interpreted it correctly. He drew out the second chair for her. 'So swift a retreat?' he murmured.

'It's cooler by the entrance, and besides, I consider I did very well,' she replied.

'Oh, you did excellently, but then you do have a talent for telling the sincere fib or two, don't you?'

'Coming from you, I think that that is a little rich, sir,' she said acidly, taking her new seat.

He didn't respond, but went to the place she had just vacated. Mrs

Fairfax-Gunn was so engrossed in observing every detail of Czar Alexander's appearance that she didn't even notice that an exchange had taken place next to her.

The orchestra began to play the overture, the sweet notes rippling out over the auditorium. The audience still chattered, although not quite so loudly, and there was a great deal of shuffling as everyone made themselves as comfortable as possible for the raising of the curtain. Then, as the final notes of the overture died away and everyone waited for the first act of the opera itself, Alison glanced across at the imperial box and was in time to see an aide whispering something to the czar. Alexander looked quickly up at him and nodded, then he left the box. A stir passed through the audience, but was extinguished almost immediately as the curtain was raised and the first scene of *Don Giovanni* commenced.

Alison sat quietly in her seat at the back of the box. She wanted to enjoy the opera, but all she could think of was the rancor of her brief exchanges with Francis since they had arrived. Suddenly she knew that she couldn't go ahead with the marriage, for to do that with circumstances as they now were would be a terrible mistake. How she was going to get out of it she didn't know, and all she could do was hope that the czar sent for Francis swiftly, so that the documents were delivered and she, Alison, could leave St Petersburg. Leave? Yes, for what other choice did she have? She couldn't stay here now and she needed to escape from Francis. Where she would go on her return she didn't know, for it was out of the question that she would now be welcome at Marchington House. Mrs Fairfax-Gunn's knowledge of events on the way to St Petersburg, and here in St Petersburg itself, meant that Pamela would never again show any sign of friendship to her former school friend, and there was bound to be a scandal.

Alison felt close to tears. She didn't have anywhere to go in England until her father returned, unless . . . There was always Miss Wright, who would surely not turn her away if she were in desperate need of assistance.

The confusion of thoughts milled bewilderingly around in Alison's head, and suddenly the box seemed almost claustrophobic. Getting up, she slipped quietly outside into the bright candlelit passage. Her reflection moved sadly beside her as she walked past the mirrors toward the inner vestibule, which was deserted now that the performance had commenced. She paused as she reached the wide area that had been such a press only minutes before.

As she stood there, she suddenly heard voices coming up the grand staircase from the outer vestibule below. One of the voices belonged to Nikolai. Her breath caught and she looked tentatively over the marble balustrade. He was slowly ascending the staircase with a number of the czar's aides. His blond hair was bright in the light from all the chandeliers, and the gold braiding on his uniform gleamed. He was laughing at something and looked supremely relaxed and confident.

Panic seized her and she turned to hurry back to the box, not wishing to run the risk of an encounter with him, but in her haste she took the wrong passage and found herself fleeing to an unknown part of the building. As she realized that there were no box curtains to her left and paused in dismay, she knew that it was too late, for Nikolai and his companions had halted in the inner vestibule to talk. She glanced around, still panic-stricken, and then heard a door open somewhere in the other direction, away from the vestibule. If someone should walk this way now she'd be seen.

Casting desperately around, she saw a slightly open door nearby, and without a second thought she hurried through it. She found herself in an unlit anteroom, small and without windows. A heavy green velvet curtain hung against the wall immediately to her right and there was a couch and a console table beneath a large gilt-framed mirror. As the passage door swung slowly to behind her, she became aware of low voices and a crack of light from another doorway leading to a second room beyond.

Slowly she went toward the other door, and through the narrow opening she saw two lovers wrapped in each other's arms. The lovers were Czar Alexander and a beautiful titian-haired woman who could only be the Countess Irina von Strelitz.

Although she knew that she shouldn't be watching such an intimate scene, Alison couldn't help lingering where she was, for there was something completely captivating about the stolen embrace. Nickolai's glorious sister was holding her imperial lover close, her muslin-clad body pressed adoringly against his. She wore a flimsy gown, low-cut and diaphanous, and it outlined her voluptuous figure to absolute perfection. There were diamonds in her lustrous hair, her eyes were closed as she returned Alexander's kiss, and there was a flush on her skin that told of sweet desire.

Footsteps sounded in the passage, and Alison swiftly hid behind the velvet curtain against the wall. She was just in time, for one of the czar's aides entered the anteroom, coughing discreetly to alert his master to his presence.

Alexander emerged from the inner room, nodded, and then waved the aide outside again. Irina came out of the other room as well, stretching out a loving hand to the czar, who drew it palm-uppermost to his lips. He gazed adoringly into her light-brown eyes, whispered something, and put his hand to her cheek, then he kissed her palm again and left her.

Irina remained where she was, her eyes closed again, as if trying to retain the moment for as long as possible. She raised the palm he had kissed to her own lips. '*Je t'adore*, Alexander,' she whispered, '*je t'adore avec tout mon coeur.*'

Alison watched secretly from behind the curtain and knew that she was looking at a woman who loved the man whose mistress she was. There was no art or guile in Irina's private moment, when she thought herself alone and unobserved. She loved Alexander with all her heart, so much so that she had to whisper it aloud, even though she was the only one there to hear.

Someone else approached the door, and Alison heard the remembered sound of spurs. It was a sound that took her back to the Dog and Flute in Stockholm and the terror that had beset her until Francis had rescued her.

Nikolai pushed the outer door open and smiled at his lovely sister. 'Are you ready?'

'Yes.'

'Another stolen moment?' He came toward her, halting only a foot or so away from Alison's hiding place.

'Would that I could always be with him,' said Irina.

'He'll never set the czarina aside for you.'

'I know.'

'You won't forget what you are to do concerning the Englishman, will you?'

Alison's lips parted. The Englishman? Francis?

Irina smiled a little. 'I won't forget, Nikolai.'

He offered her his arm, and as she moved to accept it, he paused suddenly. 'I didn't know you'd taken to wearing lavender water.'

'Lavender? I never wear it, Nikolai.'

'I thought . . .' He gave a slight laugh. 'I could have sworn that I detected lavender.'

They left the room and Alison leaned her head weakly back against the wall, remaining in her hiding place. Of course he could smell lavender, for she was wearing it, and she had been so very close to him, had he but known it.

She was about to step out from behind the curtain when suddenly the door opened again. She froze, her heart thundering in her breast. In a mirror opposite she could see Nikolai standing in the doorway. He remained in the doorway for a long moment, a motionless, menacing silhouette, and then Irina called along the passage behind him.

'Nikolai, please come on, for I wish to take my seat.'

'I'm coming.' With a final glance around the dark room, he turned and walked away again, leaving the door open so that the light from the passage lay in a bright shaft across the floor.

Alison's heart was pounding so swiftly that she couldn't have counted its beats. Her mouth was dry and she felt ice-cold in spite of the heat that permeated the entire building. She was too afraid to move, in case Nikolai returned again, and so she remained behind the curtain. The sound of the opera echoed from the auditorium, and then she heard a burst of applause and the music come to a halt for a moment. She knew that Nikolai and the Countess Irina would now be taking their seats, and hesitantly she emerged from her hiding place.

She went to the door, peeping out into the passage. It was deserted; there didn't seem to be anyone in the vestibule at the far end. Gathering her skirts, she retraced her steps, not pausing in the vestibule but almost running down the correct passageway toward Count Vorontzov's box.

Her thoughts were still on Prince Nikolai, and she glanced frequently over her shoulder, afraid that he would be behind her. She wasn't paying attention to where she was going, and would have run right into Francis if he hadn't caught her by the arms.

The cry of alarm died on her lips as she found herself staring into his angry blue eyes.

He shook her. 'Where in God's name have you been? I looked around and you weren't there.'

'I just needed a breath of air.'

'Don't just leave like that without telling anyone. If you need fresh air again, then I will escort you, is that clear?'

'Perfectly.'

'Then let us return to our places.' He offered her his arm.

Slowly she took it, but it was like touching a stranger. She wanted his comfort and the feel of his arms around her, but there was no gentleness in him now where Alison Clearwell was concerned.

They returned to their places, Alison reluctantly taking the seat next to Mrs Fairfax-Gunn. The czar had resumed his seat, and Nikolai and the Countess Irina were in a box about halfway around the auditorium. Alexander's attention wasn't upon the stage, for his glance kept wandering to his beautiful mistress, who smiled each time she met his dreamy blue eyes.

Alison couldn't help observing the exchanged smiles. There was no doubt in her mind that the czar and Nikolai's sister were very much in love and that perhaps if one was slightly more committed than the other, that one was Irina. The glow that Alison had observed so closely permeated her still and made her so gloriously beautiful that she seemed to have been touched by magic.

So intent was Alison upon the two lovers that at first she didn't realize that she too was under scrutiny. She noticed quite suddenly when her glance encountered Nikolai's. His dark gaze had been upon her ever since she had taken her seat, and it didn't waver now that he knew she had perceived his interest. He leaned a little closer to his sister, putting his hand briefly on her arm and whispering something.

Irina looked immediately toward Alison's box. The softness in her light-brown eyes turned to a malevolent glitter as her gaze rested upon Francis, and her cold hatred was so intense that it was almost tangible.

Francis felt nothing, for his attention was upon the stage, but Alison was only too conscious of the malignity that was being so silently directed toward him.

14

The carriage had long since returned to English Quay with the party of operagoers, and the few dark hours of the St Petersburg night would soon be at an end, but the dawn would be postponed a little by the heavy mist that came up suddenly from the Neva. A cloak of gray enveloped the city, swirling silently around the many islands of the delta and drifting clammily past the magnificent buildings lining the waterfronts. Golden spires and cupolas rose eerily out of the gloom, and on English Quay itself the streetlamps were muted between the trees.

Across the water the wharves of Vassily Island were busy, invisible through the mist but still audible, and a trickle of carts and people continued to cross the pontoon bridge as those who had to work through the night went about their business.

Sergei Mikhailovich Golitsin's stealthy greatcoated figure hastened along the river side of St Isaac's Square, past the bridge, and then paused to look toward the statue of Peter the Great in the center of the square. The bronze horseman reared out of the swirling vapor, for all the world as if the long-dead czar was alive once more. Sergei shivered, for he was a superstitious man and there were legends about the horseman coming to life and riding around the city under cover of darkness. Pulling his shako well forward on his head and thrusting his hands deep into his coat pockets, he hurried on toward English Quay. A sharp communication from Nikolai concerning his IOUs had reminded him of the pressing need to successfully conclude the matter of the Englishwoman's abduction.

He didn't know how to go about this most unwelcome and

unwanted of tasks, especially if the lady concerned didn't conveniently sally forth on her own. What if she only went out in company? It seemed to him that there was more likelihood of her walking alone in the grounds of the Clearwell house than there was of her going out unaccompanied, and so he felt that it might be profitable to examine the gardens. He had already perceived that the servants came and went frequently through the gate in the wall, which meant that there was a strong chance that the last one to use it might forget to lock it for the night. If that were so, then he would be able to enter the gardens and look them over carefully, just in case his only recourse was to snatch the lady from her uncle's property.

With a heavy sigh he halted beneath the trees opposite the house, looking toward the wrought-iron gate in the wall. He could see the shadowy garden beyond, but then the mist obscured everything so that he couldn't see as far as the coach house and stables backing on to Horseguards Boulevard. He was about to cross the street to the gate when he heard a carriage approaching from the direction of St Isaac's Square, which was itself now invisible through the swirling vapor from the river. At last Sergei saw the lamps shining like two amber eyes as the vehicle made its way slowly toward him. Then, just as he could make it out clearly, it drew in to the curb outside the next mansion. Giggling and laughter emanated from behind its lowered blinds, for the gentlemen inside were enjoying the company of some rather flighty ladies, and no move was made to open the doors for the occupants to alight.

Sergei gazed irritatedly toward the stationary vehicle, for the coachman was facing in his direction, as was the small boy riding the rear pair of the team of four. They would see him if he crossed the street to test the gate, and so there was nothing for it but to remain where he was and hope that the carriage drove on shortly.

As Sergei was forced to wait beneath the trees outside, Alison was asleep in her bed. She hadn't meant to sleep because she had wanted to eavesdrop upon Francis's meeting with the British ambassador's private secretary, but as soon as her head had touched the pillow, she had drifted off. Something awakened her now, however, and her eyes suddenly flew open. It was one of those strange moments, with no transition between sleep and alertness, and from her dreams she was immediately and clearly in the present.

She sat up, pushing her hair back from her face. A night-light cast a soft glow over the room, and the fire had burned low. The scent of hyacinths filled the air, and the clock on the mantelpiece whirred and then struck the half-hour. She couldn't make out the time, and the curtains and shutters were closed, so that she had no idea whether it was light or dark outside.

Slipping from her bed, she hurried to the nearest window, drawing the curtains aside and then folding back the shutters. She found herself gazing out at a misty darkness where she could make out the shadows in the gardens, but beyond the wall she could only see as far as the lamps and trees lining the embankment. Of the Neva itself there was no sign, and the islands on the far side might not have existed at all. She couldn't see the *Irina*, which had still been lying at anchor in the middle of the river when the carriage had returned from the opera house.

She was a little startled by the mist, for when they had come home, everything had been quite clear. She shivered slightly, her gaze drawn to the trees and lamps in the street, and suddenly she saw the motionless shape of a man in a greatcoat and military shako. He seemed to be looking toward the house, but then he pressed back behind a tree trunk as the sound of a carriage echoed through the mist. Coach lamps pierced the gloom as the vehicle came up to a smart speed, passing the house and driving on down English Quay. As the sound dwindled away again, the shadowy figure by the trees came stealthily out of hiding, slipping across the street to the wrought-iron gate in the garden wall.

Alison's lips parted on a silent gasp as she watched him test the gate and then open it. He came swiftly inside, closing the gate behind him, and then he hurried away from her toward the summerhouse, vanishing inside it. In those few seconds she recognized him, for she had seen him often enough on board the *Pavlovsk*. She knew it was Nikolai's spy. Her pulse quickened with dismay and for a moment she was uncertain what to do, but then a second figure moved into view in the garden below. It was Francis, and he had just left the house to make his way to the meeting in the coach house. He must be seen by the man in the summerhouse, for he walked quite openly along the gravel path leading toward the rear of the grounds, and as he passed out of sight among the mews buildings, the Russian moved surreptitiously out of hiding and began to follow.

There was no time to wonder what to do, for she knew that at all costs she had to prevent the Russian from overhearing what might be said in the coach house. Dashing into her dressing room, she hastily donned a cloak and her ankle boots, then she made her way down through the house and out into the gardens.

The chill night air made her breath catch, and she could feel the touch of the sea mist on her face as she hurried down the path. She caught a fleeting glimpse of a figure some way ahead of her, then it was gone, melting away into the bushes to the right of the path as her approach was detected. She hurried on, pushing the coach-house door open and stepping into the inky shadows beyond.

Everything was absolutely silent. She looked anxiously around but could discern nothing in the pitch dark. She called Francis's name, and after a moment a lucifer flared into life and she saw him standing alone by the carriage that had earlier conveyed them to and from the opera house.

'Alison? What in God's name. . . ?'

She ran toward him, and the lucifer went out, engulfing the coach house in darkness again. She spoke in an urgent whisper. 'The man who was watching us on the *Pavlovsk* is outside right now. I saw him follow you, and I had to warn you.'

She turned toward the door, which she had left open, and, incredibly, the figure was standing there, framed against the misty night outside. The man obviously hadn't realized that he could be seen, for he stood there quite deliberately, trying to hear what she was whispering.

Francis was nonplussed for a second, but then took a step toward the door. 'Hey, you!'

The man whirled about and fled back along the path. Francis gave chase and Alison heard their footsteps dying away into the mist; then the gate closed loudly, the sound echoing through the night. After a moment she heard Francis returning and at last he came back into the coach house.

She went toward him. 'Has he gone?'

'Like a hare. What happened, Alison? How did you see him?'

'I woke up, went to the window, and saw him standing under the trees in the street. He seemed to be looking toward the house; then he came into the garden and hid in the summerhouse. You walked along the path and he followed you. I came to warn you before he heard anything he shouldn't.' She glanced around the dark coach house. 'Are you the first to arrive?'

'Yes. Alison, do you think Naryshky's spy knew about the meeting in here?' he asked, wondering about the unknown spy at the embassy.

She looked quickly at him. 'I don't know. It's possible, I suppose.'

Another voice spoke from the shadows behind them. 'No, Miss Clearwell, it's quite impossible, for we three are the only ones who know about this meeting.' It was the young man from the opera house. He stepped closer, his figure visible in the pale-gray light from the open doorway, and he bowed as he introduced himself. 'Charles Gainsborough, private secretary to Lord St Helens.'

Francis inclined his head. 'And how can you be so certain, Mr Gainsborough?'

'Because Lord St Helens instructed me to speak to you as quickly as possible, and I haven't yet had the opportunity of telling him what I had arranged. I certainly haven't informed anyone else, which means that we three can most certainly be the only ones who know. Unless, of course . . .' He looked at them both.

Francis exhaled slowly. 'Unless Miss Clearwell and I have told someone?'

'Have you?' asked the ambassador's private secretary quietly.

Francis shook his head. 'No, I haven't.'

'Nor have I,' said Alison.

Mr Gainsborough's glance rested quizzically upon her, and Francis smiled. 'Sir, you may take Miss Clearwell's word for it. If she says she hasn't told anyone, then she hasn't. We may trust her.'

The ambassador's secret agent smiled ruefully. 'Forgive me, Miss Clearwell, but you are something of an unknown quantity to me. However, I have heard that congratulations are in order for you and the earl.'

'Thank you, sir,' she replied.

He looked at Francis. 'The fellow you've just chased away is named Golitsin, and our sources tell us that Naryshky holds a great number of his IOUs, which places him well and truly under the prince's thumb. From what you said at the embassy earlier today, when you and I were alone and Miss Clearwell's uncle was speaking to the ambassador, Naryshky's interest in you both cannot be ignored.'

'Well, it may still be simply and solely due to his keenness upon Miss Clearwell, but I doubt it. We made errors over which ship we were sailing on from Stockholm, we also slipped up a little about arrangements at the inn, and then he definitely set Golitsin to watch us on the *Pavlovsk*, and the fellow searched our cabins. On top of that there was the fact that Naryshky was waiting for us at Kronstadt . . . No, Mr Gainsborough, we may not ignore his interest, for that interest is rather intense.'

The other nodded a little heavily. 'I wish it were otherwise, my lord, because what I have to tell you now makes Naryshky the very last soul on earth whose interest should in any way have been aroused. You see, we now know that it isn't the naval and military commanders at Kronstadt who have been supplying Bonaparte with vital Russian secrets, but Naryshky himself.'

Alison gasped, her eyes flying toward Francis, whose face remained still. 'Is there any doubt?' he asked the ambassador's secretary.

'None at all. Our man in Paris, the clerk close to Boney, sent another communication after sending the documents and maps you have. He had found out that the prince had made a secret visit to France, and about certain extravagant promises the Corsican has made to him concerning future rewards. Naryshky found out about the clerk, however, or at least he suspected the man was up to something and he had him dumped in the Seine. Naryshky believed he had prevented any awkward information from being sent to London, but the unfortunate clerk was more prompt than he thought.'

Francis gave a slightly incredulous laugh. 'And you're absolutely sure about this?'

'Absolutely.'

'But why would he do it? What reason is there for—'

'We've been making discreet inquiries, and I think we can accurately say that he's acting out of pique and a sense of personal insult.

He wished to marry the czar's sister, the Grand-Duchess Helen, but Alexander refused to countenance the match. And then Alexander took the Countess Irina as his mistress, and Naryshky masked his resentment over both matters, but got drunk one night and said what he really thought. He thinks he owes Alexander a grudge or two, and this is his way of doing it. If it succeeds, Alexander will pay very dearly indeed for spurning Naryshky and then bedding his sister. Begging your pardon, Miss Clearwell,' he added quickly for having spoken so frankly in front of her.

'That's quite all right, sir,' she replied, still shaken by what he had said concerning the prince's astonishing treachery.

He turned to Francis again. 'It's now more important than ever that you see the czar without delay, for he must be told the identity of the traitor. Naryshky is in a position to wreak untold damage upon Russia, and he is known to be gathering a court party around him, consisting of a number of malcontents. Alexander hasn't rewarded all those he should have rewarded, I fear, and there have been too many past czars who've been disposed of in favor of a successor.'

'And Alexander's successor would be. . . ?' prompted Francis.

'The Corsican.'

'That's what I was afraid you were going to say.'

'I know you've already left your name at the palace, but I think it would be wise to repeat the exercise daily until the required audience results.'

'As you wish.'

'We have to use you, my lord, because to attempt to make an open diplomatic approach to the czar is still a little tricky. We haven't yet unearthed the informer at the embassy, and we don't want anyone to get wind of anything. If the informer has any contact with Naryshky . . .'

'I understand, Mr Gainsborough.'

Alison looked at the ambassador's secretary. 'Sir, do you know if the Countess Irina is party to her brother's plot?'

'We can't be certain, Miss Clearwell, but I believe she is. She and Naryshky are very close; indeed, they dote upon each other.'

Alison shook her head, remembering watching Irina alone in the anteroom at the opera house. 'No, Mr Gainsborough, I think you are wrong. If you'd said that you had irrefutable evidence that she was as guilty as he, I'd have to concede that my judgment is in error, but in the absence of any evidence of her involvement, then I have to say that I believe she is innocent.'

He smiled. 'Miss Clearwell, it would be most agreeable to think that the countess isn't part of her brother's scheme, but it would be very unwise to bank upon such being the case.'

Alison said nothing more, but in her heart she knew she was right about Irina. The czar's mistress might love her brother, hate the British, and support the French, but she wouldn't do anything at all that would hurt or endanger Alexander, whom she adored with all her heart. '*Avec tout mon coeur . . .*'

Mr Gainsborough took out his fob watch. 'I think it's time I left. I'll leave the way I came, via Horseguards Boulevard. If you need me, you have only to send a message to the embassy. Good night.'

'Good night,' replied Francis, and they watched him slip away toward the far end of the coach house. They didn't see or hear the outer door open and close, they only knew that everything went very quiet.

Francis turned to her. 'It seems I am in your debt, Alison.'

'If I have prevented the prince's man from overhearing anything he shouldn't, then perhaps I've redeemed myself a little, since it was all on account of me that you have difficulty with the prince in the first place.'

'Perhaps.'

Was now the time to attempt to repair the damage done by her outburst of earlier? 'Francis—'

'I think we should return to the house, don't you?' he interrupted coolly.

The apology and plea for forgiveness died on her lips. His gratitude for what she had done now hadn't removed his anger. Nothing had changed.

Resignedly she accepted the arm he offered and they walked back through the misty gardens toward the house. The faint glow of dawn marked the eastern sky, and soon it would pierce the cloak of vapor enveloping St Petersburg. On the Neva a ship's bell sounded and somewhere the first sea gull called.

As they entered the silent house and walked to the staircase through the hyacinth-scented hall, Alison knew more than ever that a match between her and Francis would be a disaster, for he felt far less for her now than he had when first they had entered this house.

Sergei didn't stop running until he reached St Isaac's Square again. The mist was luminous and the pontoon bridge was ghostly as it led away into the haze. He could just make out the *Irina*, her hull wraith-like and indistinct, but Vassily Island was still lost from view.

He looked back toward English Quay, half-afraid that he would see the Englishman, but there was no one behind. He exhaled with relief, walking slowly on. If only he didn't face certain ruin if Nikolai called in all the IOUs . . . But he did, and ruin was something he dared not contemplate. He simply wasn't the man for something as daring and dangerous as an abduction; why, even his initial reconnaissance had almost ended in disaster. What a fool he had been to stand so openly in the doorway. If his legs hadn't found wings he would be in the Englishman's furious clutches now. Plague take Nikolai! What was it about these two that interested him so? Why was he so convinced that they weren't lovers at all? What difference did it make if his ultimate purpose was to kidnap the lady and force her to submit? Besides, it was quite obvious that Nikolai was wrong about them, for they were lovers, as he, Sergei, had seen every time he had watched them.

Sergei paused, looking toward the bronze horseman in the center of the square. Soon Nikolai would be meeting the unfortunate daughter of the even more unfortunate Leon Razumov in the shadow of the statue. He would threaten and frighten her in order to learn the truth about her two guests, but there wasn't anything new to learn, for she would merely confirm what was obvious to everyone except Nikolai Ivanovich himself. Lord Buckingham was in love with Miss Clearwell, and she was in love with him. That was the end of it.

15

By midday the mist had gone and the sun was shining as Natalia waited nervously by the statue. She wore a dark-green cloak trimmed with black fur, the hood pulled over her head. The thoroughfares surrounding the square were busy now, and ships were arriving and leaving on the tide. Vassily Island shone across the water, its wharves a hive of activity, and on the *Irina* there were some sailors scrubbing the decks. The schooner rocked gently on the flow, her figurehead bright and arresting.

Natalia gazed toward Prince Nikolai's beautiful vessel, and she shivered with nerves. She didn't hear the prince approaching and so gave a start when he suddenly spoke to her.

'How punctual you are, *madame*.'

She turned swiftly.

He smiled a little, his dark eyes calculating. She was already afraid, just as he meant her to be, for if she was afraid, then she wouldn't lie very well, not if she thought her father's well-being was at stake. 'I will not waste time, *madame*, but will come directly to the point. I wish to know all there is to know about your two new guests.'

She looked at him in confusion. 'But, highness, there isn't anything to tell that you do not know already.'

'Do you honor your father, *madame*?' he asked softly.

'Of course I do, highness,' she replied, her face growing more pale and anxious.

'Then if you wish me to consider his case fairly, I advise you to tell me anything that maybe of interest. For instance, why is it that Lord Buckingham is really here in St Petersburg?'

She stared at him. 'I don't understand, highness—'

'It's really very simple, *madame*,' he snapped. 'I do not believe that he is here to be married or to purchase a horse from the imperial stables. I believe he has an ulterior purpose.'

Natalia was bewildered. 'Ulterior purpose? Highness, I don't know of anything other than the two things you've already mentioned. Some time ago he arranged to approach the czar about a colt from the imperial stud, and then matters with my husband's niece reached a point and they decided to use the visit here in order to be married. The special license has been applied for at the British embassy, and the wedding is to take place in about a week's time. Why, you are to be invited, highness. As to the purchase of the colt, Lord Buckingham has already left his name at the Winter Palace and now awaits the call to the czar's presence.'

Nikolai studied her. Was she a truly consummate actress, or could it be that she really was telling the truth? She was very convincing, and the look of anxiety and bewilderment in her eyes could surely not be false. 'Remember your father, *madame*,' he warned, 'for his future hangs upon your veracity.'

'I am not lying, highness, I swear it. I do not know what you suspect about Lord Buckingham and Miss Clearwell, but they are only lovers who wish to be together. They've sought my husband's blessing and assistance, and he has agreed to their request. He believes them, and so do I, for I cannot imagine that they are dishonest about their feelings for each other.'

'And you would stake your father's future upon it?'

Slowly she nodded. 'Yes, highness.'

A nerve fluttered at Nikolai's temple and he waved her away. 'Very well, that is all.'

'Highness, about my father . . .'

'Yes?'

'He has always served you faithfully and has managed the estate more than profitably.'

'I am aware of that, *madame*.'

'Then you will hear his case with—'

'I will treat the case on its merits, *madame*, and if I think that Bragin's nephew is more suitable, then I will choose him.' Tears filled her eyes. 'Please, highness—'

'That is my final word on the matter.'

As Natalia hurried tearfully away, afraid of provoking him if she pleaded anymore, Nikolai drew a long thoughtful breath. He glanced up at the bronze horseman. Suddenly he felt more secure, for it seemed that his fears might be groundless after all. Leon Razumov's daughter was too frightened to be lying, and the fact that there was indeed to be a marriage, to which he himself was to be invited, went a long way toward allaying the suspicions that had flared so disquietingly into being that night in Stockholm. He had allowed his fear of discovery to get the upper hand, and had seen threats and danger where there were none.

Well, it was too late now to prevent the canceling of the audience with the czar, but that wasn't of any consequence. Lord Buckingham could look elsewhere for a suitable horse. Nikolai smiled a little, relieved too that there would no longer be any need to effect the Englishman's convenient 'disappearance,' with the consequent implication that Irina was the person behind it. If the devil had driven, however, he, Nikolai, would have had no compunction about pointing the finger of suspicion at his sister, for she no longer deserved anything but his contempt. She was blissfully ignorant of his true feelings toward her; she was his adoring sister and believed that he returned her affection ounce for ounce.

Nikolai strolled away from the statue toward the carriage that was to take him across the pontoon bridge to the boat that would row him out to the *Irina*. He felt as if a weight had been lifted from his shoulders, and he inhaled deeply of the invigorating air. Ah, St Petersburg, most matchless of cities, soon you will be free of the Romanov yoke. The greatest ruler in the world, Napoleon Bonaparte, is to occupy the Winter Palace, and at his right hand, sharing the glory, will be Prince Nikolai Ivanovich Naryshky.

The liveried black postilion was waiting by the carriage door, opening it the moment he approached. Nikolai climbed into the sumptuous fur-upholstered vehicle and sat back, his thoughts returning to Lord Buckingham's bride. Before she became the wife of a lord she was going to be the unwilling mistress of a prince.

As Prince Nikolai's carriage drew away from the curb in St Isaac's Square, Alison was descending the staircase from the bedroom at her uncle's house. She was dressed in a pale-blue muslin gown with long sleeves and a square neckline that was trimmed with a rufflike pleated lace frill. Her hair was arranged in a side knot from which tumbled several plump ash-blonde ringlets, and there were simple drop pearl earrings trembling from her lobes. She had taken care over her appearance this morning, because they were all about to drive to the Hermitage, next to the Winter Palace, to look at the fabulous collection of treasures on display there. It was an excursion that was considered *de rigueur* for all visitors to St Petersburg, and Francis meant to combine it with a second call at the palace to leave his name.

She was a little early and so meant to wait in the grand salon until the others were ready as well, but as she reached the landing above the entrance hall, she saw Natalia come quickly in through the main door below. Alison paused by the balustrade, for it was immediately obvious that her step-aunt was upset about something. As she watched, Natalia hurried across the hall to the staircase, gathering her dark-green cloak to ascend quickly. Her face was tearstained and she didn't see Alison until she reached the landing, when she halted with a guilty start.

'Alison, I didn't see you there.'

Alison was anxious. 'What is it, Aunt Natalia? What's wrong?'

'Wrong? Why, nothing.'

'But you've been crying—'

'No!' The word came out sharply, but then was repeated more controlledly. 'No, Alison, I just have a bad headache, that's all. I'll be all right when I've rested for a while.'

'But, the visit to the Hermitage . . .'

Natalia shook her head. 'I can't go, I don't feel well enough. Please give my apologies.' With that she gathered her cloak once more ready to go on up the second flight of the staircase to the floor above, but then she paused, meeting Alison's eyes. 'You do love Lord Buckingham, do you not, Alison?' she asked.

'Yes, of course I do,' replied Alison honestly, wondering why such a thing should be asked. A cool finger touched her spine, a finger of warning, for there was something very strange about Natalia.

'And apart from the purchase of a colt from the czar, his lordship's sole purpose here in St Petersburg is to make you his bride?'

Alison managed to meet her eyes without wavering. 'Yes, of course,' she said again, but the cool finger had now turned to ice.

'I trust that you are telling me the truth, Alison, for if you are not . . .' Natalia didn't finish the sentence.

Alison took a step closer. 'Aunt Natalia, won't you please tell me what's wrong?'

'There is nothing wrong, Alison, not if you are being honest with me. But if you are lying, and if my father suffers . . .' Again Natalia didn't finish the sentence.

Alison stared at her, suddenly realizing. 'Has the prince spoken to you?'

'The prince? Why should you think that?' Natalia asked swiftly, her eyes intent.

'Because he is the only one who could make your father suffer,' replied Alison, again managing to meet the other's gaze without giving anything away.

'You are right, Alison. He could indeed hurt my father, and maybe he will anyway, but if he should do so because of something else, something to do with you and Lord Buckingham, then I will never forgive you. Never!'

Turning, Natalia hastened up the second staircase, not glancing back once as she reached the top. As her footsteps died away along the passage on the floor above, Alison lowered her eyes unhappily. She remembered how Francis had warned that Nikolai would turn his wrath upon Leon Razumov if he discovered the truth, and how she, stung by her own guilt, had accused him of cynical self-interest and insincerity.

With a heavy heart she walked on toward the grand salon. Please let all this be finished as soon as possible, let the documents be safely delivered, and let Nikolai pay the price for his unbelievable treachery to his country and his czar. And let Alison Margaret Lydia Clearwell return to England, where everything was calm, uncomplicated, and safe. She pushed all thoughts of the marriage to the back of her mind, for it was something she still hoped at all costs to avoid, but she knew in her heart of hearts that it might not be possible to avoid it, that events might force her to go through with a ceremony that she knew would be wrong.

She entered the grand salon and went to the windows facing toward the Neva, brushing past her uncle's telescope as she did so. Her step-aunt's words kept returning to her, and her spirits, already low, sank still further.

Outside, the sunlight sparkled on the Neva, and the vista of St Petersburg stretched gloriously all around. Beyond the pontoon bridge, where the Neva was at its widest before parting into two channels, she could see the forbidding ramparts of the Peter-Paul Fortress, and the slender golden spire of the cathedral that nestled within its walls. Behind the fortress was Peterburg Island, and beyond that, invisible in the sunny spring haze, was Krestovsky Island, where the Countess Irina resided.

In the foreground, Nikolai's schooner still lay at her midriver mooring, and as Alison looked, she saw the prince himself standing on the deck. She turned to the telescope, directing it toward the vessel and bending to look through. Suddenly she was looking straight at Nikolai, his figure caught in a circular frame, for all the world like a miniature. She could see the golden shoulder knots and braiding, the crimson cuffs of his black tunic, and the light-blue cordon of St Andrew across his shoulder. She could even see the miniature of Alexander at his throat, a miniature on a miniature. There was nothing on his head, so that the light sea breeze ruffled through his blond hair, and he was standing with his hands on the deck rail, gazing pensively down at the rippling waters of the Neva.

As she looked, he straightened, his glance moving directly toward her. He seemed so very close through the telescope that she drew back with a gasp, for his eyes had seemed to meet hers, but then she realized that he couldn't see her properly, any more than she had been able to see him properly before looking through the telescope.

She bent to look again, but he was walking along the deck now, toward the doorway that led to the stateroom at the stern of the vessel. As he vanished from view, Alison continued to look through the telescope, training it on the busy pontoon bridge and then upon the quays of Vassily Island opposite. She was searching for the *Pavlovsk*, but there was no sign of the brigantine. Then she remembered Captain Merryvale's words. 'The *Pavlovsk* is due in tonight, and she will leave again on tomorrow's midday tide for St Petersburg, for she stays for only one tide.' The brigantine was already on her way back to Stockholm.

Alison studied the busy wharves and then paused as the telescope came to rest upon a strangely familiar vessel, a British merchantman that hadn't been there the day before. It was the *Duchess of Albemarle*. Alison stared through the telescope as if at a ghost, but then suddenly realized that it wasn't the sunken vessel that she was looking at, but her sister ship, the *Duchess of Clarence*. Evidently Captain Merryvale hadn't had very long to wait in Stockholm, after all. She wondered if he had definitely sailed with the new vessel, and even as she wondered she saw him standing on the quay with several of the ship's officers. He was smiling and nodding, but he looked heavyhearted, as well he still might be after losing his ship in such a way. To have had her founder in a raging storm was probably acceptable, but to lose her because of a fire in the calm sheltered waters of Stockholm harbor was such an unnecessary and pointless accident.

Her uncle's carriage was waiting outside, ready to go to the Hermitage. The doors of the grand salon opened behind her, and she straightened, turning to see that Francis had come in. He wore a chestnut-colored coat and close-fitting cream corduroy breeches, and rich golden tassels swung at the front of his Hessian boots. His waistcoat was dark green, and its topmost buttons had been left undone to show off the crisp frills on the front of his shirt. An emerald pin reposed in the folds of his starched neckcloth and he carried his top hat and kid gloves, which he placed on a table before coming toward her.

'Francis . . .' she began.

'Yes?'

'You were right about the danger we might pose to my aunt's family.'

His eyes were incredibly blue as they met hers. 'I didn't for a single moment believe otherwise, Alison. What has happened that you suddenly accept that I was right?' he asked.

'I was coming down here when Aunt Natalia returned to the house. She was upset and had been crying, but when I asked her if anything was wrong, she denied it. Then she asked me if I really did love you, and if, apart from acquiring a horse from the imperial stables, your sole purpose here was to marry me.'

'Did she, indeed?' he murmured.

'The prince had been speaking to her.'

'Did she say so?'

'She didn't deny it in the end, for I guessed it when she said that if her father suffered because of us, then she would never forgive me.'

'She was that much to the point?'

'Yes.' Alison turned to look out the window. 'I wish it was all over, Francis.'

'You aren't alone in that. I'm sorry that I've had to force so much upon you, Alison, but I really haven't had much choice in the matter.'

'I know.'

'Do you?' There was a dry coolness in his voice, almost a taunt.

'Yes, I do know. You're justified in being angry with me for all that I said, for I realize how stupid, insulting, and downright childish I was to speak like that.'

'There certainly was a good deal of Miss Wright's academy about you,' he replied, his tone offering no hint of a softening toward her.

She lowered her eyes to the street outside and the trees and lamps silhouetted against the Neva. 'I wonder if even a woman of the world would carry all this off with aplomb,' she murmured.

'Alison . . .' he began.

Her gaze had become fixed upon something outside. 'Look,' she said softly, 'down there close to the steps to the water. Do you see him?'

Francis stepped forward, following her pointing finger. A burly Russian was standing there, apparently waiting for someone. He was of medium height and was very thickset, with a short wiry beard and a bull neck. He wore a pale-blue caftan tied at the waist with a leather belt, and his baggy trousers were tucked into heavy boots. There was a brown fur hat on his head and his gloves were gauntlets that covered his forearms.

Francis studied him for a moment and then looked at her. 'What about him? I see nothing remarkable.'

'He's watching the house.'

'Watching the house? Oh, Alison . . .' Francis breathed out slowly. 'The man is simply waiting for someone, he hasn't looked this way once. I think that you're allowing last night's events to cloud your judgment.'

'Even green schoolgirls have intuition, sir,' she replied. 'He's watching this house, and that carriage farther up the street is his.'

'Carriage?' He looked from the window again and saw the vehicle drawn up at the curb, facing toward St Isaac's Square and the pontoon bridge. Its blinds were down, and by the way the horses stood, they had been waiting for some time.

Alison was still studying the man. 'He's there to replace the man who came into the garden last night, I'm sure of it. I know that he doesn't appear to be watching the house, but every so often his glance comes this way. There, he's seen us watching. As she spoke, the man turned and walked away in the direction of the carriage. He climbed quickly into it and it drove away.

Francis bent to use the telescope, following the vehicle until it vanished in the bustle of St Isaac's Square. Then he straightened, looking apologetically at her. 'You were right. Naryshky's concern with us is far too keen for comfort now that we know what he's really been up to. I wish to God I knew exactly what was in his mind.'

'Francis, you must do all you can to see the czar.'

'I know. I'll leave my name again when we go to the Hermitage, but if nothing happens, I really don't know how to approach him. Protocol is everything here in St Petersburg. I vow it's worse than in London, if such be possible.' He ran his fingers through his hair.

Alison found the gesture oddly affecting, for it made him appear boyish and almost vulnerable.

The salon doors opened again and her uncle entered, looking very splendid in a damson coat embroidered with black, and white silk pantaloons. 'Ah, so I'm not the first to be ready,' he said, glancing around. 'Where's Natalia?'

Alison went quickly to him. 'Oh, Uncle Thomas, I'm afraid she's a little indisposed with a headache. She begs to be excused.'

'A headache? Oh, dear. Is she all right? I mean, should we send for a doctor?'

'She was quite adamant that she would feel better after resting for a while,' Alison said, avoiding Francis' eyes.

'Very well. It's just the three of us, then. Come along, there's no point in delaying. The carriage is waiting outside.' He ushered them both from the room.

As they went down the entrance hall, where Mackay was waiting with their outdoor garments, there was a sudden loud knocking at the front door. The butler put down Alison's cloak and hastened to see who was there.

A messenger in the czar's scarlet livery was standing outside, and he handed the butler a sealed note before hastening away again.

Alison's heart surged with hope. Surely it must be a summons to an imperial audience.

Mackay closed the door and returned to give the note to Francis. 'For you, my lord, from the Winter Palace.'

Francis broke the seal and read quickly. It was written in French, and was very brief. 'Lord Buckingham's presence in St Petersburg is not welcome. He will not be received, and is requested to leave Russia within the week.'

Disbelief swept over Francis; he read it again, but there was no mistaking the blunt message. Without a word he handed the note to Alison.

She scanned the two short sentences and then looked at him in dismay. 'Oh, no, it can't be!'

Mr Clearwell was much concerned. 'What is it? What's happened?'

Francis met his eyes. 'I'm not to be granted an audience with the czar, sir. In fact, I'm ordered to leave St Petersburg within the week.'

Mr Clearwell stared at him. 'Surely not.'

'I fear so.'

'But . . . Is there no explanation, no reason given?'

'None.'

The older man's eyes were shrewd. 'And you have no idea why this has happened?'

Francis hesitated and then looked frankly at him. 'I have no wish to involve you, sir.'

For a long moment Alison's uncle remained silent, and then he nodded. 'Nor will I probe deeper, sir, for I have suspected since yesterday that there was more to all this than you've been saying. Is the czar's refusal to receive you a great blow?'

'Catastrophic.' Francis glanced at Alison. Neither of them said it aloud, but both knew in their hearts that Nikolai's hand was behind this latest development. His suspicions had lingered, after all, and he had taken the one precaution that had been feared from the outset: he had seen to it that Lord Buckingham did not have the chance of speaking to the czar.

16

It was almost dark again, and another mist had arisen from the Neva. Alison sat in her nightgown by the fire in her room, gazing into the glowing logs. The house was quiet, for everyone had retired for the night.

The visit to the Hermitage had been abandoned, and Francis had gone alone to the Winter Palace to try to plead his case, but he had been turned away the moment he gave his name. He had had no option then but to go to the British embassy to report what had happened. He was closeted alone for some time with Lord St Helens and Charles Gainsborough, who were already somewhat disturbed because the ambassador himself had that very morning received a sharp rebuff from the Winter Palace, and the French ambassador had been cordially welcomed there. It seemed that Nikolai and the Countess Irina were beginning to triumph where the czar was concerned and that the French cause was advancing while the British were in forced retreat.

They had deliberated throughout the afternoon on what to do next, for the all-important documents must still somehow be placed in Alexander's hands, but no solution inspired their gloomy talks. Francis had left the embassy with the documents still in his possession, for it wasn't felt wise to keep them at the embassy when the unknown French agent was still at large. Impasse appeared to have been reached, and already the hours were ticking away toward Francis's unwilling departure from St Petersburg.

Dinner at the Clearwell residence that evening had been an uncomfortable affair, for Natalia had been very strained and quiet. She had offered the excuse that she was still suffering the tortures of a bad headache, but Alison and Francis knew better, for signs of the strain she was under increased perceptibly when she learned of the unexpected snub from the Winter Palace. She obviously concluded, as they had before her, that Prince Nikolai was somehow responsible.

Mr Clearwell said very little, but was plainly aware of all the undercurrents. He didn't attempt to bring any of it out into the open, however, and when at the end of the meal his wife declared that she would return to her room, he wasn't long in announcing his own wish to retire.

Alison and Francis remained in the grand salon for a while. His manner toward her was no longer quite as cold, and they sat together almost amicably as they tried to think of a way out of the seemingly impossible situation. But an answer evaded them, and soon they too retired to their rooms for the night.

Now Alison sat in the chair by the fire, the flames reflecting in her eyes as she mulled the difficulty over and over in her mind. She wished desperately that she could solve everything, but there didn't appear to be a solution. Her feeling of frustration turned to anger, and it was directed at Alexander for acting at Nikolai's scheming instigation. The czar didn't deserve to be saved from the French; he deserved to suffer the consequences of trusting Nikolai, but to let French plans proceed without challenge meant danger for the rest of Europe – and for Britain in particular.

Her thoughts returned to the opera house and the intimate embrace she had unwittingly come upon when she had taken the wrong passageway. She could see Alexander and Irina now, their faces warm with love as they had kissed and caressed. Alison sighed heavily. It was quite impossible to believe that Irina was party to her brother's treachery, for a woman as deeply in love as she would surely never put her lover so much at risk.

A woman as deeply in love as she . . . Alison sat up slowly, her loose hair spilling over her shoulders as the germ of an incredible idea suddenly formed in her head. Who adored Alexander with all her heart? Who could always gain access to him? The Countess Irina von Strelitz.

Alison got up from the chair, her mind racing. Could it be that the countess was the solution to the problem? Was she the one to place the documents in the czar's hands? Irina loved her brother, but would she put him before Alexander? Would she? Alison's pulse had begun to quicken. Oh, it was a preposterous thought, for how could they possibly take the chance that the countess would put lover before family? But what if she would? What if those words she had whispered when she thought herself alone were the absolute truth and she did love the czar with all her heart?

Pausing by the window, Alison gazed out into the gathering gloom of the misty twilight. Soon it would be dark, and the short northern night would engulf St Petersburg. Already the Neva was obscured by the vapor that rose from its chilly waters, and the lamps along the embankment of English Quay were faint orbs of light on the very edge of visibility. She could see a carriage drawn up at the curb, and a too familiar shadowy figure standing near it. The house was still under observation.

But Nikolai's spy from Stockholm and the Pavlovsk was of no interest to her at the moment, for her thoughts were still upon the Countess Irina. When she had watched the countess from behind the curtain in the anteroom at the opera house, she had known she was observing a woman who was completely in love. Her intuition had told her so then, and it told her again now. Irina would never put Nikolai before Alexander, and should be approached, even though she despised the British.

The thought swirled in Alison's head, so strong and clear that it almost urged her to act. But she must consider it from every angle. What if she was wrong about Irina? What if she told Nikolai? Alison stared out at the mist. She was sure she was right about Irina, and what other answer had presented itself? Was it really as preposterous as all that? Hadn't she, Alison Clearwell, been prepared to do a great deal for Francis? Why, then shouldn't Irina von Strelitz be equally prepared to do a great deal for her imperial lover and lord?

On impulse, Alison turned from the window, pausing only to pick up her pink woolen robe and put it on before hurrying from the room. In the passage outside she encountered Katya, who was coming to see if she required anything more before retiring finally to her bed.

Alison halted. 'No, thank you, Katya,' she said in French, 'that will be all.'

'Yes, Miss Clearwell.' Katya bobbed a curtsy and turned to go, but then Alison had second thoughts.

'No, wait a moment, Katya.'

'Miss Clearwell?'

'Please wait in my room, for I may require you, after all.'

'Yes, Miss Clearwell.' Curtsying again, the maid did as she was asked, and Alison hurried on toward Francis's room at the rear of the house, facing toward Horseguards Boulevard.

She knocked hesitantly at the door, but there was no sound from within. She knocked again, but still the room remained silent, and so she tentatively pushed the door open and peeped inside.

Candlelight swayed over the gray-and-blue bedchamber, and a fire glowed red in the white marble hearth. Francis had fallen asleep in the armchair by the fire, his lashes dark and still. A glass of cognac stood on the little table by his right hand, and he was still fully dressed.

She went softly into the room, intending to awaken him, but as she reached the chair, she saw that the glass of cognac was not the only thing on the table beside him, for a leather wallet lay there as well. She knew without telling that the wallet contained the secret documents. It was a measure of how tired Francis was that he had fallen asleep without hiding the vital papers away again.

Alison stood by the chair, gazing down at him as he slept. She longed to bend down and kiss him on the lips, and her heart ached to feel his arms around her. She didn't want to wake him up, especially when he would most probably think her scheme too outrageous and dangerous for words, but she had to tell him what she had thought of. She reached down toward him, meaning to shake his shoulder, but then her hand halted. She suddenly found herself thinking of the opera house again and the moment she had returned to the box and observed Irina looking at Francis. There had been no mistaking the malevolence in her gaze, the absolute hatred. It hadn't been directed toward anyone else in Count Vorontzov's box, just at Francis.

Alison straightened again, a confusion of thoughts milling around in her head. Irina despised Francis, for what reason could only be guessed, and so perhaps he was the last person who should approach her. Perhaps, just perhaps, this was a matter that should be conducted woman to woman. Alison's gaze moved to the little table and the wallet, lying there just waiting to be taken. Her pulse, already swift, now quickened almost unbearably. Should she do it? Should she act upon her intuition? What if she was wrong? What if she delivered the documents into the hands of the enemy? Her heart pounded like a hammer in her throat. She wasn't wrong! Irina was the answer! Snatching up the wallet, she hurried toward the door.

Behind her, Francis stirred a little in his sleep. A single word escaped his lips, a name, Pamela. It was a word that finally and irrevocably said everything to Alison. There were tears in her eyes as she closed the door softly behind her. By the fire, Francis slept on, unaware that she had even been there.

Alison hurried back to her own room, where Katya was waiting. The maid looked at her in surprise on seeing the flush on her cheeks and the nervousness that pervaded her.

'Miss Clearwell?'

'Katya, do you know how to get to the Countess Irina von Strelitz's residence on Krestovsky Island?'

The maid stared at her. 'Why, yes, everyone in St Petersburg knows her house, but—'

'I want you to take me there.'

'Now?'

'Yes.'

'But, Miss Clearwell, it's dark outside and so very late!'

'I must see the countess without delay, Katya. If you will not take me, perhaps you can tell me how to get there. Do I take a boat?'

Katya hesitated and then gave a small smile. 'I will take you, Miss Clearwell. There are always boatmen waiting before the Admiralty,'

As Alison dressed in a long-sleeved gray velvet gown, she was afraid that at any moment Francis would awaken and realize that the wallet was gone. Katya combed and pinned her hair as quickly as possible, and shortly afterward both maid and mistress were tiptoeing down through the silent house in warm cloaks, the hoods raised over their heads.

They left through the gardens, which were in darkness now, silently opening and closing the wrought-iron gate in the wall. It wasn't until they stepped outside that Alison suddenly remembered the man watching and waiting by the carriage. She remembered as she saw the shadowy silhouette of the vehicle opposite, and without explaining, she swiftly caught Katya's hand and hurried her on. She glanced back over her shoulder and was just able to see the man's startled reaction. She heard his brief order and the clatter of hooves as the carriage began to follow.

The mist eddied around as she and Katya reached the corner of St Isaac's Square, and she almost made the maid lose her footing by catching her cloak suddenly and drawing her back into the shadows of a doorway. They pressed back against the cold marble columns, listening as the carriage approached. Katya's eyes were wide and frightened, for she didn't under-stand what it was all about, but she knew enough to remain absolutely silent as the silhouette of the vehicle emerged from English Quay, reining in as the coachman tried to listen for the sound of their fleeing footsteps.

In the carriage Sergei was cursing beneath his breath. He had been thinking about Nikolai's decision to replace him with Bragin during the day. If the overseer captured her, then the estate at Novgorod would go to his nephew; if he Sergei, succeeded, then his IOUs would be returned. The thought of Bragin winning had distracted him, and he had allowed his concentration to lapse for a moment. He lowered the window glass and leaned out.

'Well?' he snapped.

The coachman leaned back to speak to him. 'They've gone, sir. I can't hear them at all. I think they must have gone into one of the houses.'

A thousand and one bitter curses trembled on Sergei's lips, then he realized that if the Englishwoman had left, then sooner or later she would have to return. All he had to do was wait and seize her as she tried to reenter the gate. 'Go back,' he said to the coachman, 'go back to where we were, but a little farther down the street this time, to be out of sight in the mist. I'll wait near the gate, and the moment I call, you are to bring the carriage, is that clear?'

'Yes, sir.'

Sergei raised the window glass again, sitting back as the carriage turned slowly to make its way back toward the Clearwell residence.

In the doorway, Alison and Katya hadn't been able to quite hear what had been said, and as the carriage drove away once more, they emerged from the shadows. 'Did you understand anything they said, Katya?' Alison asked.

'No, Miss Clearwell, they weren't speaking loudly enough.'

They hurried on past the square and the pontoon bridge and on toward the magnificent fire-damaged façade of the Admiralty, which was in the process of being rebuilt. Steps led down to the water, and a number of small boats were moored at the jetties. The boatmen were standing in groups, talking in low voices, and they fell silent as the two women descended the steps.

Katya spoke to one of them, and he nodded immediately, beckoning them toward a slender rowing boat of some age. He handed them both into the little craft, steadying it as best he could because it rocked alarmingly from side to side, and then he cast off and stepped in himself, taking up the oars to push the boat away from the jetty. As they slid away on the shining dark water, the lights of the embankment disappeared in the mist, then the jetty was lost from sight as well, and they were out on the Neva.

The boatman rowed strongly, not seeming to need landmarks to guide him. He was a burly man, wearing a coarse gray linen shirt beneath one of the ubiquitous blue caftans that so many of the Russian men favored. Bearded and rough, he rowed with a strength that was almost fearsome, making the boat skim across the water.

The pontoon bridge was far behind them now and they were moving around the spit of Vassily Island, where the Neva was at its widest before parting into two of its main channels. The Peter-Paul Fortress was invisible to their right as the rowing boat moved northwest along the channel known as the Little Neva. Vassily Island was to their left now and Peterburg Island to their right. Nothing was visible in the mist, but the boatman still seemed to know exactly where he was, for suddenly he turned the boat to the right, rowing directly toward Petersburg Island. He was unerringly accurate, for the boat entered a narrow canal and then turned northward again, rowing between high embankments that were so close that they could be seen towering out of the water. Then, quite suddenly, they emerged from the narrow waterway into a broad channel. It was the Little Neva, another of the four main arteries of the Neva. On the northern side of this, bounded to the west by the Gulf of Finland and to the east by Kamenny Island, where Czar Alexander had a private residence, lay Krestovsky Island.

As the rowing boat slid across the Little Neva toward a jetty that protruded into the water, voices drifted out through the mist.

Katya gave a quick gasp. 'There are guards, Miss Clearwell.'

'Can't we go ashore somewhere else? The island is surely as flat as all the others.'

The maid nodded and spoke swiftly to the boatman, who immediately maneuvered the boat to the west. The sound of the voices died away into the mist again, and they heard nothing more. Alison could hear the water lapping against the shore, and then she saw the island, a tree-dotted silhouette that was barely above sea level. There was a small creek, and the rowing boat entered it, nudging the shore close to some barberry bushes.

The boatman grinned at Katya in the darkness and muttered something as he jumped ashore to make the boat fast.

'What did he say?' asked Alison.

'That he knows the island like the back of his hand because he comes here to steal hares.'

As the boatman handed them both on to the land, he spoke again.

Katya turned to Alison. 'He wishes to know if he is to wait for us, Miss Clearwell.'

'Tell him that if we are not back in two hours, he is to tell Lord Buckingham where we are. He will be rewarded for his trouble.'

Katya did as she was asked, and the man nodded, but then pointedly held out his hand.

Katya was a little embarrassed. 'He wishes to be paid now, Miss Clearwell.'

'But he will still wait?'

'Oh, yes, Miss Clearwell.'

Alison gave him some coins from her reticule, and then he pointed through the mist.

Katya followed the direction he was indicating. 'The countess's house is that way, Miss Clearwell. He says that there is a path of sorts and that it will bring us to the edge of the countess's park. There are guards since robbers broke in last summer and stole some of the countess's jewels. We must watch out for them.'

'You can stay here if you wish, Katya, for it isn't fair that you should be put in danger as well.'

'You are my mistress now, Miss Clearwell, and so I will go with you.'

'If you're sure . . .'

Katya smiled. 'I am sure, Miss Clearwell. Come.'

They followed the path through the misty darkness, their cloaks brushing against the barberry bushes that were so prolific on the island. Tall lime trees rose in the gloom, their trunks covered with moss, and from time to time they heard the call of a peacock from the estate that lay unseen in the night ahead.

Doubts beset Alison now that she was close to her destination. What if the countess wasn't alone? What if Nikolai was with her? The determination that had swept her along when first she had thought of her plan now began to falter, and she could only think of the many dire consequences that might result if this all went wrong. She was British, and she carried on her person some plans and other documents containing highly sensitive and secret Russian military and naval information.

The sea mist swirled and eddied, and briefly they glimpsed the lights of a large house a short way ahead. They walked more slowly, straining to hear any guards who might be near. Gradually the house became more discernible and Alison could make out a Roman portico of white columns, a green cupola, and a particularly handsome conservatory built against the wall. The conservatory was lamplit, the warm light shining through the abundance of tropical foliage inside.

They halted by some lilacs, from which they could observe the nearby house for a moment. As Alison gazed at the conservatory, she could hardly believe her eyes when she saw Irina herself enter it from the house. Nikolai's beautiful sister wore a flimsy, revealing, low-necked white muslin robe, and her magnificent red-gold hair tumbled freely about her creamy shoulders. She walked alone through the conservatory toward a secluded corner where a white wrought-iron table and chairs had been set out. There she picked up a small dish and began to feed tidbits to a monkey on a perch.

Alison stared at her. Would there ever be a more opportune moment than this? Irina was all alone, without even so much as a maid.

Katya touched her arm. 'I do not know why you wished to come here, Miss Clearwell, but if it is to speak to the countess, then you must do it now. I will wait here.'

Alison's heart had quickened disagreeably and she felt very cold suddenly. Was it madness to proceed now? There was still time to turn back. She could return the document wallet to Francis and all would be well again ... All would be well? No, it wouldn't be well, for Nikolai would still be an undetected traitor and Russia would still be in grave danger from Bonaparte.

Taking a deep breath, she slipped from the shelter of the lilacs, crossing the lawn toward the conservatory. She paused, listening again for any sign of the guards, but there was nothing. She reached the conservatory door, and as she put her hand on the handle, it turned easily. The door opened softly and the warm, humid air breathed over her. Then she stepped inside, closing the door quietly behind her.

17

The atmosphere in the conservatory was almost oppressive after the coldness of the night, and Alison could hear the gentle splashing of water. Moths fluttered among the leaves, and the scent of earth and exotic plants filled the air.

From the door it was impossible to see as far as the secluded corner where Irina was feeding the monkey. The light from a number of lamps cast leafy shadows in all directions, and high above, the glass reflected all the foliage, as if there was another conservatory stretching out into the night.

Tossing back her hood, Alison hesitated, unsure of how to approach Irina, but then she heard footsteps coming from the house, and with a gasp she hid among the leaves. A maid entered the conservatory, her starched white apron crackling as she walked. She passed within a foot or so of Alison as she went toward the private corner where her mistress was to be found. She paused respectfully before presuming to enter Irina's presence.

'Begging your pardon, my lady,' she said in the French of a true-born Parisienne.

'What is it?'

The maid entered the secluded little area and passed out of Alison's sight, but she could still hear what was said.

The maid spoke again. 'Begging your pardon, my lady, but a messenger has been sent from his imperial majesty.'

'A messenger?'

'Yes, my lady. His imperial majesty will be yet another hour.'

'Very well.'

'Do you require anything, my lady?'

'No, I will take supper when his imperial majesty arrives.'

'Yes, my lady.'

'You may go.'

'My lady.'

The maid's footsteps sounded again, and she reappeared through the greenery, retracing her path past Alison and returning to the house. Silence fell over the conservatory, and then Alison heard Irina's soft voice. 'Well, Mischa, I must wait another long hour before I am with my love. I am unfortunate, my little monkey, but you are not, for now you can have more strawberries.'

The monkey chattered, and Irina laughed.

Alison remained hidden among the leaves, her nerve almost deserting her again. The czar would be here in an hour, which meant that it was possible for the documents to be given to him then. Oh, please, please let all this be the right thing to do.

Summoning the vestige of her courage and crossing her fingers, Alison emerged from her hiding place, stepping firmly on to the barely discernible brick path and walking slowly toward Irina.

The monkey stopped chattering suddenly, and as it did so, Alison's steps were plainly heard.

Irina turned, her green eyes raking the crowding leaves. 'Who's there?'

Alison walked more quickly, pushing the overhanging branches aside and standing at the edge of the light from the lamp on the wrought-iron table. Irina stared at her and then became alarmed, reaching out for a little silver hand bell on the table.

Alison hurried forward to stop her, putting her hand over the bell. 'Please, don't, for I mean you no harm,' she said in English. Then she repeated it in French, for she didn't know if Irina spoke English.

Irina froze, her eyes luminous in the light from the lamp. 'You're English?' she asked in that language.

'Yes, but I still mean you no harm.'

'I've seen you somewhere.'

'At the opera house, in Count Vorontzov's box,' replied Alison.

The green eyes hardened. 'Ah, yes, you were with Lord Buckingham.' Francis's title was uttered with loathing.

'I must speak with you, my lady.'

'I have nothing to say to you, for I know that you are to marry Lord Buckingham.'

'Why do you hate him so? What has he done to you?'

'Come now, my dear, don't let's play games. You know perfectly well why I despise him, for he was at the Battle of the Nile and was on the very ship that sank the *L'Orient*, killing my husband.'

Alison stared at her. 'That isn't so,' she breathed. 'It simply isn't so.'

'How very innocent you look, my dear. I can see why my brother thinks you are so desirable.'

Alison drew back. 'I am not interested in your brother, my lady, for I love Lord Buckingham.'

'I wish your handsome lord in perdition, my dear, and if you insist upon loving him, then you may go to perdition as well. I don't know why you've come here, unless it is to plead for your lord to be allowed an audience with the czar. You are wasting your time, for I have seen to it that Lord Buckingham is soon forced to leave St Petersburg altogether.'

'Why? Because your brother told you a lie?' Alison asked quietly, suddenly knowing that it was from Nikolai that Irina had heard the tale of Francis's so-called part in the sinking of the *L'Orient*.

Irina was cold. 'Have a care, my dear, for I love my brother very much.'

'More than you love the czar?'

Irina's eyes flashed. 'You are impertinent. Leave immediately, before I have you thrown out.'

'Please, my lady, I am here because I believe you love the czar above all else, and because I think you will wish to do all you can to help and protect him. He is in the gravest danger, I promise you, and not from Britain.'

'What nonsense is this? Do you honestly expect me to believe that you, a woman, would be sent on such an errand?'

'I haven't been sent, my lady. I've come on my own accord, because I know that you love the czar. I know the risk I'm taking, because you might not be what I believe you to be, but for Russia's sake and the sake of all Europe, I must try to convince you. Lord Buckingham is here in St Petersburg to give certain documents to the czar, documents that came into our hands from a British agent in Paris. Now that the audience with the czar is to be denied, he can't give him the documents himself, so I've taken them and brought them here to you. You must give them to him, my lady.'

'Me? Assist the British? You've taken leave of your senses, my dear.'

'Deny the czar the chance of seeing these documents, my lady, and you may be putting his life and the safety of Russia in peril. I'm not speaking theatrically, embellishing it all to impress you; I'm telling you the truth. There is a traitor here in St Petersburg, someone who is prepared to give Russia's military secrets to the French. That someone, your brother, was in Paris recently.'

Irina stared at her. 'What are you saying?' she asked sharply. 'Are you implying that Nikolai. . . ?'

'Yes, my lady.'

'How dare you!'

Alison put the document wallet on the table. 'These papers were in Bonaparte's possession, my lady. Please look at them.'

'I have no desire to read your documents or to assist you in your machinations.'

'If you love the czar, you will look at them,' replied Alison, meeting her gaze.

'I love the czar and I love my brother.'

'But does your brother share your love for the czar? Can you put your hand on your heart and swear that Prince Nikolai is loyal to the House of Romanov?'

Irina stared at her, more than a little shaken as an echo of conversation returned to her: 'If it were not for the czar's intransigence, Irina, I would by now be married to the Grand-Duchess Helen. It is good enough for him to bed you outside his marriage, but it isn't good enough for me to make his sister my princess. That is an insult I cannot and will not forgive.'

Alison looked at her and saw that her face was suddenly a little pale. 'You aren't certain of Prince Nikolai's loyalty, are you?' she said quietly.

'Of course I am—'

'No, my lady, you have doubts. May I ask if he told everyone here that he was going to Paris? Or was it something that he confided only in you, so that you would know where to reach him?'

Irina turned away. 'He was considering purchasing an estate in the Bois de Boulogne, but felt that it was prudent for the time being not to broadcast it too much, for the czar did not trust the French,' said Irina, her voice lowered almost to a whisper. She turned away, her hands trembling, and she went to feed strawberries to the monkey again. She was trying to distract herself, but the truth was beginning to stare her in the face, and she didn't want to recognize it.

'My lady, please look at the documents in the wallet.'

'No.'

'For the sake of the man you love. You have the czar's love, and you will keep it if you do the right thing now. Do the wrong thing, and not only might the czar forfeit his throne with his realm, but if he should survive a French invasion, then he may well think that you were party to your brother's treachery.'

Irina turned quickly, the dish of strawberries falling from her fingers. 'I would never be party to anything that—'

'Then look at the documents, I beg of you,' cried Alison, pushing the wallet across the table.

Reluctantly Irina picked it up, taking the documents out and laying them carefully on the table. The oil lamp cast a revealing light over the detailed analysis of Kronstadt's defenses and over the intricate maritime chart of the approaches to St Petersburg. Irina stared at them.

'You know what they are, don't you?' Alison said gently.

Irina nodded, 'Yes, but I cannot believe that Nikolai—'

'I cannot prove that he has done anything, my lady, but I tell you that it is true. He has been promised great rewards by Bonaparte, and for this he is prepared to sell the czar and Russia into French hands.' Alison looked sadly at her. 'Forgive me, my lady, for the last thing I wish to do is make you sad, but somehow those papers have to reach the czar, and you are the only one who can see that they do. I know the sacrifice I'm asking you to make, but you will make a far greater one if you refuse to act. You've already loved and lost, so how much greater will the pain be this time?'

Had she gone too far? By reminding Irina of her husband, had she tipped the scales the other way?

Irina touched the wedding ring on her finger and then looked at Alison. 'You are either very brave or very foolish, Miss Clearwell.'

'You know my name?'

'Nikolai told me.' Irina still toyed with her wedding ring. 'You are right, the pain would be intolerable if I lost the czar. I do love him, more than life itself, and if I can do anything to protect him, even if it means sacrificing Nikolai, then I will do it.'

An unutterable relief swept over Alison, and she had to steady herself on the table. She bowed her head for a moment and then looked at Irina again. 'I'm so very sorry that I have had to bring this to you, my lady, for I know how you must be feeling now.'

'Do you?'

Alison nodded. 'We may be from different nations, my lady, but we are both women who have to make terrible decisions in the name of love.'

'And what decision do you have to make, Miss Clearwell?'

'The decision not to marry Lord Buckingham.'

'Not to marry him? But why? If you love him—'

'He doesn't love me; he loves someone else.'

Irina studied her. 'Then why is he marrying you?'

'To protect my reputation. He feels it is his duty to do the right thing by me.'

'Are you quite sure he loves this other woman?'

Alison nodded, remembering how he had murmured Pamela's name in his sleep. 'I'm quite sure.'

'Perhaps I am the wrong person to speak to of reputations, Miss Clearwell, for I am the czar's mistress and the whole of Russia knows it. I don't have a reputation to protect.'

'No, but you have the czar's love, and that is everything.' Alison glanced down at the documents and the wallet. 'I will go now. Once again, I'm sorry for what I have had to tell you.'

'I believe you are, Miss Clearwell.'

Alison smiled a little. 'I pray only that the czar will be able to act upon the knowledge he is about to receive.'

Irina took a long breath. 'He will act, Miss Clearwell. I will see to it that he understands fully what has been going on.'

Alison raised her hood and then paused before leaving. 'Will you warn Prince Nikolai?'

'No, Miss Clearwell, I will not, for if he is a threat to the czar now, then he will be again. He may be my brother, but he will never take precedence over the czar, any more than I believe I would ever have come before his ambitions. You have accomplished what you came for, and now I think you should go.

Alison nodded. 'Goodbye, my lady.'

'Goodbye, Miss Clearwell.'

Alison turned, but then Irina spoke again. 'Miss Clearwell?'

'Yes?'

'Lord Buckingham is a fool if he doesn't love you.'

The cold night air came almost as a shock as Alison left the conservatory again and hurried back to where Katya was waiting by the lilacs. As they made their way back toward the creek, Alison knew that she had done the right thing by giving the documents to Irina. She had taken an enormous risk, but she had followed her intuition and in a short while now Alexander would be in full possession of facts that would enable him to save his realm and his throne.

St Petersburg was still enveloped in mist as the rowing boat returned to the jetty by the Admiralty. There was hardly anyone abroad as they walked swiftly toward St Isaac's Square and the pontoon bridge, so that it came as something of a shock when a tall man loomed out of the mist right in front of them and addressed Alison by name.

With a gasp, Alison came to an abrupt halt, staring at him. Then she gave a relieved smile. 'Captain Merryvale?'

He removed his hat and bowed.

'How good it is to see you again. I knew you were here in St Petersburg, for I saw the *Duchess of Clarence* at her berth.'

'She arrived in Stockholm on the very day the *Pavlovsk* left. I'm relieved to say that I am not held to blame for the loss of the *Duchess of Albemarle* and that on my return to London I am promised a new command.'

'I'm very pleased for you, sir.'

'Thank you, Miss Clearwell.'

'Will you be returning to England on the *Duchess of Clarence*?'

'Yes, tomorrow afternoon. I've just been making final customs arrangements for part of her cargo. I'm afraid that such things have to be done whether it is night or day.' He smiled. 'May I escort you home now, Miss Clearwell?'

She returned the smile. 'If you wish, sir.'

Accepting the arm he offered, she walked at his side, with Katya following a step or so behind. Nikolai's spy had completely slipped her mind.

Sergei was waiting beneath the trees opposite the Clearwell residence and the carriage was drawn up at the curb farther long the street, out of sight in the mist. He was tired, cold, and angry that he had allowed his prey to elude him earlier. If Bragin had succeeded where he, Sergei Mikhailovich Golitsin, had failed, then ruin would no longer be merely a threat, it would be a reality.

He heard footsteps approaching from the direction of St Isaac's Square and he looked intently toward the sound. Then he made out a woman's voice speaking in English.

Turning, he gave a low whistle and immediately he heard the carriage stir into motion, the team's hooves slow and steady. He ran softly across the street to the shadows by the gate in the wall, pressing back out of sight as the approaching footsteps grew louder. The carriage was close now and would be alongside at the very moment the Englishwoman and her maid reached the gate. As their figures became discernible in the mist, Sergi leapt out to seize Alison. Too late he saw that there were three figures instead of two, and he was almost caught completely off-guard, but his instinct saved him. He lashed out blindly, catching the unfortunate Captain Merryvale a brutal blow to the jaw. Katya began to scream for help and for her pains was thrust so hard against the wall that she was winded, falling to the ground like a sack.

Alison was too frightened to do anything but back away. She couldn't cry out and she couldn't run away, her strength and willpower had deserted her. Sergei seized her and dragged her roughly toward the carriage, which had now drawn up beside them. In his panic to accomplish the task as expeditiously as possible, he flung the carriage door open, and it struck Alison on the forehead. She lost consciousness immediately and knew nothing as she was thrust into the vehicle.

Sergei clambered in as well, slamming the door behind him, then the whip cracked and the team struck sparks from the street as they strained to come up to speed.

Katya scrambled to her feet in dismay, staring at the carriage as it drove swiftly through the eddying mist. The whip cracked again, the sound seeming to echo all around, and then gradually silence returned and the mist swirled slowly again, like the gentle billowing of a fine muslin curtain.

Tears filled Katya's frightened eyes as she bent to shake Captain Merryvale, but he didn't stir. She straightened, running to the house and up the steps to the door. She hammered on the lion's-head knocker with so much force that the sound reverberated through the house like an echoing thunderclap.

Lights began to appear as candles were hastily lit inside, and voices were heard as Mackay and several of the footmen came from their beds.

In his room, Francis at last stirred as the noise penetrated his sleep. His thoughts were scattered for a moment and then he sat up, running his fingers through his hair. He heard the confusion as the servants went to investigate. What in God's name was going on?

Then his glance moved to the table where the precious wallet should have been lying . . .

18

Alison lay on a soft bed swathed with golden satin. The sheets and pillows were satin and so was the tentlike canopy, and the scent of roses hung in the dawn-lit room. It was a seductive perfume, caressing her senses as she began to stir.

She still wore her gray velvet gown, and her hair had come loose from its pins, spilling in confusion over the pillows. Her eyes opened and she gazed up at the golden canopy. Where was she? She couldn't collect her thoughts because her head seemed to be swimming, and as she slowly sat up, a sharp pain lanced behind her eyes, making her feel suddenly and violently sick. She held her breath, closing her eyes again. The room seemed to be swaying and she found herself gripping the satin sheets in a futile effort to make everything be still again. Then, very gradually, she realized that it wasn't her imagination, or the pain in her head, for the room really was rocking gently from side to side. It wasn't a strong motion and wasn't even particularly unpleasant, but added to the sickening pain behind her eyes, it made her feel very unsteady and ill.

After a long moment she opened her eyes again, looking around the room. There was damask on the walls and a sable-covered ottoman couch against the foot of the bed. The scent of roses came from an open potpourri jar standing on the floor next to the stove that was warming the air. There were damask curtains at the single window and another curtain tied back beside the door. Her gaze moved over everything. She had never been in this room before, and yet somehow it seemed familiar. How had she come here? She couldn't remember anything.

She put a hand tentatively to her forehead and winced as her fingertips brushed the bruise. Again she had to close her eyes as a wave of nausea washed over her. Oh, if only everything would stop swaying . . .

Without warning her memory returned. Suddenly she could see Captain Merryvale falling to the ground and hear Katya's screams for help. She saw the maid being flung against the wall and she felt herself being seized and thrust toward a carriage. She had been abducted by Nikolai's creature!

Her heartbeats quickened and she was trembling as she got up slowly from the bed, steadying herself against the post for a moment to look around the room again. She must escape! She went to the door, but it was locked. Turning, she went to the window, but that too was impossible to open. She gazed out at the mist, which was luminous now that the first light of dawn had begun to drive away the darkness. Where was she? Was she still in St Petersburg? The mist drifted impenetrably, weaving back up itself. She listened carefully and gradually became aware of the familiar sound of the wharves on Vassily Island. The sound was clearer than it had been from English Quay. Was she on Vassily Island?

She stared out at the mist again, willing it to draw back so that she could see, but it remained stubbornly where it was, obscuring everything so well that she couldn't even see the ground. Then, as she was beginning to despair, a rowing boat glided past, its oars shipped as the ebbing tide carried it downstream. In a moment it had passed out of sight again, swallowed by the mist.

Alison's heart had stopped. She was on the *Irina*! Suddenly the swaying sensation was explained and the strange familiarity of the room, which she now remembered was very similar to the stateroom where she and Francis had been entertained by Prince Nikolai. Trembling, she backed away from the window and then turned to run to the door, beating her fists against the wood and screaming as loudly as she could.

'Let me out! Let me out!'

At first there was no response, but as she continued to make as much noise as she could, she at last heard voices. One was high-pitched and almost singsong, and the other was deep and monosyllabic, and she knew immediately that they belonged to Nikolai's servants, the dwarf in the golden robes and the huge black man. Then she heard another sound that made her pull back swiftly from the door; it was the disturbed and agitated growl of the lynx, Khan. The sounds were at the door now and the key turned in the lock.

The door swung open and the dwarf came in. Behind him, blocking the doorway, was the black man, and he was holding on firmly to the lynx's turquoise-studded collar. The animal's amber eyes were wide and dangerous, its tufted ears were flattened, and its mouth was drawn back in a snarl that revealed its sharp teeth.

The dwarf swaggered farther into the room, his little hands thrust arrogantly over his belt. 'It will do you no good to make such a noise, Miss Clearwell,' he said in singsong French, 'for no one will hear you.'

'You can't imprison me,' she replied in the same language.

'But we can, for we do his highness's bidding. He will be here soon, and you will await him.' The dwarf grinned, his glance moving deliberately and suggestively toward the bed.

'Please let me go. I'll make it worth your while—'

'We do his highness's bidding,' he repeated, and then nodded at the lynx. 'It would be very foolish if you tried to escape, Miss Clearwell, for Khan will see that you remain a prisoner.'

'Please help me,' she begged, but she knew it was futile.

'Make yourself beautiful for his highness, Miss Clearwell, for that will avail you of much more. Please him, and he will grant you many things; displease him, and you will find that the Neva is very deep.' Turning, he went out again and the door was locked behind him.

Alison was panic-stricken, running to the door and beating at it again, but she could hear the dwarf laughing and Khan growling. Tears filled her eyes and she left the door again, hurrying to the window, but the mist still coiled and writhed silently outside, white now as the dawn grew brighter with each passing minute.

The tears wended their way down her cheeks as she went to sit on the bed. She was filled with a sense of hopelessness. No one knew she was here, and so no one could help her. By now they would know that she had been taken, but they didn't know who by. Unless . . . Francis would guess, surely? But what could he do about it? This was St Petersburg, and the prince was a powerful man. Her only hope was that by now Irina had given the wallet to the czar and that events were in motion to put a halt to Nikolai Ivanovich's treachery.

She stared down at the crumpled satin in her hands, and then her eyes wandered to the soft uncompromising expanse of the rest of the bed. She could see the suggestive grin on the dwarf's face. 'Make yourself beautiful for his highness, Miss Clearwell. Please him and he will grant you many things; displease him, and you will find that the Neva is very deep.'

Her thoughts went unwillingly back to Stockholm and those terrifying moments before Francis had rescued her. Nikolai had made no attempt to hide his desire. 'Don't be foolish, Miss Clearwell, for there is so much pleasure to be had. I intend to possess you, and I will do so whether you struggle or whether you consent. Of course, it would be so much better if you consented, because it would please me to introduce you to the delights of making love.'

There was no one to save her now, no one to snatch her from his grasp. When he entered this room, he would be able to take her as he chose, and there was nothing she could do to prevent him.

Fresh tears stung her eyes and she lay down on the bed, curling up tightly and hiding her face in her hands. Her whole body shook with sobs and there was a cold band around her heart. She was at Nikolai's mercy, and when his pleasure was done, what then? What would become of her when his desire was slaked and she was of no further interest?

At the house on English Quay all was still in confusion. Katya had tearfully explained all that had happened and Captain Merryvale had been brought in and a doctor sent for.

Natalia was so upset that she had virtually collapsed and had had to be taken to her bed to be looked after by her maid. Alison's uncle had at last been told the full truth about Francis's purpose in St Petersburg.

He and Francis were in the grand salon, where all the chandeliers had been lit, the brilliant light flooding out of the windows into the mist.

Wearing a blue paisley dressing gown, Mr Clearwell stood before the fireplace, his face grim. 'I wish I'd been told from the outset, sir.'

'It seemed wiser not to involve you, Mr Clearwell.'

'Look where all this has brought us now! We think, but we can't be sure, that Alison has given those damned documents to the Countess Irina, and now we have no idea at all where Alison herself is, except that it seems likely that Naryshky has abducted her. Dear God, what a scrape.' With a sigh, he went to a table to pour himself a glass of cognac. Swirling his amply filled glass, he turned to face Francis again. 'What do you intend to do now?'

'Find Alison.'

'One might as well search for a needle in a haystack. If Naryshky's taken her, he'll make sure his tracks are covered, you may be sure of that. And as to expecting any assistance from those you question, you might as well bay to the moon. Naryshky is a man of influence and power, and no one in St Petersburg is going to risk his displeasure by informing on him.'

'Sir, I know from the ambassador's secretary that the man who has been watching this house, and the man who most probably kidnapped Alison, is someone by the name of Sergei Mikhailovich Golitsin, and that he, like Naryshky, is in the Preobrazensky Regiment. If I have to tear the truth out of him, I promise you I will.'

'The officers in that regiment are the elite, sir, and if you imagine that you can simply walk into the barracks and confront him—'

'There must be a way, Mr Clearwell.'

'If there is, my lord earl, I do not know it. Alison could be in any one of a thousand different places, and we may never see her again.' The older man blinked back sudden tears. 'I feel so utterly helpless,' he said quietly, 'but there is one thing of which I am certain: I hold you to blame for all that's befallen my niece – you, Lord Buckingham, and I trust that she will forever be on your conscience.'

'I hold myself to blame, sir,' replied Francis. 'For the moment, however, I can do nothing other than report to the embassy, to let them know what we think has happened to the documents.' He ran his fingers through his hair. 'She must have given them to the countess, for why else would she have gone to Krestovsky Island? She mut have taken leave of her senses to give such information into the hands of Naryshky's sister. Unless . . .'

'Unless what?' prompted Mr Clearwell, looking at him.

'Oh, I was just thinking of something Alison said when it was suggested that the countess was as culpable as her brother in the plot with Boney. She was quite convinced that Irina was innocent, although I don't know why.'

Mr Clearwell drew a long breath. 'Innocent or not, I hardly think the countess is likely to hand her beloved brother over to the czar. She and Naryshky dote on each other, everyone knows that.'

Francis's mind was racing. 'But what if the countess dotes more on the czar?' he murmured, crossing to the windows that faced over the Neva. His hand rested on the telescope as he stared out at the luminosity of the mist. Had Alison perceived the one certain way of seeing that Alexander received the vital information? Had she understood that Irina's love for the czar by far outweighed her love for her brother?

As he looked, the mist seemed to thread a little, thinning so that he could see the trees on the embankment and then the river beyond. The pale light of early morning shone on the water, and he could make out the white hull of the *Irina*, still lying at anchor in midriver. A rowing boat was coming alongside and there was a familiar uniformed figure seated in the stern.

Francis bent to train the telescope on the rowing boat. Yes, it was Prince Nikolai, and he was just getting to his feet to step out of the boat on to the wooden staircase that was against the side of the schooner. As the prince went swiftly up to the deck, Francis moved the telescope along the vessel. A pale, tearstained face was peeping out of a window near the stem. It was Alison, her hair in disarray, her eyes frightened. Then she'd gone.

Francis straightened and turned quickly to Mr Clearwell. 'Alison's on the *Irina*. I've just seen her.'

'The *Irina*? Man, it's thick mist out there, you can't possibly see the—'

'The mist thinned for a moment and I saw her looking out of a cabin. I also saw Naryshky going on board. There isn't any time to be lost, I have to get to her before he has time to . . .' Francis didn't finish the sentence, but ran from the room.

In the entrance hall he saw Captain Merryvale seated on the sofa by the fire, his head bandaged because he had struck it as he fell. He was sipping a tot of Mackay's precious Scottish whiskey, and the butler was waiting to replenish the glass.

Both men turned as Francis hurried down the staircase, and Captain Merryvale rose to his feet. 'Is something up, my lord?'

'How fit are you, Captain? Are you well enough to help me get Miss Clearwell off the *Irina*?'

The captain's eyes were hard and bright. 'I'm game to do anything you wish, my lord, for I don't take kindly to being set upon, nor do I take kindly to those who mistreat ladies. I'm your man if you want me.'

'I want you, sir. We'll take a boat.'

Mackay spoke up quickly. 'Just one minute, my lord, I beg of you.' The butler hurried away, returning in a very short while with a pistol, which he pressed into Francis's hands. 'You may have need of this, my lord,' he said quietly.

Francis nodded and looked at the captain. 'Let's get on with it then.'

Mackay hastened to open the doors for them and they hurried out into the misty morning. English Quay was deserted as they ran downstream to the next jetty and then swiftly descended the stone steps to where a number of rowing boats and barges were moored. A moment later they were rowing out on the mist-covered Neva, pulling strongly in the direction of the *Irina*.

Alison backed slowly away from the door as she heard footsteps approaching. She could hear the soft jingle of spurs and knew to whom those steps belonged. Her pulse had quickened and she could hear her terrified heartbeats as the key turned in the lock. She could press no farther away, for she had reached the wall. A choked sob rose in her throat as the door swung open and Nikolai stood there.

His dark glance raked her from head to toe and then he entered the room, closing the door behind him. 'Good morning, Alison,' he murmured.

She didn't reply, but remained pressed against the wall, her gray eyes huge and afraid.

He came toward her. 'We have some unfinished business, do we not?' he said softly, halting a foot or so away.

She was so frightened that she couldn't move even an inch away from him. She felt like a fly, trapped in the web of a clever, hungry spider, and her heart was thudding so loudly now that she was sure he must be able to hear it.

He put a hand out, taking a lock of her hair and parting the strands between his fingers. 'You are so very beautiful, my dear,' he said. 'Even now, when you are so very pale and afraid, you are quite the most lovely of creatures. I won't be denied my pleasure this time, you may be sure of that, and even though you've been so very elusive and difficult, I still offer you the choice.'

'Choice?' she whispered.

'Yes. Either you come to me of your own volition, or I take you by force. Which is it to be?'

'I'll never come to you,' she breathed.

'As you wish. It's really of no importance, for in the end I will possess you anyway.' He came closer, suddenly taking her face in his hands and bending his head forward to force his lips over hers. He could smell the lavender she wore.

She began to struggle then, beating her fists against him and trying to kick. He gave a low laugh, as if her resistance excited him more, and he lifted her from her feet, carrying her toward the bed.

Her struggles redoubled, but he was far too strong for her. He flung her on to the bed and then almost leapt upon her, pinning her down before she could even think of scrambling away. He pressed his body against hers, his hands sliding over her. His lips were hungry, kissing her so demandingly that he hurt her. As she writhed beneath him, striving with all her might to pull free, he became more and more aroused. He tore at her gown, and as the delicate gray velvet ripped, his fingers slid to cup her breast. With his other hand he pulled up her skirt, his hand caressing her thigh, and all the time he was kissing her, his mouth stopping her breath.

She refused to surrender and continued to struggle, but she was growing weaker because his strength was so great, made greater by the force of his lust. Her cheeks were tearstained and her lips bruised.

She couldn't cry out and she couldn't prevent him from violating her. A silent scream rang through her.

Someone help me, please. Oh, dear God, someone help me!

19

At last the rowing boat came alongside the steps that led up to the *Irina*'s deck. Francis got out and made the boat fast, and then he and Captain Merryvale went quietly up on to the schooner. They paused at the top, glancing both ways along the deck. Everything was misty and deserted.

Beckoning to the captain to follow him, Francis went softly toward the stern of the vessel. Halfway along, they came upon an open door giving on to a hatchway that led down into a hold. Lamplight shone out and they heard laughter and voices. Looking inside, Francis saw what appeared to be most of the schooner's crew indulging in the Russian passion for gambling. Some were playing cards, others throwing dice, and another group was laying odds on a race between some cockroaches.

Francis drew back out on to the deck, closing the door very quietly. Casting around, he saw a broom resting discreetly in a corner, and quickly he wedged the handle silently through the handle on the door. When it was firmly in place, he gave the captain a quick smile.

'That would keep them contained for a while if the alarm is raised,' he said. 'Come on.'

They continued to make their way toward the stern of the *Irina*, listening all the while for any sound that might tell them Alison was in immediate danger, but all remained quiet.

They reached the door that gave on to the sandalwood-scented passageway. Francis pushed the door softly open, and it swung away at his touch, revealing the passage to be quite as deserted as the deck behind them. Francis led the way inside toward the beautiful door of

the stateroom. As they reached it, it suddenly opened and the dwarf
came out. His jaw dropped as he saw them, and he turned to scuttle
back inside, but Francis seized him by the collar. His companion, the
black man, who had been following him with the lynx, was so taken
by surprise that he released Khan's collar.

With a snarl the big cat leapt forward. Francis let go of the dwarf
and pressed hastily behind the stateroom door, dragging the startled
captain with him.

The dwarf gave a squeal and ran along the passage toward the
deck, the lynx in pursuit. Once outside, the dwarf could think only of
complete escape, and he dashed down the steps to the rowing boat,
fumbling with a rope in his haste to get away from Khan, who was
hesitating at the top of the steps, putting a tentative paw down to test
the way. Pushing the rowing boat away, the dwarf scrambled to take
up the oars, and he was still attempting to put them into the rowlocks
as the boat slid away into the all-enveloping mist. Khan remained on
the deck, padding impatiently up and down, his amber eyes eager, for
he wasn't used to being free.

Meanwhile, in the stateroom, the black man had lost his footing,
stumbling back as he released the lynx and falling heavily to the floor.
With the danger from the lynx past for the time being, Francis wasted
no time but leapt upon the fallen man, knocking him out with a sharp
upper cut to the jaw. Captain Merryvale wisely hurried back along the
passage, closing the outer door so that Khan could not make an
unwelcome reappearance.

In the bedroom, Nikolai Ivanovich had frozen at the first squeal
from the dwarf, and as he heard the ensuing sounds from the adjoining stateroom, he leapt away from Alison, who lay bruised and
silently weeping on the bed.

The door burst open suddenly and Francis came in, followed by
Captain Merryvale. Nikolai reached immediately for the pistol he
always carried, but the one in Francis's hand was already leveled at
him. The prince's face drained of color and his tongue passed
nervously over his lips as he began to back away from Francis, his
hands raised in swift and craven submission. Like so many bullies, he
was a coward who could never take on his victims face to face, unless
they were weaker than he.

Francis's glance flickered toward Alison and his eyes darkened with anger as he saw what had been done. He pressed the pistol into the captain's hand. 'Keep an eye on him,' he said briefly, nodding at Nikoali, then he went to Alison.

She lay with her head turned away, her face hidden by her tangled hair. Her body trembled with stifled sobs and she had curled up defensively, her arms across the torn bodice of her gray velvet gown to hide her breasts. Her skin was bruised and scratched from the violence of Nikolai's assault and her skirt had been wrenched up to reveal her thighs.

Francis felt close to tears himself to see her like this, and he reached out gently to smooth her hair away from her face. She flinched at his touch, giving a frightened whimper, and he rested his fingertips against her tearstained cheek. 'It's all right, Alison. It's me, Francis. You're safe now.' He took off his coat, placing it gently over her, and then he pulled her gown down to hide her legs. 'Alison, did he. . . ?' He couldn't say the words.

Fresh tears welled from her closed eyes and she shook her head. She felt so ashamed and defiled that she couldn't look at him, but kept her face averted.

A deep rage swept through Francis and he turned sharply about, striding across to seize Nikolai around the throat. 'You damned animal,' he breathed, his voice shaking with loathing.

'She wanted me. She invited me,' cried Nikolai.

Francis's fingers tightened their grip. 'One more word and I'll put an end to your foul life right here and now,' he said in a menacing whisper that struck abject terror through Nikolai.

'Don't hurt me. Please, don't hurt me.'

'Hurt you? I'd like to tear your bestial throat out with my bare hands for what you've done to her.'

Suddenly there were shouts from the deck and Nikolai's terrified eyes brightened with a glimmer of hope. His crew! There were too many of them for these two. But almost immediately his hope was extinguished, for men burst into the stateroom, and they weren't his crew, but wore the czar's scarlet livery.

Dread seized Nikolai Ivanovich then, and he broke free from Francis, whose attention was momentarily diverted. Dashing toward the door in a vain attempt to rush past the new arrivals, Nikolai very swiftly found himself seized and thrust against the wall.

'Unhand me immediately,' he cried, trying to force some authority into his terrified voice. 'Do you know who I am? I'll have your necks for this.'

The man in charge stepped forward. 'Nikolai Ivanovich Naryshky, you are under arrest and are to be taken immediately to the Peter-Paul Fortress.'

Nikolai's face was ashen. 'The Peter-Paul Fortress?' he whispered. 'There must be some mistake, for I have done nothing. With what am I to be charged?'

'High treason against His Imperial Majesty Czar Alexander, and against Russia. You have been an agent for France and will now pay the penalty.'

'No! I'm innocent,' cried Nikolai, his knees giving in beneath him.

The czar's men held him, and the officer in charge looked at him with contempt before nodding for him to be removed. Then he turned toward Francis and Captain Merryvale, not seeing Alison on the bed.

'Identify yourselves, gentlemen,' he commanded.

Francis bowed low. 'Francis, Lord Buckingham.'

Captain Merryvale bowed as well and gave his name.

The officer's eyes cleared. 'Lord Buckingham? Ah, how very fortunate that I should find you like this, for my orders are that as soon as Prince Naryshky has been arrested, I am to call upon you at English Quay to tell you that his imperial majesty is very grateful and appreciative of the great service you and Miss Clearwell have done him and Russia, and he wishes you both to call upon him at the Winter Palace at midday.'

Francis inclined his head. 'I am more than pleased to obey such a command, sir, but I doubt very much if Miss Clearwell will be able to do the same.' So saying, he went to the bed again, sitting on the edge of it and taking Alison's hand.

The officer stared toward her and then looked at Captain Merryvale. 'Naryshky did this?' he asked.

The captain nodded.

'Now he will pay more dearly than ever, for she is now greatly in favor with both Czar Alexander and Countess Irina. Please tell Lord Buckingham that I will place a boat at his disposal, and the moment he feels Miss Clearwell is sufficiently recovered to go ashore, you will all be conveyed back to English Quay.' The officer hesitated. 'Russia is very grateful to you all, Captain, and your efforts will not go unrewarded, you may be sure of that.'

Captain Merryvale withdrew from the cabin with the officer, and Francis was left alone with Alison. He drew her hand to his lips. 'Alison?'

Slowly she turned her head, meeting his eyes.

'It's over now,' he said gently. 'Naryshky is under arrest—'

'I took the documents, Francis,' she interrupted, trying to sit up. 'I took them when you were asleep and I went to her. I know I took a great risk.'

'You did well, Alison, for the countess must have given the wallet to the czar.'

'But if it had gone wrong . . .'

'It didn't, did it?' He smiled. 'I think your judgment was better than mine in this instance, Alison, for by doing what you did, you accomplished everything at a stroke.'

'How did you know I was here?'

'I was looking at the *Irina* through your uncle's telescope, and I saw you looking out of the window.' His gaze moved over her bruised, tearstained face. 'My poor darling, you've suffered so very much, haven't you?' he said softly.

The words of endearment brought her no comfort, for she could remember how he had whispered Pamela's name in his sleep. What he felt for her now was pity, no more and no less.

'Do you feel able to go back to the house?' he asked.

She nodded. 'Yes, I think so.'

'Let me help you up.' He rose to his feet and assisted her to put on his coat, to hide the savage tears in her gown, but as she stood, the room began to swim and everything faded into darkness. Her legs wouldn't support her and she would have fallen if he hadn't caught her. Without a second thought he lifted her into his arms and carried her from the room.

The deck was a scene of confusion. Khan had been eventually

caught, lured by a cold roast chicken from the galley, and the crew
was still confined in the hold, having been unable to break open the
door when they had heard the czar's men arrive. The black man still
hadn't come around from the blow Francis had given him; he lay on
the deck where he had been dragged. His hands and feet were bound,
and he would soon be carried down to one of the many boats that
now lay alongside the *Irina*. Of the dwarf there was no sign at all, for
he alone appeared to have escaped.

Assisted by Captain Merryvale, Francis carried Alison down to the
boat that had been put at their disposal, and within a few minutes
they were being rowed ashore through mist that was beginning to thin
fast as the morning sun rose higher in the sky.

As the boat reached the jetty, Francis immediately stepped out with
Alison, who hadn't come around. Followed by Captain Merryvale, he
went swiftly up the steps to the street and then across to the house,
where Mr Clearwell, Natalia, Mackay, and several other servants
were waiting anxiously beneath the portico.

Mackay was immediately dispatched to bring the doctor, and
Francis carried Alison to the couch in the entrance hall, laying her
gently down by the fire. Natalia was distraught, sending a footman to
bring Katya immediately and then ordering another to see that the
fire in Alison's bedroom was properly stoked.

Francis was hardly aware of what was happening around him; his
attention was fully upon Alison's ashen face. He pushed her hair away
from her forehead, his fingers lingering on the bruise left by the
carriage door. Then he took her limp hand, raising it softly to his lips
and kissing the palm.

An hour later, Alison came around, to find herself in her bed. Sunlight
was streaming in through the windows and Katya was hovering
anxiously by the bedside.

'Miss Clearwell? Oh, Miss Clearwell, you're awake again.' Without
waiting for her reply, the maid hurried from the room.

Alison stared up at the canopy of the bed. She had been dreaming,
and the dream still clung to her. She had been about to give her
marriage vows and Francis's ring was just going to be slipped on her
finger. She wore a gown of white satin and silver tissue, and there was

a wreath of roses in her hair. But then Francis tilted her face toward his, his eyes cool and distant. He told her he would never love her, that she would always be second best to his love for Pamela, but that he would try not to make her unhappy. His voice sounded hollow, and there wasn't any warmth or even affection in his eyes. She turned to run from him, the vows unsaid. Captain Merryvale had been waiting to take her away from St Petersburg. Then she had awakened.

Now she lay there thinking about the dream. It was telling her that everything was over now, and she could indeed go back to England with Captain Merryvale if she wished. There would be gossip – Mrs Fairfax-Gunn would see to that – but maybe it would be possible to explain the truth to Pamela. Pamela was the one Francis should marry, and if she, Alison, could put things right, maybe there would still be a marriage between the Duke of Marchington's daughter and Lord Buckingham.

The bedroom door opened suddenly and Natalia hurried in, followed by Alison's uncle. Natalia bent quickly to kiss Alison's pale cheek. 'Oh, my dear, my dear, I feel so very ashamed that I was so worried about my father that I couldn't see how worried you were too. To think that you and Lord Buckingham were on such secret business. But now it's all going to be all right; the prince has been arrested and his lordship is going to ask the czar to give the estate at Novgorod to my father.' Natalia blinked back tears and smiled a little ruefully. 'Forgive me again, but I cannot believe that all these weeks of worry are over at all, and it's all thanks to you.'

'To me, Aunt Natalia?'

'Yes, my dear, because you were so very clever in taking those papers to Countess Irina. Now the French plot is foiled, the prince's vile treachery is revealed, and everything is going to be all right.'

'Yes,' murmured Alison, 'everything's going to be all right.'

'The doctor examined you and said that although you struck your head very badly, you will soon be all well again. He has left some laudanum for you to take if you have a bad headache, but he doesn't think you will need it. As to your terrible experience at the prince's hands, he says the bruises and scratches will soon heal and you will not suffer any lasting distress.' Natalia squeezed her hand. 'Soon you will marry Lord Buckingham, my dear, and you will know the happiness you truly deserve after all this. I'm so sorry that I ever doubted that you loved him.'

Alison slowly drew her hand away, glancing at her uncle. 'Where is Francis now, Uncle Thomas?'

'At the embassy, but he'll be returning shortly to prepare to go to the Winter Palace. I know that you are invited as well, my dear, but perhaps you don't feel up to it. . . ?'

'Uncle Thomas, I don't intend to go to the Winter Palace with him, but I do intend to leave this house. I mean to return to England this afternoon with Captain Merryvale on the *Duchess of Clarence*.'

Her uncle stared at her, completely taken aback, and Natalia sat down on the bed with shock. It was Natalia who spoke first. 'Return to England today? Oh, my dear, we won't hear of it, for you simply aren't well enough.'

'Aunt Natalia, I mean to leave. My mind is made up.'

'But what of Lord Buckingham and your marriage?'

'There's isn't going to be a marriage, Aunt Natalia, for although I love him, he most certainly does not love me. He's marrying me because he feels obliged to, not because he wants me as his wife. He loves Lady Pamela Linsey, and I mean to do all I can to see that he still marries her.'

Startled, Natalia exchanged a glance with her husband and then looked at Alison again. 'You're wrong, you know, for Lord Buckingham does love you.'

Alison shook her head. 'I wish it were so, Aunt Natalia, but it isn't.'

Her uncle took her hand. 'Are you quite set on this, my dear?' he asked gently.

'Yes, Uncle, I am.'

'You do understand the grave consequences such actions will have upon your reputation, don't you?'

'Yes.'

'And you are prepared to face that?'

Tears filled her eyes. 'I have to face it, Uncle, because I love Francis too much to marry him. I know how dearly he wishes to make Pamela his wife, and that means that it would be very wrong indeed for me to accept his offer.'

Natalia rose concernedly. 'We cannot permit her to leave like this,

Thomas, for we would be gravely failing in our duty.'

Mr Clearwell put an understanding hand on his wife's arm, but shook his head. 'It will do no good to try to change her mind, my dear. I fear we have no sensible option but to let her go and to at least see that Katya accompanies her so that she doesn't travel alone. Please go and tell Katya, so that she has time to prepare.'

With a sigh Natalia gave in, but as she went to the door, she paused again. 'Alison, I suppose you only mean to take some hand luggage with you? There is no time to pack everything else.'

'Most of my things can follow later on, Aunt Natalia.'

'Very well.'

'Aunt Natalia?'

'My dear?'

'I'm truly sorry to cause you any further anxiety.'

Natalia smiled and then went out.

Alison's uncle bent to kiss her pale forehead. 'I cannot approve of what you intend to do, my dear, but I do understand your motives, which are very noble, if misguided. I cannot believe that once he was married to you, Lord Buckingham's love for Lady Pamela would persist for long, if indeed he still loves her at all, but if your conscience weighs so very heavily upon you . . .'

'It does, Uncle Thomas, for Pamela is my best friend.'

He nodded. 'Then the matter is closed. Katya will go with you and Captain Merryvale will be charged with your safe-keeping. When you reach England you are to stay with William, is that clear? By complete coincidence a letter arrived from him this morning, and in it he tells me that his mother's aunt is staying with him for the rest of the summer, which means that she can act as your chaperone until your father returns. His great-aunt usually resides in Scotland, but a fire at her home means that she has unexpectedly foisted herself upon her favorite great-nephew. I've only met the lady concerned several times, many years ago, and she seemed agreeable enough, although, according to William, she has become a veritable dragon in her old age.'

Alison smiled. 'I will do as you wish, Uncle Thomas.'

'My dear, I don't think Lord Buckingham will receive your news at all well, for he is determined to do the right thing by you, whether or not he still loves Lady Pamela.'

She met his eyes. 'I don't mean to tell him, Uncle. I mean to leave as soon as he has gone to the Winter Palace.'

'Oh, Alison, my dear—'

'It's the best way, Uncle Thomas. When he returns from the embassy in a little while, I would like you and Aunt Natalia to tell him that I'm all right but that I'm sleeping. Tell him that I'm really not up to accompanying him to the Winter Palace and that he must go alone. Then, when he's left, I will go to the *Duchess of Clarence*, which will have sailed by the time he returns. I know I'm asking you to be party to something of which you do not approve, but I wouldn't dream of making such a request unless I felt it was the best way.'

Her uncle sighed and nodded. 'You really have given this some thought, haven't you?'

'Yes.'

'If you became Lady Buckingham, you'd be very happy, I know you would, and so would his lordship.'

'No, Uncle.'

'What if your aunt is right and he does love you?'

'It isn't my name he whispers in his dreams,' Alison said quietly, turning her head away.

Her uncle said nothing more, but withdrew sadly from the room.

Alison closed her eyes, which stung with all the tears she had wept. She didn't weep now, though, for she had gone past crying. The complicated sequence of events that had commenced in Stockholm had come to an almost perfect ending; for the ending to have been absolutely perfect would require Francis and her to live happily ever after, but that could never be, not when his heart was given to Pamela.

Now she, Alison, had to at least try to make the ending perfect for one of them, and that meant telling Pamela the complete truth. Once the tale of all that had happened in Stockholm and here in St Petersburg reached London, it might never be possible to explain, and so she had to reach Pamela first. There was nothing more she could do.

20

As Alison lay there contemplating what her conscience dictated she must do, Francis was leaving the British embassy. Behind him there was jubilation at the satisfactory outcome of events, especially as not only had the czar been successfully warned of the danger around him, but also the identity of the French agent in the embassy had at last been discovered. The aide concerned, a gentleman who had been somewhat reticent about his mother's French origins, had immediately been bound hand and foot and conveyed across St Petersburg to the French embassy, on the steps of which he had been left like a rather ignominious parcel. Mr Gainsborough, a wickedly talented cartoonist when the spirit moved him, had drawn an extremely witty and derogatory lampoon of Bonaparte being kicked by John Bull, and this had been pinned to the unfortunate agent's coat. The fury with which both agent and cartoon would be received by the French ambassador could well be imagined and was the source of much sly British glee.

As Francis entered the Clearwell residence, however, his thoughts were not of the success of his mission or the imminent audience with the grateful czar, but of Alison, who had still been under examination by the doctor when he had felt obliged to report to the embassy.

He handed his hat and gloves to Mackay. 'How is she?' he asked without ceremony.

'Miss Clearwell is sleeping, my lord. The doctor assures us that she will soon be fully recovered and that she hasn't come to any lasting harm.'

'He is confident of that?'

'Most certainly, my lord.'

'Thank you, Mackay.'

'My lord.' The butler bowed and withdrew as Francis hurried up to the staircase to the grand salon, where he found Mr Clearwell studying the river through the telescope.

The older man straightened and turned as he entered. 'Ah, you've returned to us, my lord.'

'Mackay tells me that Alison will soon be well again.'

'Assuredly so, my boy, for apart from the shock and stress of her ordeal, she has suffered no major injury. The bruises will soon be gone, and once she has rested . . .' Mr Clear-well's voice died away, for rest was the one thing Alison intended to deny herself; what rest could there be on an imminent voyage back to England?

Francis went to stand beside him, gazing out at the sunlit Neva. 'I only hope that she will be able to forget what she suffered at Naryshky's foul hands.'

'So do I, my boy, so do I,' agreed Mr Clearwell with feeling. 'If you hadn't reached her when you did, I can hardly bear to think what would have happened to her.'

Francis' blue eyes were cold and hard. 'I would have torn his monstrous heart out for what he did, but he was saved by the very czar he had been endeavoring to bring down.'

'Saved? My dear sir, Naryshky's life is forfeit anyway, and perhaps it is better that the czar takes it than you.'

'There would have been a certain grim satisfaction in having extinguished him personally, Mr Clearwell, for if you had seen her lying there in that cabin . . .' Francis swallowed, lowering his eyes for a moment. 'I would give away my fortune for five minutes alone with him, and I wish to God I had squeezed the trigger when I had my pistol trained upon him.'

Mr Clearwell put a quick hand on his arm. 'Your concern and anger do you credit, my lord.'

'Concern and anger?' Francis gave a dry laugh. 'Mr Clearwell, you seem surprised that I should express such emotions, and yet you know that I am about to marry her. Should a bridegroom not feel rage against the man who tried to violate his bride?'

Mr Clearwell was silent for a moment. He didn't know what to say, for he knew that the marriage was no longer going to take place. Turning, he bent to look out of the telescope again. 'I, er, see they've removed the *Irina*,' he murmured a little lamely.

Francis couldn't help but be conscious of the rather clumsy change of subject. 'Is something wrong, sir? Is there something I should know?'

'Everything is quite in order, my boy. Er, when will you be leaving for the Winter Palace?'

'I'm just about to change into my court togs.'

'You do realize that Alison will not be able to accompany you?'

Francis smiled a little. 'I didn't expect that she would, sir.'

'Er, no, of course not . . .' Mr Clearwell gave a slightly awkward laugh as he continued to apparently find the view through the telescope of the utmost fascination.

Francis looked curiously at him. 'Mr Clearwell, are you quite sure that everything's all right?'

'Mm? Oh, yes, quite all right,' murmured the older man. 'Shouldn't you be putting on your finery?'

'Yes, of course.' Francis bowed a little and then left him. At the door of the grand salon he paused, looking back at the figure by the telescope. Something was wrong. But what? With a long breath he went on out, closing the door quietly behind him.

Mr Clearwell straightened once more. His face was sad. If only he felt sure that he was right to support Alison now. Maybe Lord Buckingham did love Lady Pamela Linsey, but like Alison herself, he too had a conscience to salve, and that conscience bade him marry Alison in order to shield her from cruel gossip. Damn it, the fellow wanted the marriage – indeed, he seemed determined on it – and yet Alison's honor was going to deny him his wish.

Mr Clearwell lowered his eyes regretfully, for many marriages survived and succeeded on far less than existed between these two.

When he had changed into his court attire, Francis studied himself in the mirror in his dressing room. He disliked the popinjay garb that was *de rigueur* for all formal royal occasions. Why was it necessary to parade in fashions that were twenty years or more out of date? He loathed the leaf-green brocade coat with its abundance of silver embroidery, for not only did it offend his taste for all that was discreetly stylish, but it also reminded him of an evening reticule once owned by his least favorite aunt. However, protocol demanded antiquated, glittering garb, and so here he was, done out in all that was required and about to set off for the meeting that until a few hours ago he had despaired of ever achieving. If it hadn't been for Alison . . . Alison. Turning, he snatched up his plumed hat and left the room, but instead of walking toward the staircase, he went the other way, toward Alison's room.

He knocked softly on the door. 'Alison?'

There was no reply.

Quietly he opened the door and went inside. She lay asleep in the capacious bed, and there was no sign of Katya. He halted by the bedside, gazing down at her. Her silver-blond hair spilled over the pillows like the most costly of silk, and she didn't stir as he put his fingertips softly to her cheek. How pale she was, like a beautiful slender ghost. So different from Pamela, whose cheeks were always flushed with becoming color and whose dark loveliness was all that was fascinating and vivacious.

'As unlike Pamela as it is possible to be,' he murmured, bending suddenly to kiss her on the forehead. Then he left, closing the door behind him.

As his footsteps died away, Alison opened her eyes. His words echoed painfully through her. She could never compare with the woman he loved, and if there had been any lingering doubt about what she must do, that doubt was now completely extinguished. She had to go back to England, to make Pamela understand the truth and to make her realize that she was the one who must become Lord Buckingham's bride, not Alison Clearwell.

Several minutes later she heard the carriage arrive for him, and then the whip cracked and the carriage drove away again, conveying Francis to the Winter Palace and out of Alison's life. The moment he had gone, she got out of bed and called for Katya, who came immediately.

The maid was excited at the prospect of going to England, so much so that in spite of her mistress's sad mood, she couldn't help chattering. Strangely, the maid's bubbling excitement was a comfort, for it was a distraction. Alison had already decided upon which things she intended to take with her, and the necessary valises were soon packed. Katya's few belongings took up another valise, and it wasn't long before they were both ready to go to Vassily Island and the *Duchess of Clarence*.

A boatman had been engaged and was waiting at the jetty as Alison bade a tearful farewell to her uncle and step-aunt. Natalia was in tears as well and begged her at the eleventh hour to change her mind and stay. Natalia was quite convinced that Francis loved her, and she kept saying so, but Alison knew the truth, and knew that she was doing the right thing.

As she and Katya left, accompanied by two footmen with their luggage, a carriage drew up at the curb outside the house and a familiar figure in vermilion stepped down. Alison didn't halt or look back, but hastened on across the street toward the steps leading down to the jetty.

Mrs Fairfax-Gunn stared after her, her brown eyes alight with the scent of still more scandal as she noticed the luggage the footmen were carrying. Without further ado she hurried to the house, where Mr Clearwell and Natalia were still watching Alison.

'My dear sir,' said the gossip eagerly, 'is it possible that Miss Clearwell is suddenly leaving us?'

Natalia turned on her. 'Oh, go away, you horrid trouble-maker, and take your clacking, spiteful tongue with you.'

Mrs Fairfax-Gunn took an involuntary step backward, almost toppling back down the steps; indeed, she would have done had not Mr Clearwell managed to seize her arm in time to save her. She was all of a fluster, for Natalia's attack had taken her quite by surprise. 'Oh, dear! Oh, dear,' she squeaked breathlessly, overcome with righteous indignation that anyone should presume to speak so cruelly to her.

Natalia gave her a glance of utter contempt and then turned and stalked into the house.

Mrs Fairfax-Gunn gaped after her, for Natalia had always seemed so meek and kindly. But then the gossip's insect antennae began to quiver, for there was obviously yet another delicious scandal in the offing. Feigning an imminent attack of the vapors, she leaned heavily on Mr Clearwell's arm. 'Oh, I feel quite faint and fear I must sit down.' Her brown eyes moved toward the invitingly open door of the house.

Mr Clearwell was having none of it. 'Then allow me to conduct you to your carriage, madam,' he murmured, propelling her determinedly down the steps.

'Oh, but—'

'Your carriage is most comfortable, Mrs Fairfax-Gunn.'

'But—'

'I'm sure you'll understand if I leave you, madam, but my wife is very distressed at the moment.'

Mrs Fairfax-Gunn drew herself up furiously. 'Sir, I am much distressed at the moment as well,' she breathed, her bosom heaving like a vermilion sea.

'Madam, I would not be concerned about you if you suddenly exploded,' he replied, ushering her into the carriage and then closing the door firmly behind her. He nodded at the astonished coachman. 'Drive on, off the end of the quay, if you wish. Just go away from here.'

As the carriage drove smartly away, Mrs Fairfax-Gunn's face was flushed with fury. They wouldn't get away with this! She would see to it that every shocking detail of their niece's conduct with Lord Buckingham was broadcast over England with a bell. Alison Clearwell and her wretched family would rue the day they decided to snub Arabella Fairfax-Gunn. Oh, wouldn't they just!

As Francis was ushered into the presence of Alexander, fourteenth Romanov Czar of All the Russias, the *Duchess of Clarence* left her mooring at Vassily Island, moving downstream out of St Petersburg toward the Gulf of Finland. When his lengthy audience was over, he departed from the Winter Palace with the czar's praises and gratitude ringing in his ears, with Leon Razumov assured of the estate at Novgorod, and with the promise that the thoroughbred colt from the imperial stables would shortly be shipped to England. By this time, the *Duchess of Clarence*, a strong easterly breeze speeding her along, was already within sight of Kronstadt.

But Francis wasn't yet able to return to English Quay, for he was summoned to another meeting, this time with Countess Irina, who wished not only to give him a pearl necklace for Alison, but also to advise him that in her opinion he would be very foolish indeed to allow Alison to slip through his fingers.

Francis stared at her. 'Slip through my fingers? I'm afraid I don't understand.'

'My lord, she doesn't intend to marry you, even though she loves you very much.'

He was very still. 'There must be some misunderstanding.'

'Oh, yes, my lord, there most certainly is, and you are the one who is doing it. She loves you, but she fears that you still love another, and she will therefore not wear your ring. Because of her, the czar I love is now safe and will continue to come to my arms; I would like to think that because of me, you will go to her arms. Forget that other woman, my lord, and make certain that Miss Clearwell becomes your countess, for you will never find another like her.'

He looked into her lovely green eyes. 'Are you quite sure she means not to marry me?'

'Quite sure, my lord, for she told me herself.'

'If you will forgive me, Countess, I believe I should return to English Quay without delay.'

'I wish you well, my lord,' replied Irina, extending her hand and smiling at him.

But the *Duchess of Clarence* had long gone when at last Francis arrived back at the Clearwell residence, and as he entered the house and saw Mr Clearwell coming down the staircase to meet him, he knew that he was already too late, for there was an atmosphere that told him Alison was no longer there.

He faced her uncle. 'Where is she?'

Mr Clearwell saw that somehow he knew. 'She sailed on the *Duchess of Clarence* just after you left for the palace.'

Francis' blue eyes were bitter and reproachful. 'Why in God's name didn't you say anything to me? Didn't I at least deserve that much?'

'My boy, it isn't what I wanted, but Alison begged me to give my word. She feels she must return to England to try to put things right for you with Lady Pamela, and once she had decided that that is what she must do, there was no changing her mind. She loves you, but it isn't a selfish love; it's the sort of love that will always place your happiness first.'

'My happiness?' cried Francis, turning away and running his fingers through his hair. 'I must go after her.'

'And what of Lady Pamela?'

Francis' eyes swung back toward him. 'Sir, if I am not mistaken, that lady is to be your daughter-in-law, for I did not lie when I said that she still had a *tendre* for your son William. Alison chose not to believe me. She thought I'd have said anything at that time in order to bring my mission here to a successful conclusion. It's true that I love Pamela, but there are degrees of love, are there not? Pamela isn't the one I wish to marry. I want Alison as my bride.'

'Then you must persuade her, my boy.'

'I intend to. I'll follow her on the first available ship.'

21

It was humid and thundery on the evening the *Duchess of Clarence* arrived in the Pool of London, just upstream of the Tower. Yellow-gray clouds hung low over the city, and the air was stifling. The Thames was as still as a mill pool, with reflections barely moving on its mirrorlike surface, and every sound seemed to travel a long way. England's capital sweltered in an unaccustomed haze of oppressive early-summer heat, and after the crispness of St Petersburg it was almost claustrophobic.

Alison said farewell to Captain Merryvale, and then she and Katya were rowed toward the northern shore of the Thames and the steps between the Customs House and Billingsgate fish market. Escorted by one of the ship's crew, they were taken to the Moor's Head Inn in nearby Lower Thames Street. The inn was one of the finest posting houses in the city and was Alison's deliberate choice, for she had no intention as yet of adjourning to William's residence in Berkeley Street, Mayfair, but meant to go direct to Marchington House, which was by the Thames at Hammersmith, farther inland.

Within half an hour of leaving the *Duchess of Clarence*, she and Katya were seated in a post chaise that conveyed them at speed across the capital. It was the custom of such vehicles to drive like the wind – indeed, the yellow-jacketed postboys were known as 'yellow bounders,' and were far from popular with other road users – but they were nevertheless the best form of transport if one did not possess a carriage of one's own.

Katya gazed out excitedly, for London was so very different from St Petersburg, and there was so much to look at. The maid sat on the edge of the carriage seat, her eyes shining. She wore a straw bonnet and a blue linen chemise gown, with a plain white shawl resting lightly around her shoulders; she had left Russia wearing a cloak to keep out the chill of the northern wind.

Alison wore a primrose three-quarter-length pelisse over a white muslin gown, and a little brimless primrose silk hat adorned with a flouncy ostrich plume that curled down to her right shoulder. Her hair was swept up beneath the hat, except for a frame of soft curls around her face, and her only jewelry was a dainty pearl brooch. Her gloved hands clasped and unclasped nervously in her lap, not only because she would soon be face to face with Pamela, but also because she knew that a violent thunderstorm was in the offing. The last thing she wished was to be out on the open road when the storm broke, but she was still determined to tell Pamela the whole truth without delay and to make her accept that she was the one Francis loved.

The church clocks were striking half-past-eight as the chaise dashed along Piccadilly. Every evening at this time there was a crowd gathered outside the Gloucester Coffee House to watch the spectacle of the West Country mail coaches, which set off in colorful convoy as the final chime was struck. Horns blowing and hooves clattering, the six gleaming maroon-and-black coaches drove off immediately in front of the chaise, which was forced to check its speed and follow them. The postboy cursed as he reined in the lead horse he was riding, but there was nothing he could do but bring up the rear of the dashing cavalcade.

Katya stared out in amazement at the coaches, for each one carried outside passengers and never before had she seen people traveling in this precarious and seemingly dangerous fashion. Surely they would be thrown off when the coach turned a corner. Or they would be catapulted into the air if there was a bump in the road.

The convoy of coaches sped past Hyde Park Corner and on toward the Knightsbridge turnpike gate, but still the outside passengers were secure in their places. As they swept through the open gate, for his majesty's mail passed freely along the highways, it was plain that traveling outside wasn't quite as hazardous as the maid had thought, and she gazed admiringly after them as the chaise was forced to halt to pay the toll.

Alison glanced up at the lowering skies, where the clouds seemed to be pressing down over the city. The air was heavy and so humid that she felt she couldn't draw breath. It was unpleasantly close, and she knew it wouldn't freshen until the storm had broken and run its course. She was afraid, staring ahead along the busy highway as the postboy urged his team on once more.

A low growl of thunder rolled across the heavens and a warm breath of wind blew across the dusty road, whipping up small clouds as the chaise dashed on its way. The trees whispered, shaking their leaves, and the air was strangely clear, as if everything was much nearer than it really was. Alison's heart had begun to beat more swiftly the moment she heard that ominous roll of thunder, and she had to clasp her hands tightly in her lap to try to maintain her composure. She mustn't give into her terror of thunder, not now . . .

The chaise drove through open countryside toward Hammersmith. The hedgerows were heavy with hawthorn blossom and honeysuckle, and lacy white cow parsley nodded at the wayside. As the wind increased, petals were dislodged, fluttering through the air like warm snow. A vivid flash of lightning lit the heavens as the village of Hammersmith appeared ahead, and the first heavy drops of rain struck the coach windows. The postboy turned up his collar and urged his team to greater effort, but he knew that he wouldn't reach his destination without getting a terrible soaking.

An earspliting crash of thunder reverberated directly overhead as the chaise drove wildly through the village, passing the famous sixteenth-century Red Cow Inn, which was the first stage out of London on the much-used road to the west. The storm intensified with each minute now, and rain sluiced down the windows as more flashes of lightning were followed by thunder that seemed to roll endlessly across the sky. Puddles formed and the chaise splashed through them, sending muddy spray over the trembling cow parsley. They had left the main highway now and were driving along the country lane that led to Marchington House and its beautiful park on the bank of the Thames.

The gates of the estate were open, the lodgekeeper having left them when he had dashed inside as the storm began, and another roll of thunder disguised the rattle of the carriage as it drove through into the park. The drive curved between rhododendrons that were in full bloom, the heavy crimson, purple, white, and pink flowers standing out against the shining dark-green leaves. Gusts of wind blustered through the trees, sometimes blowing so strongly that branches bent to and fro as if trying to break free from the trunks. Leaves spun through the wild air, and lightning stabbed brilliantly through the gloom, each bright flash followed almost immediately by another thunderclap.

Alison's heart was pounding in her breast now, and despite her determination to remain calm, the past had begun to move around her. She could hear those other hooves, driving along that Wiltshire lane, and she could see her mother's face smiling at her in the window glass. Tears were wet on her cheeks and she turned her face away so that Katya wouldn't see. The maid was unaffected by the storm; indeed, she appeared to find it as exciting as she had everything else since setting out on this first great journey of her life. Nothing had alarmed her and nothing had tired her; she was carried along by the sheer exhilaration of seeing and experiencing things she had never dreamed she would ever know. She didn't glance at Alison and so didn't know that her mistress was now close to breaking point, driven there by a storm that was the final straw after everything else that had borne down upon her in recent weeks.

The postboy urged his team on along the gravel drive as it wound between the trees of the park. The house was nowhere in sight yet, for the rhododendron drive was deliberately long so that its magnificence could be enjoyed to the full. By now the rain was so heavy that it washed rapidly down the carriage windows, distorting the view into a blur of bending, twisting shapes. Alison didn't see the park, but instead saw the Wiltshire countryside during a long-gone storm, and she heard her mother's gentle voice trying to soothe her. But she couldn't be soothed; she was too frightened. She stared at the rain on the glass, her breath catching as yet another jagged line of forked lightning split the sky outside. This time it didn't drain harmlessly into the ground, but struck an oak tree that hung directly over the drive a little way ahead. The tree shattered as if riven by a gigantic axe, and with a splintering groan it crashed across the way, barely giving the postboy time to rein his terrified horses in.

A wild uncontrollable hysteria surged through Alison. As the chaise drew to a sharp standstill, the horses tossing their heads within a few feet of the still-trembling branches that blocked their path, she flung the door open and alighted. She felt the wind tugging at her hem and the lash of the rain against her face. The smell of wet earth mingled with the sweet fragrant balsam trees, and torn leaves whirled away on the storm as another thunderclap split the sky overhead. The earth seemed to shudder and the rain fell even more heavily as the clouds burst.

Katya had been flung to the floor of the carriage by the force of the halt, and the postboy was preoccupied with trying to calm his terrified horses, so that neither of them saw Alison push her way around the fallen tree and then gather her skirts to run on along the drive, ignoring the storm. Her white muslin gown was soon drenched and mud-stained, and her pelisse was torn by the jagged branch she had caught it on while pushing past the tree. The ostrich plume in her little hat was soon a very sorry sight, hanging low and dejected over her wet shoulder as she ran tearfully along the drive, determined to somehow reach the house. Her panic was overhwelming and all she could think of was getting to Pamela and telling her the truth.

Sobs rose in her throat as she ran blindly through the storm, her little shoes offering no protection to the soles of her feet as she hurried over small stones amid the gravel. The wind soughed impatiently through the trees, and the clouds raced menacingly overhead. Lightning flashed again and was followed by thunder, but all she could hear was the pounding of her own heart and the accusing whisper of her own conscience. She had had no right to fall in love with Francis, no right to think even for a moment that she could marry him; he belonged to Pamela and must still make her his bride . . . Lady Pamela Linsey was meant to be Lord Buckingham's bride, not Alison Clearwell. Not Alison Clearwell. Not Alison Clearwell. The three uncompromising words were repeated over and over again in her head, and fresh tears stung her eyes as she ran on through the wildness of the storm. Her heart was in turmoil, tightening accusingly within her breast, and she was soaked to the skin as at last the drive led out of the trees and across the open park toward the house, which stood splendidly on a small hill above a bend in the Thames.

Marchington House had been built in 1762 by Robert Adam, and was a perfect example of his design. It faced grandly across its deer park, standing out sharply as another flash of lightning stabbed the surrounding countryside with electric blue. Alison stumbled on through the wind and rain, the sight of the house spurring her on. She had to reach Pamela, she had to tell her how and why everything had happened. Pamela had to believe her, and had to turn a deaf ear to Mrs Fairfax-Gunn . . .

Lights had been lit in the house because of the gloom of the storm, and as she drew nearer, she could see the elegant ballroom, which was built to one side of the main house. She could see the dazzling chandeliers and the beautiful mirrors lining the green-and-gold walls, and she could see a man and a woman, elegantly clad, dancing alone together. Their faces were flushed and smiling as they looked into each other's eyes, she so dark and lovely, he so tall, manly, and protective, with sandy hair and brown eyes.

Alison's steps faltered, and she stood in the rain staring at them as they danced. Her clothes clung wetly to her body, and a wild confusion of emotion was still swirling enervatingly through her as she watched Lady Pamela Linsey gazing adoringly up into William Clearwell's dark eyes. Pamela wore a pink silk gown that plunged low over her curvaceous bosom, and there were diamonds at her throat and in her ears; she looked breathtakingly beautiful. They paused in their seductive dancing and he drew her closer, his arm slipping around her slender waist. Then he bent his head, kissing her on the lips, and she did not hesitate before linking her arms around his neck and returning the kiss.

The rain washed coldly over Alison as she stared at them. It was all a dream, she wasn't really here at all . . . She looked toward the house, taking a hesitant step, but then her legs wouldn't support her. Everything was spinning – the storm, the ballroom, the earth – and day turned to night as she sank to the wet grass. She was only vaguely aware of shouts from the doorway as some footmen emerged to see if there really was someone there, as a frightened maid had claimed she had seen from an upstairs window. She heard their steps and then felt them gathering her up from where she lay. She didn't see the two in the ballroom draw guiltily apart as the servants' voices carried from the house. Another flash of lightning illuminated the gathering gloom of the stormy evening, but Alison was barely aware of it.

Then she heard the echo of a vast entrance hall and Pamela's anxious voice asking the butler what had happened.

'It's a lady, my lady, the maid saw her outside in the storm.'

Pamela hurried closer, looking anxiously at Alison's pale face. Her breath caught in surprise. 'Alison?'

Alison's eyes filled with tears of wretchedness. 'Forgive me, Pamela,' she whispered brokenly, 'forgive me for everything. It's you that he loves, not me, you must believe that.'

'What do you mean, Alison? I don't understand.' Pamela took her cold, wet hand. 'What on earth are you doing here like this? I thought you were in St Petersburg. Where is your carriage?'

Alison tried to concentrate upon her, but it was so very difficult. 'You must believe me, Pamela. Francis doesn't love m-me, he l-loves only you. He was just being honorable toward me by saying he would marry me. You m-must still marry him; you mustn't l-listen to Mrs Fairfax-Gunn.'

Pamela stared at her, the diamonds she wore flashing with a brilliance that was almost as dazzling as the lightning outside. She spoke again, but Alison didn't hear. The light was fading. It was as if she was slipping into a dark tunnel, leaving Pamela farther and farther away. Her heartbeats echoed through her whole body, and she felt suddenly as if she were on fire. Her clothes were wet and cold, but her skin was aflame, and she knew nothing more except the lingering, relentless pang of guilt that reached past her heart and into her very soul.

Pamela turned quickly to the butler. 'Send someone for Doctor Arrowsmith and tell my maid that she is to attend Miss Clearwell in the Italian room without delay.'

'My lady.' He hurried away.

She nodded at the footmen who had brought Alison in. 'Take her to the Italian room. I'll be there directly.'

As they did as she ordered, she stood alone in the center of the entrance hall's red-and-white-tiled floor. The hall was in the Roman style, with black marble columns and white marble statues on plinths. The statues were of emperors, gods, and goddesses, and the floor was laid out in the classical key pattern.

William emerged from the ballroom entrance and paused by a statue of Juno. 'Did you say Miss Clearwell? Is it Alison?'

Pamela turned to face him. 'Yes.'

'But she's supposed to be in St Petersburg.'

'She's very much here and is apparently without a carriage. She's been soaked through and is quite delirious. William . . .'

'Yes?'

She went to him, slipping her arms around his waist and resting her head against the rich blue brocade of his waistcoat. 'The things she was saying, about Francis and about Mrs Fairfax-Gunn of *all* people . . .' She looked up into his eyes. 'She said something about Francis still loving me. What's it all about, William? Why is she here like this, and so distressed? Do you think that Francis and she. . . ?'

He kissed her on the lips. 'I hope so, my darling, oh, how I hope so, for there is nothing that would suit us more than for Francis to fall in love with my little cousin. Just think of the wonderful *fait accompli* we could present to your parents on their return from Paris.' He smiled. 'If it is so, Pamela, we've suffered tortures of conscience for nothing.'

'I can't believe that things could work out quite as neatly as that,' she replied, glancing toward the staircase.

'I love you, my darling, and I don't mean to ever lose you again, no matter what your parents might think. You and I were meant for each other, and if I've behaved basely in deliberately seeking you out the moment they and Francis are out of the country, then I make no apology.'

'If you've behaved basely, then so have I. My parents left me in the safekeeping of my old nurse, who would have seen to it that you weren't admitted tonight when you called. But she is unwell and confined to her bed and I have admitted you, a fact that is known to all the servants and that will compromise me beyond redemption. Tonight I have committed myself to you, my dearest William, and nothing is going to change that.' She paused, lowering her lovely eyes for a moment. 'Besides, I don't think it will come as a great surprise to Francis, who I'm sure suspects anyway.'

'Suspects?'

She nodded. 'When he was about to leave England, he and I had a terrible disagreement. Oh, it was about something and nothing, but it brought certain problems to the forefront. He said that he trusted I would have made up my mind completely when he returned, and I pretended not to know what he was talking about. But I did know, for he was referring to my feelings toward you, feelings he knew had not been eradicated. I let him depart on that note, which I would not have done if my heart was involved. I didn't even inquire about his plans. I've learned them subsequently from you. I must go to Alison now.'

'Pamela, what exactly did she say about Francis?'

'That he didn't love her and was only being honorable when he said he would marry her. And something about Mrs Fairfax-Gunn, who I know is in St Petersburg now. I don't know what's been going on, but something has, and that something involves Francis having asked Alison to many him. She says he was doing it out of a sense of duty, and she's distraught that I must accept that he still loves me.' Pamela drew a long breath. 'No doubt she'll tell me in due course.' Gathering her soft pink silk skirts, she hastened away toward the staircase.

Outside, the storm raged on, with lightning blazing blue white across the rainswept countryside and thunder echoing over the dark sky.

The sun was shining as Alison opened her eyes. She was in a room with walls painted with Italian scenes and there was a beautiful Italian crystal chandelier suspended from the golden coffered ceiling. Katya was standing by the window.

Someone spoke. 'Alison? Are you awake?'

It was Pamela. She was seated by the bed, a cup of tea in her lap. There was a dainty lace day bonnet on her dark head and she wore a frilled blue-and-white-striped lawn gown. She put the cup of tea on the tray on the table and then leaned forward to put her hand over Alison's. 'How are you feeling?'

'I don't really know. I can't remember . . .' The storm. Her breath caught. 'There was a terrible storm, a tree was struck by lightning.'

Pamela squeezed her hand reassuringly. 'Poor Alison, how unkind fate is to repeat itself like this. But you're all right, truly you are, and the storm has been gone a week now.'

Alison's eyes widened incredously. 'A week?'

'You were delirious and suffering with a fever, but then last night you slept easily and the doctor said you would be better this morning. And so you are, for you know me now.'

Alison swallowed. 'I don't deserve your kindness, Pamela.'

'And you don't deserve to suffer with guilt, for you haven't done anything that I haven't done myself. You said many things when you were feverish, so that I know all that happened in St Petersburg. You love Francis, don't you?'

Alison couldn't reply.

Pamela smiled. 'Would it help if I told you that I love William, and that I mean to marry him?'

Alison stared at her.

22

L ondon was just stirring into life for another day as the chaise drew up at the curb in Berkeley Street. Mayfair was quiet, except for the milkmaids with their heavy yokes, and the night mist that had cloaked everything with silver was already beginning to thread and disperse.

Francis alighted wearily from the chaise, pausing on the pavement to toy with the frill protruding from his cuff. He wore a charcoal coat, wine-red silk waistcoat, and cream corduroy breeches. His Hessian boots boasted handsome golden tassels, and his top hat was tipped wearily back on his hair. He was tired, and he knew that dawn was not the time to call upon William, but he was not in the mood to wait upon a more civilized hour.

He nodded at the postboy. 'Wait for me,' he said, then he went quickly to the door of the elegant red brick house that faced toward Lansdowne Passage opposite.

A maid had been attending to the fire in the kitchen, and at the peremptory knock at the front door she hastened to answer it. She recognized Francis, who had visited the house before. 'Why, my lord, it's you,' she said rather unnecessarily, for she was taken by surprise by such an early call.

'Is Mr Clearwell in?' he asked, entering the cool gray-and-white hall without invitation.

'Yes, my lord, but he's in his bed.'

'Is Miss Clearwell here?'

'Miss Clearwell?' The maid looked blankly at him. 'No, my lord, there's no Miss Clearwell here. Mr Clearwell's aunt, Lady Lowthes, has been staying . . .

'Has she been here at all?'

'Miss Clearwell? No, my lord.'

He removed his hat and tossed it on a table, then he teased off his gloves. 'Have Mr Clearwell awakened straightaway, for I must speak to him.'

The butler had appeared, his coat donned swiftly over his night-shirt, for he hadn't intended to rise for another half an hour. 'What is it, Kitty?' he asked, coming down the staircase, but then he halted in surprise on seeing Francis. 'My lord?'

'I wish to see Mr Clearwell.'

'But—'

'Now,' snapped Francis.

'Yes, my lord.' Turning, the butler hastened away again, returning a moment or so later to say that Mr Clearwell would be but a minute.

Then William appeared, still tying the belt of his green silk dress-ing gown. He paused at the top of the staircase, his eyes wary. 'Francis?'

'William.' Francis waited until the butler and the maid had with-drawn, then he looked at William again. 'Where is she? Marchington House?'

'Yes.' William knew from the butler that Francis sought Alison.

'I take it that you and Pamela know all that went on?'

'Yes.' William came down the staircase toward him.

Francis smiled a little. 'Just as I know all that has been going on between you and Pamela. It was plain to me before I left the country.'

'I love her and she loves me.'

'Do you mean to marry?'

'Yes.'

'Without parental consent, I take it?'

William nodded. 'If necessary. Francis, I—'

'Don't apologize, my friend. If I were an innocent party, and if I still loved Pamela, then I might feel it necessary to call you out, but since neither criterion applies in my case, then I cannot with any honesty complain about the situation.'

'You bear us no grudge?'

'How can I when I am far from guiltless myself? I wish you well, William, for I know that you and Pamela were meant to be together. Just as Alison and I . . .' He broke off. 'What has she said about me, William?'

'That you feel honor-bound to marry her.'

'She still thinks that?'

'Isn't it true?'

Francis met his eyes. 'No.'

'Then you must tell her, Francis.'

'That's why I've followed her. How is she, William?'

'On the road to recovery at last.'

Francis' eyes sharpened. 'Recovery? She's been ill?'

'She drove to Marchington House by chaise on arriving in England, and there was a terrible thunderstorm. Lightning struck a tree, which fell across the road in front of the chaise, and Alison walked the final mile or so to the house in the rain. She was soaked through and took a fever. She was ill for a week, and only began to recover yesterday.'

But Francis had already snatched up his hat and gloves and was running to the door.

William hurried after him and was in time to see him get swifly into the waiting chaise, which immediately drove away into the thinning mist. William stared after it, and then a slight smile curved his lips. All was indeed going to end well . . .

Pamela was informed that Francis had arrived, and she received him in the magnificent crimson drawing room, where priceless paintings adorned the silk walls. She wore a simple white muslin gown embroidered with coffee-colored spots, and a shawl trailed on the floor behind her as she came to greet him. She hesitated a moment and then extended her hands.

'Hello, Francis.'

'Pamela.' He took the hands, smiling at her. 'It's good to see you again.'

'Is it?'

'You know it is. You and I would have made a very bad match of it, whereas you and William will do very well, I fancy.'

'You knew about William before you left, didn't you?'

'Yes.'

She smiled. 'And now it is you and Alison?'

'I trust so.'

'She loves you, Francis, but she thinks that you feel only a sense of duty toward her.'

He drew a long breath. 'It was never a mere matter of duty. Pamela, does she know about you and William?'

'Yes, I've told her everything.'

'So she knows that if she and I were to marry, she would not be hurting you?'

'Yes, Francis, she knows.'

'Where is she?'

'The rose garden. Go to her, Francis, and tell her that you love her. That's all she needs to hear.' Pamela hugged him suddenly. 'I'll always love you, Francis, but as my dearest friend.'

He dropped a kiss on her dark hair. 'The affection is mutual,' he said softly, then he left her, hurrying through to the rear of the house and the terrace overlooking the sunken rose garden, where Alison sat on a shady seat beneath an arbor of sweet-scented pink roses.

He paused, watching her for a moment. Her ash-blonde hair was loose about the shoulders of her cream lawn short-sleeved gown, and there was a blue silk shawl over her bare arms. Her face was very pale and she looked so fragile that he longed to put his arms around her and protect her. She was leafing through the book on her lap, but she wasn't reading it. Her thoughts were obviously elsewhere, for occasionally she stopped idling through the pages and gazed at the rose beds in front of her.

At last he went to the steps leading down into the garden, and she heard him, looking up swiftly. She stood, the book slipping from her lap, and as he neared her, he saw that there were tears shimmering in her lovely gray eyes.

He put his top hat and gloves down on the seat and then turned to face her. 'How are you? William said there was a storm and a tree struck by lightning . . .'

'I'm all right, Francis.

'Oh, Alison, if only you'd waited—'

'I had to come back here. I couldn't bear feeling the way I did.' She met his eyes. 'Please forgive me for all the things I said to you. When you told my uncle that you believed Pamela and William were—'

He put a finger to her lips. 'There is no need to say anything, my darling, for all recriminations and misunderstandings must be put in the past. I've wanted to tell you how much I love you, but somehow the words have never been said.'

She gazed at him through her tears. 'You love me?' she whispered.

'How can you doubt it? In the beginning we pretended to be lovers, but I found it only too easy to keep up that pretense. When I kissed you, I meant it, and when I held you close, I wanted to make you mine. My desire and love have almost been the undoing of me because they've been so very strong. And then, before the opera, when I tried to tell you and make you confess your feelings too, what should have been a moment of sheer joy and honesty became a nightmare of misunderstanding and accusations. I retreated into my wounded vanity, and became cold and distant. I responded poorly, Alison, and mishandled everything, but I didn't stop loving you. I know that I said I wished to marry you because I felt I had compromised you and because your family had to be considered, but that was always only part of it. I should have told you that I loved you, but I didn't, and for that I will always blame myself.'

'I've been as much at fault,' she replied, her voice trembling with incredible happiness. He loved her! Tears of joy wended their way down her cheeks and she reached out to him.

He took her hand, drawing her gently into his arms and holding her close. He closed his eyes. 'I love you, Alison, and that is why I wish to many you. Be my bride, my darling. Let me make you Lady Buckingham.'

She slipped her arms around him. 'Nothing would give me greater happiness,' she said softly.

He put his hand to her chin, tilting her lips toward him. He could taste the salt of her tears and feel how her body quivered against his. The kiss was long and lingering, and all the sweeter for being utterly honest. There was no pretense now, no guilt and no danger. They were in England now, not Russia, and hazardous government business was a lifetime away. They did not need to glance over their shoulder to see if Prince Nikolai's spies were watching, and they did not need to give others the impression that they were something they weren't. This kiss was the truth, painfully sincere and filled with a love they had both tried to deny.

Francis drew back, cupping her face in his hands. 'You know there will still be talk, don't you? We all four will be at the center of much gossip and speculation, for society is going to be much surprised when it learns which lady is to be Lord Buckingham's bride.'

'I know.'

'Do you mind?'

'I mind nothing in this world as long as you love me,' she whispered.

'I will always love you, Alison,' he said softly, kissing her again.

Also by Sandra Heath
and soon to be published:
LORD KANE'S KEEPSAKE

Gerald Kane made Miss Emma Rutherford an offer
unthinkable to refuse. The handsome lord had both title
and wealth to support his suit, plus Emma's father's
emphatic approval. He had even given Emma the fabulous Kane diamonds to seal their troth.

How then could Emma let Lord Kane's affair with the
most stunning beauty in London interfere with her
engagement? How could she listen to the seductive
suggestions of Lord Kane's archrival, the irresistible if
infamous Lord Avenley?

And how could she possibly hold out for the one thing
that Lord Kane neglected to pledge?

His love.